To Ann-Marie

Hope you enjoy the read

All the best

Ray

Murder In Manfield Road

Raymond Draper was born in Northampton England and still lives in the town. This is his second novel. The first, Millars, was published in 2000 and was well received.

Also by Raymond Draper

MILLARS

ISBN *978-1-4092-0764-1*

Published in 2008 by Lulu.com

Copyright © **2008** *Raymond Draper*

The right of Raymond Draper to be identified as the author of this work has been asserted by him in accordance with the Copyright Designs and Patents Act 1998

All rights reserved. No part of this publication may be reproduced, stored in or introduced into a retrieval system, or transmitted in any form or by any means (electronic, mechanical, photocopying, recording or otherwise), without the prior written permission of the Raymond Draper. Any person who does any unauthorised act in relation to this publication may be liable to criminal prosecution and civil claims for damages.

This book is sold subject to the condition that it shall not, by way of trade or otherwise, be lent, resold, hired out, or otherwise circulated without the publisher's prior consent in any form of binding or cover other than that in which it is published and without a similar condition including this condition being imposed on the subsequent purchaser.

All characters in this work are entirely fictitious and any resemblance to any person living or dead is purely coincidental.

Raymond Draper

MURDER IN MANFIELD ROAD

A THOMAS & GREY MYSTERY

Murder In Manfield Road

Introduction

She was trying to breathe but as fast as she was sucking in air it was escaping out of the gash in her throat. She had winced when she'd felt the sharp tug of her hair and her head had involuntary jerked back, but she'd hardly felt the blade when it had sliced easily through her carotid artery and jugular vein. Yet when that same blade had plunged into her back, propelling her headlong forward along the hallway, she had opened her mouth to scream out in pain. That had been when she had tried to breathe.

She stumbled towards a wall and put a hand out to try to balance herself, but it slipped on her own hot slick blood and she lurched into it like a drunk. As she bounced and reeled across the hallway from one wall to another she watched her life-blood spurt from her throat onto the floor and walls with a kind of detached fascination, as if she was somehow outside herself.

She didn't feel her arm break when her full weight fell on it after her legs had given way and she collapsed onto the carpet in her lounge. In life she had often dreamed that her dying words would be something profound or witty, but in her moment of death she couldn't speak and her last conscious thought was nothing weightier than 'what is happening to me?'

It took less than two minutes for her to die.

Chapter 1

Brian Thomas was sitting on his favourite bench in the peaceful grounds of St. Andrew's Private Hospital, Northampton. Built in the early nineteenth century to serve lunatic paupers, the hospital boasted over a hundred acres of tranquil parkland and from where he sat he had a good view of the croquet lawns and beautiful sandstone Chapel which had been designed by the famous Victorian architect Sir Gilbert Scott. Scott had earlier designed St.Pancras Railway station and his son had once been a patient as had the Northampton born poet John Clare who found inspiration for many of his great works while strolling around the grounds.

Thomas had a lot on his mind. He was wondering how he could balance the demands of his job with the ever increasing support his wife needed in nursing her father who was suffering from Alzheimer's.

It had begun innocently enough; he'd forgotten a few words, where he had put things, what he'd said only moments earlier. It had been a family joke, a few laughs about 'senior moments', but it soon turned to serious concern for his well-being.

He began to lose his sense of time and space and often he would lash out when he didn't know where he was. For someone in his mid-seventies he could be surprisingly aggressive and things had come to a head when one day Thomas's wife Alice had found him sitting naked on his bed, sobbing pitifully. He had forgotten how to dress himself. Horrified she had dressed him as best she could and driven him straight to his doctor. His preliminary diagnosis had been confirmed after weeks of extensive tests and it had been as crushing as it had been certain.

So, with his father-in-law slowly degenerating into full-blown dementia he had put in for a transfer from the Metropolitan Police to Northampton where he hoped he would find more time to help Alice. Before then he had been working quite happily as an on-call major crime Senior Investigating Officer.

For a while the change had worked well; from regularly putting in a seventy hour week in the MET he found he could comfortably get away with about fifty, and he was home most evenings by around six. The job itself was fine too; although there was less major crime in Northampton than he had been used to, there was enough to keep him interested.

But Bill, his father-in-law, was getting worse. He needed full time care and Alice had already quit her job so that she could look after him all day long. The problem Thomas was mulling over was what to do about Bill's increasingly violent behaviour. His ability to recognise who he was with and where he was had begun to decline by the day and it was impossible to predict how he would be from one day to the next. Out of frustration he could kick and bite anyone close to him at any time without warning, and Alice was not strong enough to cope with his violent outbursts alone. She needed help but they could not afford full time private care. Despite that, from what he had been able to find out from the baffling NHS guidelines, he earned too much to qualify for government assistance.

He was distracted from his thoughts when a pigeon fell from a nearby tree and thumped onto the grass directly in front of him. Clearly distressed it seemed to panic when two crows swooped in low and landed close by, settling either side of it. It tried to drag itself clear of them, puffing out its chest and flapping its wings in a feeble attempt to scare them away, but they were unimpressed and began to circle it, one to the right, and the other to the left.

Fascinated, he watched as the pigeon dragged its injured body around in circles to ward off the attack it sensed was coming, but it was moving far too slowly to worry the crows. Instinctively knowing when to strike the crow to the left distracted it and the one to the right pecked out its right eye. Blinded, it screamed, blood pouring from the vacant eye socket, wings flailing helplessly. Quickly both crows moved in and pecked its throat until they were certain it was dead. Then they began to eat it.

He shook his head in bewilderment. He'd been too absorbed in how the crows had worked as a pair and despatched their prey to shoo them away.

Just then his air-raid siren ring-tone went off and he pulled his mobile out of his pocket and put it to his ear.

'DCI Thomas'

'Sir, we have a sudden death in Manfield Road; it sounds bad' DI Sheila Grey announced, urgency in her voice.

Thomas stood up quickly, took the full address from her, buttoned his coat and headed for his car.

Chapter 2

Thunder clouds were gathering over Northampton as Thomas steered his black Ford Focus through the tortuous late-morning traffic towards Manfield Road. Selecting shuffle on his IPOD as he drove he was treated first up to Pink Floyd's Comfortably Numb, his favourite Floyd track. Ramping up the volume a few notches he had soon forgotten about the traffic as his mind was swept away on Gilmour's soaring guitar solo and his hands began drumming out the beat on the steering wheel.

Alice had bought him the IPOD some months earlier together with a gadget that allowed him to tune it in to a channel on his car stereo. Fully expecting it not to work when he'd tried to install it, he had been ecstatic when it had begun pumping out music on the first attempt. Now what had once seemed to be a piece of mysterious modern technology was contemptuously easy for him to handle and he had recorded all his favourite music on it.

All the houses in Manfield Road were basic red bricked terraced boxes yet when they had been built in the early twentieth century it had been strictly with middle class families in mind. The factory managers and directors of the nearby Manfield's shoe factory had lived there. In those days people tended to live within walking distance of where they worked and Thomas pictured in his mind Manfield Road in the early mornings and evenings thronging with men in suits busily making their way back and forth to work, each with their own worries, their own families.

Today it was bed-sit land; the large interior rooms and cellars, most of which had been converted to bedrooms, were magnets for students. The local college was within easy walking distance and the rooms were big enough to accommodate a bed and a sofa and TV or computer, and that's all most students needed. Rents were attractive to landlords and tenants alike; less than one hundred a week per room with shared facilities. A few families still survived, but they were few and far between and as quickly as they moved out buy-to-let landlords moved in.

When she had called earlier D.I. Grey's tone had left Thomas in no doubt that what he was approaching was going to be serious. She had said the body of a young woman had been found earlier that morning; it looked like violent death.

Northampton did not suffer many murders and Thomas reckoned to Grey this would be an exciting incident, she had certainly sounded pumped up on the phone. He hoped it wasn't for the wrong reasons. The discovery of a dead body was not something to feel excited about in his book, but he imagined Grey, with her overt ambition and limited experience of major crime, was the type that might see one as a career enhancing opportunity.

He preferred to approach crime scenes on foot; it allowed him get a feel for the neighbourhood and become accustomed to the surrounding area. Approaching his destination he parked his car in an empty spot on the Wellingborough Road about one hundred yards west from the turning into Manfield Road and as he walked towards the address Grey had given him he could see that already there was a lot of activity; a crowd had gathered around the cordon she had had organised and uniformed officers were struggling to keep them at bay. As he closed in nearer he could see an ambulance, a few squad cars, and a Scientific Support Unit van parked nearby. Thomas expected the medical examiner would already be inside.

He could see DI Grey approaching him as he showed a constable his card and ducked under the 'Police No Entry' tape. Grey always reminded him of a rugby prop forward.

Aged around forty, she was a tall thick-set blonde with what he thought was a ridiculous habit of wearing designer label power suits, the trousers of which seemed to be forever on the verge of splitting open at the seams as they stretched precariously over her colossal thighs. He was sure she would have looked much more natural and feminine wearing a blouse and skirt, but then when he looked in the mirror it reminded him that he was no fashion guru either.

Grey was suited up in a clear film overall, blue latex gloves, and pale blue plastic shoe covers. Beneath the overall Thomas could see that she was wearing her usual power two piece in charcoal, a blue blouse, and deeper blue tie. The suit was meant to look elegant, but in his eyes under the shrink-wrap it looked like something she'd bought in a hurry from The Red Cross.

She noticed him approaching and greeted him cheerfully 'Morning Sir.'

'DI Grey.' Thomas nodded. 'What have we got?'

'A female sir, in her early twenties from the look of her; her throat has been cut and a there's a wound in her back. Probably done with a sharp instrument, a knife or something similar, but as yet we've found no weapon. Her body is in the lounge; there's no evidence of forced entry.' She had said it all without pausing for breath and Thomas deliberately spoke very quietly and slowly when he replied.

'Is the Medical Examiner here?'

'Yes sir, inside now.'

'In that case I'll go and see what he can tell us and then you can give me more details when I've finished with him.'

'Yes sir, I should have something for us to start with in the next half hour or so. By the way the M.E.'s a she.'

'OK thanks, you carry on then. Oh, and extend that perimeter will you, I don't want this to become a circus. Keep the crowd far enough back so they can't see anything important. I'll catch you once I've spoken to the M.E.'

'Sir' Grey replied, accepting Thomas' implied criticism and striding off towards a group of uniformed constables. Thomas turned away and headed towards the house. On his way he pulled on a protective overall, gloves, and shoe protectors.

Stepping into the hall he could tell immediately that it was not a college student's house. A student pad would be stark and sparse, containing no more no less than what the landlord had to provide by law, but this place was tidy and homely, possibly a married couple's home. The hall light had a lampshade, something absent in most bed-sits, and there were a couple of framed Constable Prints hanging on the wall. Recently someone had taken the trouble to put up ceiling coving, a job he knew from painful experience not to be undertaken by the faint-hearted. The walls looked freshly painted in eggshell, and judging by the spongy feel of it, there was a reasonably good quality plain green carpet covering the floor. Under other circumstances it would have been quite welcoming.

Two rooms and a staircase led off of the hallway, but he could already see what he was looking for. A bloodstained foot, toes pointing towards the ceiling, was protruding from the room at the far end of the hall. He walked slowly towards it but stopped abruptly when he saw blood splashes directly in front of him and on the walls. He called out for the Medical Examiner, and a mid-thirties brunette clad in SOC overalls peered around the corner.

'DCI Thomas.' He announced, smiling. 'Are you the M.E.?'

'Yes, Jane Edwards; I'll come out, but you can have a look around if you like. It's been cleared.'

'Thanks, but I'll wait.' He decided. Often forensics were crucial to a case and he had always been wary of fouling scientific evidence at crime scenes, even after he'd been given the all clear. In his experience murder investigations could take weeks or even months of hard graft, and the last thing he needed after all that effort was some smart arsed lawyer destroying his case because he'd inadvertently managed to somehow corrupt damning forensic evidence through his own over-eagerness. With that in mind he decided to defer a decision whether to inspect the body here or at the morgue until after he had spoken to Jane Edwards.

Edwards carefully stepped over the bloody foot and walked along the passage towards him, seemingly unaware that she was stepping in fresh blood as she walked. 'Shall we go outside?' She suggested. 'I could do with some fresh air.'

'Yes, of course.' Thomas agreed, turning to walk towards the front door.

Edwards followed him outside and took a deep breath. 'Ah that's better.' She said exhaling loudly.

'Not wishing to hold you to anything but any preliminary thoughts?' he asked.

To his pleasant surprise Edwards did not hesitate; most pathologists he'd met had been very wary about giving off-the-cuff opinions. 'Well, we will have to wait for the results of the autopsy to be certain, but I would say she hasn't been dead very long, perhaps a couple of hours judging by her temperature. It's about mid-day now so that would put time of death somewhere around ten or ten fifteen; definitely no earlier. There's a deep gash across her throat and blood spatters from the hall into the lounge which runs off of the far end of the hall. The body is in the lounge as I think you could see. There's also a wound to her back below the left shoulder, but I don't think at the moment that it was fatal. My guess is she was slashed in the hallway, possibly from behind, and then stabbed. She probably staggered around a bit then collapsed in shock; blood would have been spraying about, and she would have lost consciousness from oxygen starvation fairly quickly. Death would have been within a few minutes. She probably bled to death. As I say all of that is preliminary and you'll have to wait for the post-mortem to be sure.'

He had been listening intently and asked. 'So you think she was attacked in the hallway?'

'Judging from the splash patterns in the hall and the fact they appear to lead to where she's lying in the lounge, it looks that way.'

'Any defence wounds?'

'None; hence why I think her attacker jumped her from behind without warning.'

'That's interesting; any idea of the type of weapon? I don't suppose there's one in there.'

'Very sharp instrument, craft knife, scalpel, something like that; the wound is very deep, but clean; severed the carotid which looks like it's recessed, and the jugular and larynx. To do that requires a very deep cut and something very sharp. I didn't hear anything from any Scene-Of-Crime-Officer about finding a weapon.'

'Anything else?'

'There are no signs of any struggle at all. No bruising, no defence cuts on the hands or arms as I've said. The assailant was probably right handed because the left carotid has suffered most damage.' Edwards made as though pulling someone's head back from behind with her left hand and slicing across the throat with her right. 'I'll have more after I've finished the autopsy. There are also some forensics; I found fibres possibly from the assailant's clothes in the blood around her throat and I imagine there could be some transference on her clothes too. SOCO have everything bagged. They might be useful to you.'

'Let's hope so. Are you sure about the attack being from behind? Could it have been an unexpected slash from the front?'

Edwards sighed wearily. 'No, I'm not sure but it's my judgement as of now. You asked and I'm giving you my best opinion based on the preliminary examination I've carried out here. If it's certainty you're after DCI Thomas, you'll have to wait until after I've had her on the slab.'

Thomas felt suitably chastised. 'I'm sorry.' He managed a rueful smile. 'Listen, I'll let you get on. You'll give me a call?'

Edwards smiled, her irritation quickly gone. 'Yes, of course.'

'Thanks.' He said giving her a warm smile. Edwards headed off towards the Scientific Support Van and he decided to head back inside.

As he approached the lounge he could see blood-spray patterns on the walls and floor. To Thomas the blood on the walls, thick crimson streams that had dripped down to the skirting boards, looked like bitter tears of outrage. Blood had gushed from her throat and he could see finger marks and what looked like hand-prints where he imagined she had staggered from side to side and put out her hands to try to balance herself before she passed out.

Stepping over her upturned foot into the lounge, he knelt down beside the body. The head was turned to the right, eyes staring lifelessly at the rear window, face gripped in agonised shock. A bloody open wound, already cleaned by the M.E., had slit the throat from ear to ear; the chest was a mass of uncongealed blood, still warm. The right arm had been fractured when she had fallen he guessed; the snapped ulna was clearly visible where it had pierced the skin. The left arm was bent upwards, the fingers of the hand pointing towards her neck. One leg was stretched straight out, the other doubled under itself. Thomas reckoned that she had collapsed, possibly after losing consciousness; once the brain had been starved of oxygen loss of motor functions would have followed very quickly. He shuddered at the thought. She was wearing a blue skirt and white blouse both blood splattered; day clothes, he decided.

He paid particular attention to the young woman's hands. He was looking for any signs of defence marks but could see none. The M.E. had probably been right; it looked as though this woman had been attacked from behind. In cases he had seen where the attack had come from the front, invariably there had been cuts and abrasions on the hands and arms where the victim had tried to ward off the blows. Here there were none indicating she had probably been surprised from behind. Her arms likewise showed no signs of bruising, but he noticed some discolouration around the veins on her wrists and his experience made him immediately turn his attention to her face. Looking closely at her nose, he could see that the membranes were showing signs of wear, and the septum was unusually thin. A cocaine addict, he guessed.

He searched around the area close to the body for a few minutes more but decided that SOCO had probably already covered everything so he backed out. Slowly treading back through the hallway, he examined the blood stains on the floor more closely. Bending to take a closer look, he noticed they first appeared about eight feet from the front door but just before they began he spotted a small tuft of hair. Kneeling to examine it more closely he could make out the blonde colour, similar in shade to the victim's hair. He called for a Scene-Of-Crime- Officer and asked him to put it in an evidence bag. The officer gave him a look that said. *'You must be joking if you think we haven't already covered this'*, but when Thomas didn't smile he sighed and did as he was asked.

Thomas considered the discovery of hair in the hallway possibly significant because he had a picture in his mind of what had happened. The victim had been heading towards the lounge with her back to the front door, the murderer behind her. Did she answer the door or was the killer already in the house, he asked himself? Then the murderer had grabbed her hair from behind, yanked back her head thus exposing her throat, and dragged the blade across, severing the carotid artery and jugular vein. In the action of grabbing her hair and yanking back her head, the assailant had pulled out a lock of hair. Or alternatively he was still holding onto her hair when he stabbed her in the back and the hair came out when she fell from the force of the blow. Either way, if his theory was right, and the hair he'd found did match the victim's hair, then it would be useful evidence when the case came to trial.

Stepping outside the house he looked around for DI Grey. He spotted her talking to two uniformed officers by the perimeter tape and walked over to her. He waited a short distance away until she had finished her conversation before approaching closer.

'So what have you found out?' He asked without preamble.

'We think her name is Susan Reed, age 22, married to Alan Reed. He's in custody. He says he found the body and so he's an obvious suspect. We know he called it in at 10.22 this morning.'

'It's just past twelve now and the M.E. says she died just over two hours ago so he must have found her very shortly after death.'

'Assuming he didn't do her in.' Grey added.

'Assuming that, yes; do we have any witnesses?'

'A woman over the road says someone approached the house just after ten and rang the bell. She didn't see him enter. Her description is vague; a white male, medium height, wearing a baseball cap and dark top, she thinks perhaps navy blue, dark trousers, again possibly navy or charcoal, and light coloured shoes.'

'What was the husband wearing when you first saw him?'

'Baseball cap, navy blue jacket, navy corduroys, and white trainers. He's five ten. Clothes are with forensics.' Grey told him.

'So it could have been the husband she saw if he'd forgotten his key and she was still alive; any other witnesses?'

'Not yet sir; we're doing door to door now. Another possible useful source is CCTV.'

'There's CCTV in this road?' Thomas asked, sounding surprised and looking around.

'No sir, but there are cameras on the Wellingborough Road at the bottom and Wantage Road at the top.' Grey explained.

'No side roads or other means of approach?'

'No sir, not by car nor on foot.'

'That is interesting; it could be significant. Make sure we get hold of the tapes.' Thomas ordered, Grey thought unnecessarily. 'Did our witness see from which direction the caller approached the house?'

'She's fairly certain he approached from the left which would be the Wellingborough Road end. Regarding the CCTV sir, it's worth reminding ourselves that these are very busy roads. There will be a lot of traffic on film.'

'Yes, but it's worth a shot and there's no guarantee that our murderer came in a vehicle; in any event there won't be so many pedestrians.' Thomas pointed out. 'Where's Mr. Reed?'

'At Campbell Square station sir. In view of the timeline and description I've put him under caution'

'Good; I'll go and talk to him. You finish up here and we'll meet up later in my office.'

Sounding slightly put out DI Grey said 'Yes sir.' and headed back to the uniformed officers.

Chapter 3

Thomas looked around for a few more minutes, taking in the scene. SOCO were still busy pouring over every nook and cranny, and uniformed officers were doing door to door, controlling residential traffic and keeping the gathering curious behind the tapes. Inside the house, the ambulance crew was preparing to remove the body and take it to Jane Edwards to perform her autopsy. It would be at least another day before forensics would finish with the house and much longer before anyone other than authorised police was allowed inside it.

Thomas decided he had what he needed and headed back towards his car. On the way he thought about how murder disrupted everyday life. Manfield Road would be closed for at least a day, which meant that residents would have to find somewhere else to park their cars and parking in this part of town was already problem enough. He chuckled inwardly; the wardens round about would have a field day. Innocent residents would be plagued by police undertaking door to door enquiries, not once but probably two or even three times over the next few days. Some of them would be pulled in for further questioning.

Then there would be the goons; the morbidly curious who would see nothing distasteful in walking around the area, knocking on doors, questioning already tired and frightened residents, taking photographs, so that they could take them back to their sad homes and add a bit of excitement to their sad lives.

The press would be professional but nevertheless intrusive. For a few days, at least while police activity was still visible, they would pitch camp in the street and take opinions from householders and passers by at every opportunity.

And there would be fear amongst residents. He tried to imagine what it would be like living in a street where a murder had just been committed; an unsolved murder, he reminded himself. Surely the first instinct would be shock, followed quickly by incredulity, then fear that the murderer was still out there and maybe you would be next.

He reached his car, pressed the remote central locking, opened the door and slid inside. He started the engine and switched on his IPOD. The shuffle selected Freaker's Ball by Dr.Hook and as he drove this was followed by Dire Staits' Telegraph Road.

So smiled Thomas, I'm Comfortably Numb from the Freaker's Ball driving along Telegraph Road. Okay.

The sun broke through the clouds as he drove across The Mounts towards Campbell Square Station. He parked his car around the back and went inside to see the Duty Sergeant who would know where Alan Reed was being held. He hated this part of the station even though he spent a lot of his time here. It was the area where suspects were searched and charged and it contained the holding cells which stank of stale urine and body sweat.

The walls in the cells were defaced with abusive graffiti, some of which had been there for years because nobody had bothered to clean it off. Inside each one was a cold metal bench on which prisoners could sit and wait until they were called. Sometimes they had to wait for a day or more. There were male and female toilets across from the Duty Desk which were used as much for suspects to throw up in after they'd been arrested as for calls of nature, and the combined stench from the cells and the toilets were enough to make Thomas retch every time he came down here. Throwing up was common after arrest and charge; it was the combination of shock and fear that did it and you could never quite get rid of the stench of stale vomit no matter how much disinfectant you used.

The interview rooms were just away from the Duty Desk and the one in which he waited for the Duty Sergeant to bring Reed was furnished with a teak desk and four low backed blue office chairs. Two windows on the far side away from the door saved it from being too claustrophobic and a single fluorescent lamp in the ceiling threw down enough harsh light to make him screw up his eyes for a few seconds. The floor was covered with worn beige cord carpet heavily stained with a variety of unmentionable substances from what looked like years of use. The standard dual tape deck was to the left of where he was sitting.

A uniformed constable stood at ease in the corner with his hands behind his back as the Duty Sergeant brought Reed out from the holding cells. Thomas stood and motioned for Reed to sit down and the Duty Sergeant closed the door behind him as he left, leaving Thomas and the uniformed constable alone with Reed.

Reed looked dishevelled and stressed. The duty doctor had already extracted DNA and the clothes he had been wearing before his arrest had been taken away for forensic examination. He was wearing a grimy police-issue boiler suit that looked two sizes too big and old vomit stains were clearly visible on the chest. He hadn't shaved and judging by the state of his eyes and hair, he didn't look as though he'd showered either. His hair, fairly long and thick and surprisingly grey for such a young man, was sticking out in all directions like some caricature of a manic professor. His eyes were bloodshot through either crying or lack of sleep, Thomas couldn't tell which. He guessed he was around twenty five, possibly five ten and two hundred pounds. He looked fit but pale, his cheeks a ghostly white.

Thomas switched on the tapes and recorded the time before introducing himself. 'You know why you're here?' He began.

'They told me I'm being held on suspicion of murdering my wife.' Reed said looking straight at Thomas.

Thomas rarely sat during criminal interviews; he liked to tower over suspects so that the guilty would feel intimidated, and at this moment he was leaning against the back wall, arms crossed. 'As I understand it, you found her. Is that correct?'

Reed was silent for a few moments, seemingly remembering the moment he had found his wife. He appeared to picture something in his mind and his eyes began to well with tears; it took him a few moments to gather himself and answer. 'I, I had been to the shop to buy a paper and some cigarettes.' He began unsteadily. 'I had been gone maybe twenty minutes. When I got back home she was on the floor in the lounge, blood everywhere.'

Thomas gave Reed a few moments to settle before continuing then asked 'Other than you and your wife, did anybody else have a key to the house? Could anybody else have got in without your permission?'

'No.'

'Can you say what time it was when you left?'

Reed thought for a moment. 'I don't know, around ten maybe.'

'And how long before you returned?'

'I'm not sure exactly; but as I said twenty minutes maybe. I walked to the shop at the bottom of the street, bought a paper and some cigarettes and walked back.'

'And can you describe what you saw when you returned home?'

Reed tried to hide his tears by shielding his eyes with his hands, but Thomas could see his shoulders shaking as he silently sobbed and it was a few minutes before he had pulled himself together. 'She was such a mess. Blood was everywhere, on the floor, on the walls, over her chest, her hands and arms. And her face, that look, that ghastly expression. Inspector I'll never forget that look on her face.' Reed said raising his eyes to look directly at Thomas; they were spread wide in horror as he pictured the nightmare scene. 'As soon as I opened the front door I could see one of her feet from the hall. I remember for a brief second thinking she must have fallen, but then I saw the blood. I ran into the lounge and that's when I saw her, saw her face.'

Reed broke down again and Thomas passed him a paper tissue. He blew his nose and dabbed his eyes, trying to calm himself. Thomas again waited until he had stopped crying before continuing. 'Did you touch her at all?' He probed.

'No. No I was too frightened.'

'Are you sure? It is important.' Thomas persisted.

'Yes, yes I'm sure.' Reed recalled. 'I remember being so scared. I didn't know what to do. I thought she was dead but I remember running upstairs into the bathroom to fetch a mirror and putting it against her mouth. There was no breath. I think that was when I called the ambulance.'

'Why didn't you call the police?' Thomas asked.

'I didn't know what had happened. I could see her throat was a mess but I just wanted help and calling the ambulance seemed the right thing to do. I didn't know what else to do.'

'Wasn't it obvious to you she had been attacked?'

'Not at first.' Reed explained and then suddenly became impatient. 'Look, I wasn't thinking straight, alright? I was in shock. She was lying there covered in blood; there was blood on the floor and walls and she looked dead. She wasn't breathing but I didn't know what had happened. I was scared to death and that's the truth. I had no idea what to think.'

Thomas decided to change tack. 'OK let's talk about earlier, before you went out to buy your paper. What happened?'

Reed lifted his head from his hands and looked sharply at Thomas. 'How do you mean?'

'I mean tell me what happened between you and your wife before you went to the shop?'

'Nothing happened. I'm sorry I don't understand what you're getting at?'

'Did you argue?'

'No.'

'Did you ever argue?'

'Well yes of course we did. What kind of a question is that?'

'When was the last time you argued?'

'I don't know!' Reed shouted, letting his irritation at Thomas' questions show.

'Try to remember. Was it this morning?' Thomas persisted, picking up the pace of his questions. In his experience quick fire questioning often produced damning answers from the guilty.

'No, I've already told you!'

'Was it last night?'

Reed appeared incredulous that Thomas should be asking such questions. Clearly rattled he shouted. 'No! Look, where's all this leading? I've told you, I went out to buy a paper. I came back home and she was dead on the floor in the lounge. She was covered in blood; that's all I know.'

'Did you kill your wife Mr. Reed?'

'What? No; why are you asking me this?' Reed cried disbelief that Thomas could even ask him such a question etched in his expression.

'Did you have an argument, cut her throat, stab her, and then leave the house to dispose of the weapon?'

'No! What weapon? What are you talking about?'

'Was it a knife? Where have you hidden it?'

'There was no knife! Will you stop this? I did not kill her. I loved her.'

Thomas pushed away from the wall and leaned on the desk, his face close to Reed's. 'Are you seriously asking me to believe that when you left her everything was normal yet when you returned twenty minutes later she was dead? According to you, in that short time your wife just happened to invite a murderer into your house who then cut her throat, and made an escape. Are you seriously asking me to believe that? Why would anyone do that? And why in that precise twenty minute period when you were out of the house? Are you seriously asking me to believe that someone knew you were going out? Do you go out for a paper and cigarettes at that time every morning?' Thomas' tone was scathing.

Reed had been listening with a look of disbelief on his face, but slowly the logic of Thomas' line of questioning seemed to dawn on him. His shoulders slumped, and his head dropped. When he replied it was in a quiet, resigned voice. 'No.'

'No, exactly;' Thomas echoed, 'how would anyone know you were out or likely to be out?'

'I have no idea.' Reed replied his voice almost a whisper.

Thomas ploughed on in his scornful tone, hoping Reed would crack. 'You have no idea because there was no-one else was there? You argued before you went out. You stabbed her, slit her throat, and then disposed of the weapon. Isn't that what happened?'

'No! I've told you, she was fine when I left her but when I got back she was dead.' Reed insisted his voice trembling.

Thomas pressed on, straightening to his full height, towering above Reed. 'You grabbed her round the neck, from behind, and slit her throat. Isn't that true?'

Reed shot up out of his chair and wagged a finger at Thomas. 'No. It's not true and I've had just about enough of this crap! If you think I killed her then you prove it, otherwise you can keep your wild theories to yourself. You have no right to accuse me like this and you can be bloody sure I'll be making a complaint against you Thomas. Who the hell do you think you are?'

'Sit down!' Thomas thundered and the uniformed officer quickly sprung into action, moving in towards Reed who sat quickly when he saw the officer hurrying towards him

There was a moment's pause before Thomas sighed theatrically. 'I'm sure you have heard of forensic science.'

'Of course I have, everybody has.'

'Then you won't be surprised to know that fibres from shirts, jackets, trousers, in fact any clothing or part of the body easily transfer from one person to another in the course of a violent attack. Now what do you think might have happened to fibres from your wife's attacker's clothes? What do you think we will find when we analyse your clothes?'

'You'll find nothing from me or my clothes.' Reed declared firmly.

'Are you so sure?'

'Certain because I didn't kill her. Please do check.' Reed said challengingly.

'Oh, have no doubt.' Thomas replied in a matter of fact tone. 'As far as you are aware, did your wife have any enemies?' He asked.

Reed thought for a few seconds. 'Not that I can think of.' It was the usual response in Thomas' experience. Rarely in murder investigations did witnesses suggest someone disliked the victim enough to commit murder; victims were invariably popular with no enemies. Yet they were dead.

'Did she have a habit?' He asked although he already knew the answer.

Reed fidgeted around in the chair. 'Habit? I don't understand.' He murmured evasively.

'Oh I think you do. Did your wife, to your knowledge, have a cocaine habit?' Thomas repeated louder.

'Not that I'm aware of.'

'It will come out in the toxicology tests from the autopsy, so don't lie to me. I'll ask you one last time. Did she have a habit?' Thomas asked again sounding tired of Reed's play acting.

'Well it was more of a social thing I'd say.' Reed admitted.

'What are we talking about, once a day, twice a day?'

'I don't know.' Reed shrugged and Thomas speared him with disbelieving eyes. 'No really, I don't.' Reed continued. 'She didn't shoot up when I was around; she wouldn't dare in my presence.'

'Do you have a habit?'

'No, I don't touch drugs.' Reed answered emphatically.

'Very wise; who was her supplier?'

'How would I know?' Reed challenged, sitting back and putting his hands in his pockets.

'Well somebody was. Why wouldn't you know? She was your wife.' Thomas persisted.

'Well I don't know.'

'Did you argue about it?'

'Sometimes.'

'Why, didn't you approve of it?'

'No I didn't,' He agreed, adding bitterly, 'and she couldn't afford it.'

'Where do you work?'

'Uh, I don't at the moment. I'm between jobs.' Reed muttered, seemingly embarrassed to admit it and averting his eyes from Thomas.

'You're between jobs. Did your wife pester you for money to feed her habit?'

'Yes, all the time.' He said bitterly as if remembering.

'Is that why you killed her? She was pestering you for money you didn't have?'

'I've told you I didn't kill her.'

'I think she got fired up, knowing she couldn't afford her next fix and blamed you. You argued, you fought, and you killed her in a fit of rage, is that it?'

'No!'

'Oh come on! Stop spinning me a line. Tell me something sensible instead of trying to make me believe this ridiculous story. Look, for what it's worth, what you've done is understandable; perfectly understandable. You lose control for that split second. You're arguing, she's telling you how useless you are because you're out of work and can't keep her in cocaine. You snap, you fight, she walks away, dismisses you. You feel useless, disrespected, and in a frenzy you grab her and slit her with the knife.'

'No! I didn't kill her.'

Thomas gave him a withering look. 'Well it's easier to imagine than someone just walking in off the street at the precise moment you were out. Frankly that story beggars belief, and if that's not enough, you're asking me to also accept that your wife let her killer in. Well I don't believe you and I don't think a jury will either, do you?'

'I don't care what it sounds like; I didn't kill her.' Reed maintained.

Thomas ignored him and persevered with his attack. 'I'll tell you what I do believe. I believe that you had ample opportunity and motive. You were with her earlier and you had argued about money; she had a habit and she needed her next fix but you couldn't afford it. When she told you that you were a waste of time, useless, you killed her. Now that makes sense to me.'

'I didn't kill her!' Reed shouted.

'Oh come on! Get real! I know you haven't had much time to come up with anything better but frankly what you're suggesting is a fantasy. Either you killed her or she happened to invite her murderer in. Which do you think is more likely?'

'I didn't kill her!'

'So you keep on saying, but I think you need to listen to yourself. I'm not stupid and neither will the jury be. Better if you admit it now.'

'How many times do I have to tell you? I didn't kill her.'

'Which shop did you go to for your paper?'

'Threshers on the corner.'

'Did you go straight to it, no diversions?'

'Yes of course. Why would I take a diversion?'

Thomas gave him another sarcastic look. 'Oh, I see.' Reed said. 'No I went straight there.'

'Did anyone see you or speak to you on the way?'

'No.'

'On the way back?'

'No'

'Are you sure; no one at all?'

'I didn't speak to anyone; but the checkout girls at Threshers all know me.'

'Did you pass anyone on the way or on the way back?'

'I don't think so.'

'What about on the other side of the road. Did you see anybody?'

'Not that I noticed.'

'We'll take a break now for an hour.' Thomas said switching off the tapes. He stood up and left the room leaving Reed alone with the uniformed officer. In fact he had no intention of speaking to Reed again that day. He had decided to let him sweat in the cells overnight before trying again in the morning. Reed had been unconvincing and the longer the interview had lasted the more he believed Reed had probably murdered his wife. He'd had motive and opportunity and Thomas suspected he had disposed of the weapon somewhere earlier that morning. Reed's confidence when he had threatened him with forensics had created a nagging doubt in the back of his mind but that could have simply been bravado. Time would tell.

Chapter 4

Out of the interview room and heading for the exit, Thomas called Grey on his mobile.

'How are things?' he asked.

Grey summarised. 'Uniforms are continuing house to house sir and there have been what could be a couple of sightings of the mystery person in the dark clothing. Conflicting information though; one witness says our suspect was heading up the street towards the house, the other down the street. The good news is the CCTV tapes are available and we've taken them in for inspection.'

'Good, well done. It sounds like there could have been two callers. I've spoken to Reed and he says he went to Threshers on the corner to buy a paper and cigarettes. I'd like you to check. Ask them if they know Alan Reed, if they can remember whether he was in there between ten and twenty past this morning. Check there hasn't been a change of shift; if there has track down who was on the tills and go and see them. We need to establish if he was in that shop as he says.'

'Will do sir.' Grey obeyed. A wave of pride had washed over her when Thomas had said 'well done'. In her opinion Thomas was quick, if not sometimes too quick to criticise her, and a 'well done' from him was like praise from Caesar. She sometimes wondered why she didn't feel rebellious against him but somehow she didn't; the more he picked on her faults the harder she wanted to impress him, and when he did throw her a morsel of approval, a warm glow of satisfaction spread over her.

'Now here's the bad news.'

'Sir?'

'If Reed murdered her then he must have disposed of the weapon somewhere close. I want a full search of that whole street, front and back gardens, fingertips, drains up, the lot.'

'I'll need clearance for the uniforms sir.' Grey pointed out, knowing that a fingertip search would cost the earth in uniformed manpower and ruin the budget.

'I know', Thomas sighed not relishing the conversation he was going to have with his Chief Superintendent. Budgets were already stretched. 'I'll get it.'

'Sir.' Grey said.

'Ok, anything significant call me, otherwise I'll see you at Campbell Square at nine in the morning.'

'Yes sir.'

Thomas rang off and called Chief Superintendent Judd, his direct boss. After ten minutes of what he put down to haggling, Judd agreed to the allocation of uniformed officers to conduct the search Thomas wanted.

Having closed his call to the Chief he headed for his car. Settling into the driver's seat he switched on the IPOD and the shuffle surprised him with the second movement of Beethoven's Emperor Piano Concerto in E Flat major. Written for Beethoven's Patron Archduke Rudolf in about 1810, this was one of his favourite classical pieces. His recording had been performed by Vladimir Ashkenazy in the early seventies, and the second movement, slow but rhythmical, always swept him away. He had read somewhere that the musical term for it was *Un poco mosso*, and that it meant 'a little motion'. The way it rolled off of the tongue that sounded about right to him. He had once bought the full musical score, believing he could probably play it on his nineteenth century upright; after all it was the slow movement and even with his limited talent he ought to be able to manage it.

He was a closet failed concert pianist who's talents on the piano did not run even to pub standard, and he would have gladly given up all of his police career, all the medals and trophies he had won at golf, squash, football, rugby, cricket, any one of which he had once been able to play to almost professional standard, for just one ounce of flair on the ivories. But alas, he had none. Nevertheless he could knock out a tune in e flat major, so he had been fairly confident he would be able to play the second movement from The Emperor.

But when the score had arrived he had been crestfallen to find that the second movement was in the key of B major, and he could not play in that key. Deflated he had put the score to the bottom of his pile of music books and never bothered with it again. He would never admit it to himself, but he did not have the application to improve his playing.

He lived in the Wootton district of town in a comfortable four bedroom detached house in a quiet cul-de-sac. Built in the late 1990's the house boasted what builders call classic buff facing bricks and rustic red roof tiles. Double glazing and cavity wall insulation kept the noise and cold out, and the separate lounge and dining room plus added study and the four bedrooms provided enough room for himself, his wife Alice, and Alice's father Bill without any one of them feeling too over crowded.

The double garage allowed them to secure both cars over night. He was not a keen gardener so he didn't mind that his back garden was smaller than most and he'd designed it so that it was virtually maintenance free; just a simple lawn surrounded by borders full of perennials. Ten minutes once a week with the mower kept the grass in order, and about twice a year he'd thin out the borders and cut them back. Alice liked to sit in a pretty garden but wouldn't lift a finger to keep it that way.

He and his wife were childless; they had discussed having children years earlier but both had been too career minded to want to devote the time they would have to, so it hadn't happened. Neither of them had regretted it. Before taking a break to look after her father, Alice had been a partner in Grant Thornton Accountants. Fortunately there was a branch in Northampton and they both hoped she would return once things had settled down with Bill.

He parked his car in his drive, unlocked the front door, went in and dropped his car keys on the hall table, a simple but elegant French mahogany antique made around 1870 that would have fetched around £2,000 at auction, but which he'd bought for a hundred pounds twenty years earlier. He walked into the lounge to see his wife serving her father a cup of tea. She smiled at him and he put his arm around her waist and kissed her cheek. 'Hi' he said.

'Hi you.' Alice said admiring her husband. Fifteen years of marriage, she thought, and he still makes me weak at the knees. Six two, fit as he was when I first met him eighteen years ago, strong chin and a mat of tightly curled black hair greying at the temples, plus ebony skin smooth as silk. A real turn on she decided for the thousandth time, and kind; strong yes, handsome yes, but above all, kind. That was why she loved him more today than ever before. 'Tea?' She asked.

'That would be nice. Hi Bill, how are things?' He greeted Alice's father who was sitting on an easy chair with a good view of the TV, still dressed in his dressing-gown despite it being late afternoon. Bill's wife had died two years earlier of a heart-attack and he had seemed to go downhill ever since. In his early seventies, physically he still looked fairly fit, back straight, eyes clear and alert, hair grey, a bit thin but not too bad for his age. Mentally things were much worse; he was on a very steep slippery slope with only slow unknowing death awaiting him.

Bill did not respond; he appeared not to hear him.

'Hi Bill.' Thomas repeated. Bill turned towards him but showed no sign of recognising him and quickly turned away concentrating again on the TV. 'He doesn't recognise me.' Thomas mouthed silently to Alice. She nodded in understanding.

'Busy day?' She asked.

'Afraid so, body in Manfield Road, probably murder.' He told her. 'Looks like I'm going to be busy.'

Alice chided him. 'Brian you like being busy. Busy is what you do. If you're not busy you're cranky.'

Thomas laughed. 'Hey, who's complaining? Bill would you like a sandwich?'

Bill ignored him.

Thomas left him alone in the lounge watching TV while he followed Alice into the kitchen. She was at the worktop busy putting tea bags into cups. He approached her from behind and put his arms around her waist, pulling her to him. 'Mm, you smell nice.' He murmured nuzzling her neck with light kisses.

He could feel himself becoming aroused. They had been married fifteen years but he had never tired of her; she was his soul-mate as well as his lover, and in his judgement, what a lover. Blonde, lithe, and tall, with legs that went on forever, full rosy lips and eyes he could drown in, he was always, even now, a little breathless in her company. When they'd first met he had been very possessive of her, feeling insecure, but gradually she had reassured him, built up his confidence and proven to him that she loved him. He was proud of her and felt privileged that he had found what he could only describe as his ideal woman.

Alice pressed back into him. 'Hello big boy, can I help you?'

'Oh yeah.'

'With what?' She teased wriggling against him.

'Oh, I've got a list.' He murmured running his hands over her hips.

'Well,' she said teasingly, 'if you like, later, we'll tick a few boxes.'

'Later?' He asked, pressing harder.

'Mmm, right now I've got to make the tea and you're making a sandwich.'

'He didn't answer me, he might not want one.' He protested.

'I know but he must be hungry, he's hardly eaten a thing all day.'

Reluctantly he let her go and set about making Bill's sandwiches. He cut them into quarters so they would be easy for Bill to manage and laid them out decoratively on a plate with some lettuce and tomato. Smiling he took them into the lounge ready to play the doting waiter. When he reached Bill he offered the plate to him but Bill became irritated and knocked the plate away. 'Get away from me.' He said threateningly.

'Bill, it's me Brian; Alice's husband.' He said in a futile attempt to help Bill recognise him but Bill waved him away again and turned his attention back to the TV. He seemed to be in a world of his own and so Thomas put the untouched plate on a nearby table. He felt helpless and mildly rejected unable to decide what to do for the best. He understood Bill's condition but it didn't make it any easier to handle and he opened his mouth ready to speak but nothing came out.

'Dad' Alice said trying to reason with her father knowing that his truculence was being brought on by his Alzheimer's. Her father was in a place where he didn't recognise her husband and felt threatened by him; his defence was to lash out in temper.

Turning to Alice Bill shouted. 'Do you know him? How dare you bring a nigger into my house?'

Alice was quickly at his side. 'Dad this is Brian, my husband. Come on Dad, you know Brian.'

Bill pushed her away in anger. 'Don't give me that; you're not married. You're cavorting with a bloody nigger. I can't believe you. After all your mother and I have done for you. You just wait until I talk to her about it.'

Thomas couldn't listen to any more. He was both angry and pitiful, but didn't know what to do or say. In frustration he turned away into the kitchen.

'Now where's he going?' Bill bawled. 'Thinks he owns the place does he? Who the hell does he think he is?'

From the kitchen he could hear his wife trying to soothe her father but he was still shouting abuse. Instinctively he wanted to help her but until now Alice had managed these outbursts well enough and Bill had not yet added serious violence to his rants; his aggression, so far, had been limited to verbal attacks and the occasional angry shove or kick born out of frustration. He decided on balance he should leave her to deal with it; there would come a time shortly when he would have to get involved but not just yet.

Despite understanding that the racial outburst was borne from Bill's Alzheimer's, it still stung. He had endured a lifetime of it and, he remembered it was one of the things that had driven him to join the MET from university. With a first from Nottingham, he could have chosen accountancy or law, or some other corporate profession, but he had opted for the MET, at least in part, because he had thought that in the police he would be best positioned to stamp out prejudice and inequality. In truth, he reflected as he tried to recover from Bill's verbal attack, he had succeeded in only a small way; yes he had reached DCI, but there was still a nagging feeling that he should have been a Superintendent by now and maybe his colour had held him back. Yet there had been nothing he could put his finger on; no overt racialism he could point to, just a feeling he had.

Shaking off his depressing thoughts he gingerly poked his head around the lounge door to see Alice holding Bill, stroking his hair and murmuring soothing words to him. Bill was crying. He decided to leave them to it.

Chapter 5

The shuffle rewarded Thomas with Peter Cincotti's On the Moon as he drove towards Campbell Square station the following morning. This raised Thomas's spirits because he was fast approaching his record for what he considered sensible strings of song titles selected by the shuffle. On The Moon allowed a continuance of Comfortably Numb having been to see The Emperor at the Freaker's Ball in Telegraph Road, and now On The Moon. In his fantasy world of song titles there was no reason why Telegraph Road couldn't be On The Moon; the Moon had to have roads didn't it? Sure it did, he convinced himself; they just hadn't been discovered yet; sensible strings didn't need sensible logic. That made five titles. His record was eight and he couldn't wait to hear what the shuffle would select next.

The rush hour traffic was remarkably light and he was trying to remember whether the schools were out as he pulled into the car park at the side of Campbell Square station.

The station was owned by the local council and leased to the police. Built on the western perimeter of the eighteenth century prison, it was opened in 1941 and until 1960 when Mereway station had opened the two storeys building had been the hub of police activities in Northampton. Now it shared first place with Mereway. From the outside it was a dour greying faceless blot on the Northampton landscape, and from the inside it was tired, foul smelling, and unwelcoming, but it had one redeeming feature; it stood next door to the local magistrates' court and was therefore handy for the swift execution of justice.

Thomas walked upstairs to his office where Detective Inspector Grey was reading her notes while she waited for him. As he hung up his jacket he smiled inwardly at Grey's figure hugging Clara Power Suit in pinstripe grey. Can't blame her for trying, he thought, but when you're built like a prop forward you shouldn't try to squeeze into a scrum-half's outfit.

'Morning DI Grey.' He said with a smile.

'Morning sir.' Sheila Grey replied, standing.

'Take a seat.' He said motioning her to the chair. 'What have we got?'

Grey organised her thoughts as she sat back down. 'Well sir, uniforms have completed house to house. Two witnesses, conflicting in some ways I'm afraid. The first is a woman who lives directly opposite. She's about sixty and says she was bringing her milk in at around ten when she spotted a mid twenties male in a dark jacket and trousers, cap and white trainers walk up the street and knock on the door. She thought nothing of it, closed her door and didn't see anything else. The second, also a woman but much younger, lives two doors up from the other witness and swears she saw someone at just after ten o clock walk down the street and knock on the door. Similar description in some ways; male she thinks, average height, dark clothing, baseball cap; but this witness thinks the person was about forty years old.'

'Alan Reed is in his twenties; he could have been the one seen walking up the street. Mind you if he did knock on the door he obviously thought she was still alive.' Thomas reminded her, sounding disappointed.

'Yes sir, but our witness says she didn't recognise who it was. She was pulling her curtains and just happened to see somebody. Again she didn't take a lot of notice and didn't see anyone leave.'

'What about the staff at Threshers?'

'The check-out girl knows Alan Reed and says she remembers seeing him in the shop sometime during the morning but she can't be sure of the exact time. However, we checked her till roll between ten and ten thirty, and there's a purchase of The Sun and twenty Bensons at 10.07a.m. She says that is what Reed normally buys.'

'Hmm, that would fit in with what he told me. He said he left the house, went to Threshers and bought a paper and some cigarettes. Cash or card?'

'Cash sir I'm afraid.' Grey told him, regret in her voice. She knew that a card payment could easily be traced back to the purchaser. 'As I say, he is a regular but the cashier can't be certain exactly when she saw him.'

'Nevertheless she says she did see him and the items purchased match what he told me. How did she say he looked?'

'She didn't notice anything unusual sir. I specifically asked her about his appearance, but she said he sounded his usual self, and there was nothing that caught her attention.'

'Hmph.' He said, sounding disappointed again. 'Have we got the search organised?'

'Yes sir, it began earlier this morning; nothing has turned up yet.'

'OK, what about the CCTV images?'

'BCC are beginning to look at them now sir; they could be significant if we can narrow down the exact time of death.'

'They could indeed; anyway let's hope so. I'm still waiting for the post-mortem report; we should have it later today, but I doubt there will be much new in it. I don't think the time of death will change much either from what the M.E. told me at the scene; the body was still warm so I think her initial stab will turn out to be fairly accurate. What about personal effects?'

Grey ignored his unintentional pun and consulted her notes. 'Mobile phone sir, we have a list of contacts from it, bank statements, the normal house bills, and a computer she shares with her husband. So far we've found nothing out of the ordinary.'

'When did they marry?'

Grey looked at her notes again. 'Two years ago. She was twenty two years old and he was twenty five according to the certificate. Talking to the neighbours they were quite a fiery couple, lots of noise and arguments, some long into the night. It seems they have lived there since they were married.'

'Twenty two's young to get married. Did the neighbours notice any boyfriends or girlfriends?'

'No sir but from the reaction we've got from the house to house they're not a very observant lot.'

'That's the trouble nowadays; people don't even know their own next door neighbours. You could be dead for a fortnight and nobody would notice until you started to stink. Anything else?'

'Not yet sir but we're still asking around plus we've put out the usual appeals on the radio and in the press.' Grey said putting down her note book.

Thomas sighed. 'Then we have to wait. Let's hope either the CCTV, Forensics, or the M.E. will give us a break but I think our best chance of a quick result will be if we can get Reed to confess. It just beggars belief to me that someone would have turned up and murdered her in exactly that twenty minute slot when he says he was out of the house. No, far more likely is that he did her first, then calmly went out, disposed of the weapon and bought his paper to cover his tracks. So far he's been very resilient, but I've had him in the cells overnight so maybe we'll have better luck this morning. I think we'll start with him then go and see your two witnesses. What are you planning?'

Grey was surprised and disappointed at his question; surprised because he was normally so assertive and methodical and for Thomas to ask her what she was planning next was a first; it was as if *he* didn't know what to do next. Disappointed because she badly wanted to be at the centre of this investigation and she felt that Thomas was sidelining her. She understood they needed to work as a team, split their efforts, not duplicate them, but she wanted to spend as much time with him as she could so that she could learn from him. After all, he had a wealth of experience in murder investigations and he came from the MET with one hell of a reputation.

She took a deep breath, trying to sound enthusiastic. 'We need to go through the CCTV sir; I thought I'd oversee that and then talk to her friends.'

'Good; yes that will become important.' He said then hesitated, weighing things up in his mind. 'But I think we need first to speak to Reed. You have some background information and this morning I think I'll change tack a little. If he did kill her in a rage something must have triggered it so I'll try to get him to admit what that was. First I think we need to build a picture of his relationship with his wife and in doing so try to establish whether there was anything bubbling under the surface that suddenly boiled over yesterday morning. Will you have time to join me?'

Grey tried to contain her excitement, apologising to him silently for misjudging him. 'Yes sir, I think so.'

'OK, let's get him up then.' He said, standing up out of his chair. At least Grey had covered everything he'd asked her to without fuss and she had not gone over the top with any wild theories, he said to himself. Grey was inexperienced when it came to murder and this would be an opportunity for her to learn the importance of team work and the adoption of a calm and methodical approach. In his time he had met many young promising DI's who had gone completely overboard when faced with a case of murder. Some of them had forgotten everything they had ever learned about investigative techniques; others had ruined promising careers after suddenly turning into their own version of Columbo. But the one thing he knew from all the years he had been working on major crimes was that there were no shortcuts, no substitutes for graft. Gather the evidence first and see where it leads you. Don't work on hunches or race headlong up blind alleys. In the end slow and methodical beat fast and intuitive every time.

Grey rang the Duty Officer and they arranged to meet Reed again in the same interview room Thomas had used the day before. Reed looked tired and puffy-eyed when the Duty Sergeant brought him in. Thomas imagined he'd had little sleep; unsurprising under the circumstances, but was it through grief over the loss of his wife or a guilty conscience? Thomas was determined to find out and switched on the tapes. First he introduced DI Grey then said 'Sorry we couldn't get to you yesterday Alan,' deliberately using Reed's first name to try to put him at his ease – and off his guard. 'Things have been a little hectic as you can imagine.'

Reed stared at Thomas with steely accusatory eyes. 'Is it usual to hold the husband of a murder victim in the cells overnight without charge?' His tone was vitriolic.

Thomas was unfazed by his tone, he had half expected it. Clearly the overnight stay in the cells had unnerved Reed; he imagined he would have been on edge all night, expecting the call from him at any moment, preparing himself, dreaming up replies to anticipated questions; so ultimately it would have been a huge disappointment when he hadn't turned up. Later that disappointment would have turned to anger. He replied calmly. 'Yes, I'm afraid it is. Like it or not Alan you are a suspect; you had motive and opportunity, and you won't be released until I am satisfied you did not kill your wife.'

'I didn't kill her.' Reed repeated tiredly.

'So you said yesterday, but you will appreciate we have to eliminate you from our enquiries, and unfortunately that takes time.' Thomas pointed out reasonably.

'You could have let me go home and grieve instead of banging me up in a stinking cell and letting me worry all night about being fitted up for her murder. What did you think I was going to do, flee the country?'

'Were you?' Thomas asked.

'Give me a break.' Reed said dismissively.

'Are you sure you don't want a solicitor?'

'I have nothing to hide.'

'Ok well, shall we get on? I want to ask you about your wife and your marriage.'

Reed shrugged, hands in his pockets.

'Can you tell me how you met?'

Reed put both his hands on the table and leaned forward. 'We met about three years ago. She was a student at the college in Booth Lane studying Business Administration. I was temping there helping with new registrations. We met in the canteen and hit it off straight away. She had no self confidence; not with her studies or with men and I offered to help her with her work; I'd done some accountancy so understood a lot of what she needed to know. Shortly afterwards we started dating and we married a year last June.' Reed looked at Thomas enquiringly, waiting for the next question.

'Did she have many friends at college?'

'Not many but she had a couple of close friends she saw quite regularly.'

'So you married while she was at college?'

'That's right; things were tight but we just about managed. Manfield Road had belonged to my parents and they left it to me so we don't have a mortgage to worry about; that helped.'

'What about after she left college; did she make new friends at work?'

'She didn't work.' Reed said, seemingly uncomfortable to admit it. His body language convinced Thomas he was being evasive; his wife's work, or lack of it, and possibly her friendships were obviously things he did not want to discuss.

'She didn't work, why not?' He probed.

'Her cocaine habit got worse; she couldn't have held down a job. She was either high as a kite when she could afford a fix or asleep when she couldn't. Mostly she slept.'

'I thought you said she was just a social user.'

'Yeah, well she was more than that.'

'Feeding that kind of habit must have been expensive; how did she manage it?'

'I, I don't know.' Reed stuttered and again Thomas was sure that he was hiding something. 'Somehow we made ends meet. When I was in work things were OK.'

'Did she bother you for money often?'

'All the time,' Reed continued, sighing, 'but I didn't always have it to give her, especially when I was out of work.'

'So what did she do for her fix when you couldn't afford it?'

'I've told you, I don't know.' Reed said defensively.

Thomas decided to store this question in the back of his mind and change direction. 'Let's get back to her friends. Did you mind that she continued to see them after you began dating?' Thomas asked.

Reed seemed relieved that Thomas had moved away from asking about his wife's cocaine habit. He sat back in the chair, his hands resting on the table, looking more relaxed. 'Not at first, but as we became closer, I admit it became an issue.'

'An issue;' Thomas repeated, thinking it was a strange word to use, 'what do you mean by an issue? Did you argue about it? Were you jealous when she went out with them?'

'Possessive, I suppose. I couldn't understand why she would want to spend time with anyone other than me. If she loved me, why would she?' He seemed convinced of his own logic.

'Who was she seeing when she went out?' Thomas asked.

'She had some long standing friends from college; people like Vanessa Vokes and Mandy Singleton. They met up once or twice a week, usually together sometimes separately.'

'No male friends, of the platonic kind I mean?' Thomas persisted and noticed a momentary change of expression on Reed's face. Was it anger, he wondered? But before he could interpret it Reed had recovered, his expression blank once again. Reed shrugged his shoulders.

'Not as far as I know; I wouldn't have put up with it if she had; it was one thing letting her go out and see her female friends but I would have drawn the line if she had wanted to see blokes.' He said.

'These friends, do you know where they live?'

'No, I didn't mix with them much when we were at college and completely lost touch after we left, but Sue still saw them.'

Thomas decided to probe another avenue. 'You were temping when you met. Couldn't you find a permanent job?' Again he thought he noticed a fleeting change in Reed's expression.

'I was between jobs.' Reed replied evasively.

'What jobs? What were you doing before you worked at the college?'

'I'd been an articled clerk at Dove's the accountants.'

'How did that end?'

Reed adjusted his position in the chair, and again, to Thomas it looked like a defensive manoeuvre. 'I left.' He said.

'Left, just like that? You gave up articles with one of the towns best accountancy firms without having another job to go to? Why?' Thomas sensed there was more to it than Reed was prepared to say.

'Well not exactly. I was fired.' Reed admitted.

'Fired; on what grounds?'

'Look is this really necessary?' Reed protested. 'What does it have to do with my wife's death?'

'Alan, we are trying to form a picture of your relationship with your wife and her friendships. Doing this could well help us find her murderer. So please, why were you fired?'

Reed shrugged his shoulders again. 'I had an argument with my boss.'

'You argued; about what?'

'I don't remember; something about not respecting his authority. I didn't understand it then and I don't now.' Reed said, his tone growing louder. He was clearly uncomfortable discussing his working life.

Thomas didn't want Reed angry just yet so he let it pass. 'Ok, so how long did you temp at the college?'

'Eight months, then I found a permanent job.'

'And where was that?'

'At Dixie's, the shoe retailers; I was their book-keeper.' Reed said. 'And before you ask I was fired from there too. I would have left anyway; I couldn't stand the manageress. She was a first class bitch.' He growled truculently.

'Sounds like you have a problem with authority.' Thomas said.

'No I don't.' Reed argued, his face twisting into an angry glare. 'Authority has a problem with me.'

'How long did you last at Dixie's?'

'A few months, that's all; I knew from day one that it wouldn't last.'

'So how many jobs have you had in all?'

'I don't know, not that many, six maybe. The last one was about two months ago. I'd been a storekeeper at McCann's Automotive, but I left after a disagreement with the manager.'

'Left or was you fired?' Thomas asked, raising his eyebrows.

Reed's shoulders slumped forward. 'Alright, I was fired.' He admitted.

'And you've been on the dole ever since?'

'That's right, but even the bastards down the Job Centre don't like me. They've cut my dole saying it was my own fault I lost my job and I'm not actively seeking work. Bullshit! I write half a dozen letters a day and fill out God knows how many application forms.' Reed bawled.

'No luck?'

'Not with my record; well you can imagine, but it's unfair. I do good work and if people treat me right then I respect them but I won't take shit from anybody.' Reed said firmly.

'So let me summarise. Your wife didn't work because she had a cocaine habit which made her incapable and so she relied on you to finance it, but you couldn't hold down a job for any length of time. On top of that you were possessive of her; you resented her going out with her friends when, by your way of thinking she should have been at home looking after you. Your neighbours say they've heard you arguing late into the night Alan. Did you argue with Susan yesterday morning or the night before?'

'No'. He countered eyes meeting Thomas' warily, sensing that Thomas was about to accuse him again. He was right.

'I think you did Alan. I think you argued. I think you hated it when she went out at night without you. Did you think she had a lover; did you sit at home while she was out wondering where she was, who she was really seeing? Did she tell you how useless you were, how you couldn't hold down a job? Was she desperate for another fix? Did she keep on and on, demand money from you, call you inadequate when you couldn't give her any, goad you, dare you to prove you were a man? Did that make you angry? It did, didn't it? She wouldn't stop even when you pleaded with her to; it was her fault, wasn't it? She got what she deserved; she wouldn't stop and you killed her didn't you?'

Reed returned Thomas' gaze, eyes pleading. 'I didn't kill her. Why won't you believe me? I didn't kill her.' He insisted.

'Alan, it wasn't your fault.' Thomas said soothingly. 'It was her fault. She made you do it. She was telling you how useless she thought you were; how you were not really a man because you couldn't finance her habit, and she was out seeing other blokes. No man would take that from a woman. I understand Alan, really I do. It wasn't your fault.'

'I didn't kill her. None of what you're saying is true.'

'Alan, I told you about the forensics didn't I?'

'Yes.'

'Well I ask you again; what do you expect us to find when we examine the fibres from your clothes and try to match them to the fibres we found on your wife's body? We both know we'll find a match don't we. Why deny it?'

At that moment Reed did something that jolted Thomas and almost stopped him dead in his tracks. He stopped crying, wiped his eyes and sat back in the chair fixing Thomas with a cool stare. 'You'll find nothing Mr. Thomas; absolutely nothing; because as I've already told you I did not kill my wife.' It was as if he had forgotten about the forensic evidence or lack of it until that moment, but now that Thomas had mentioned it again, he had suddenly found some inner confidence.

Thomas took a second to recover his composure. The way Reed had made his denial had been absolutely convincing, but Thomas had been fooled before. 'What did you do with the weapon Alan?'

'What weapon? You're not listening to me. I didn't kill her.'

Thomas gave him a disdainful look. 'Alan I know you did it so let's stop playing games. Now where did you hide it? Was it a Stanley-knife?'

Reed covered his eyes with his hands in frustration. 'Oh God, this is a nightmare. I've told you I didn't kill her! I want a solicitor. I think I should have a solicitor here with me right now.'

'Where did you hide it Alan?' Thomas tried one last time, but Reed seemed not to hear. Thomas sighed, recorded the time, and switched off the tape. He had to accede to Reed's request immediately or risk prejudicing a case against him in the future.

He was disappointed he had been unable to break him down and still a little shaken at his show of confidence when he'd threatened him with forensics. He arranged to have Reed escorted back to the Duty desk where he could telephone his solicitor or have one allocated to him and Grey and Thomas were left alone together in the interview room.

'Impressions?' he asked.

'Well he became defensive when you hit on his work record and his wife's college friends. Plus he didn't like it when you touched on her cocaine addiction. There's obviously something there he's not telling us and we'll have to work on it to get it out of him. Yet he seemed absolutely sure we would find nothing from forensics, and he denied killing his wife. I don't think he'll crack sir unless we can face him down with evidence.'

'Hmm, me neither.' Thomas agreed reluctantly, showing his disappointment. 'One thing that bothers me is the weapon.'

'Where he disposed of it?' Grey asked.

'Not only where he might have disposed of it, but where he could have got it from.' He explained. 'If he did kill her I don't think he had planned to do it; no, it's more likely he killed her in a fit of rage. So if we assume for the moment that he lost control and then slit her, he would have needed either to already have the weapon in his hand or very close by where he could've grabbed hold of it quickly, otherwise I suspect he would have had time to have cooled down and he'd have pulled himself together. But she was attacked in the hallway and there was nowhere obvious in there for a weapon to have been handily placed, so unless he had already been holding it he would have had to have gone and fetched one before he did her. Now the most likely places to find one were the lounge or kitchen; so to believe that theory we have to imagine that they had an argument of some kind, he lost his temper, went into the kitchen or lounge, took hold of the weapon, returned back into the hallway, and then slit her throat. That somehow doesn't quite fit.'

'He *could* have been already holding it sir; maybe he was going to use it for something else before they started to argue.' Grey suggested.

'Hmm, maybe; anyway' He sighed, 'let's pay your witnesses a visit shall we?'

Chapter 6

Thomas and Grey drove back to Manfield Road in Grey's Vauxhall Astra. As Grey concentrated on weaving her way through the late morning traffic, Thomas reflected on the progress they had made so far.

In some ways he was disappointed but he felt comforted that they did at least have the CCTV forensics and M.E. report to move onto if Reed did not admit to the crime. But the more he thought about Reed, the more uneasy he felt. On the one hand he was the obvious suspect; he had motive and opportunity; he was jealous of his wife and probably had a very low self-esteem because of his inability to hold down a job, and his wife would have made him feel worse when they argued. Thomas could imagine how vicious her drug-fuelled vitriol would have been when she railed at him because he couldn't finance her addiction. Drug addicts had scant regard for sensitivities when they couldn't get what they wanted, and judging by the marks on Susan Reed's wrists, she had been a heavy user. He was sure she had been an addict and finding her supplier might yet prove to be important to the investigation.

On the other hand Reed had been confident, almost arrogant, when threatened with forensics, and he had protested his innocence time and time again. Plus the business with the knife bothered him. If Reed had done her in a fit of pique, then it didn't make much sense that he'd taken the time to go and find the weapon and then wait for an opportunity to jump her from behind. Grey might have been right, he might have already had the weapon in his hand, but somehow he doubted it; it didn't quite feel right.

Then there was the lack of defensive wounds. If the pathologist had found cuts and bruises on her wrists or forearms then that might well have pointed towards a frontal attack carried out in a fit of rage, but an attack from the rear was a coward's way; the sort of method a professional might use.

Take it slowly and methodically, he reminded himself; don't get carried away with theories; let the evidence lead you.

Grey parked the Astra at the bottom of Manfield Road and they walked up the street together and knocked on the door of the first witness, Mrs. Elsie Stephens, who lived opposite the Reeds' house.

Mrs. Stephens answered the door by opening it a few inches which was as wide as her security chain would allow, and peering around it. Thomas showed her his card and she undid the chain with a rattle and let them both in.

She led them into her lounge, a triumph of floral opulence that took Thomas' breath away. Fresh carnations and pinks adorned a mahogany drop leaf table that stood in the centre of the room; another arrangement, this one in purple and yellow tulips was the centre-piece of the window looking out over the back garden, and the walls were papered with climbing red roses on deep green stems. The sun beamed through the window onto the sofa, vibrant in purple dendrobium orchids. Thomas was almost dazzled and his eyes were grateful when they looked down to see the carpet was plain ivory.

'Would you like some tea? Mrs. Stephens asked.

'Mm, that would be nice.' Thomas said. 'No sugar for me.'

'Thanks, yes please.' Grey said. 'Two sugars for me.'

'I'll just go and make it then.' Mrs. Stephens said heading for the kitchen.

She returned carrying a tray and Thomas and Grey took their cups and sat down on the sofa. Mrs. Stephens set the tray down on the mahogany table and sat in an easy chair by the side of the TV.

To Thomas she looked as though she was in her mid-sixties. She was dressed in a floral dress with pink carnations against a pale blue background, and blue carpet slippers decorated with red roses. *'What else?'* Thomas asked himself.

'Sorry to bother you again Mrs. Stephens', He said. 'We just need to go over the statement you gave earlier to the constable.'

'Oh I do hope there's not a problem with it officer.' Mrs. Stephens said, blushing slightly. 'You see I'm afraid I wasn't taking that much notice at the time. I didn't realise you see…'

'No, no problem at all.' He interrupted. 'There are just a couple of things we need to get clear in our minds, that's all.'

Mrs. Stephens seemed relieved. 'Oh, well then, that's good.' She said and took a sip of her tea before setting her cup back on the table.

'You said you were bringing the milk in when you noticed someone approach the house where Mrs. Reed lived and you saw that person knock on the door?' He asked.

'Yes that's right. The milkman had been late you see and I had telephoned the dairy to enquire where he was, but then I heard him arrive and went out a few minutes later.' Mrs. Stephens explained.

'Can you remember what time that was? It would help us immensely if you could.'

Mrs. Stephens furrowed her brow. 'Let me see. I telephoned the dairy when the news was on the radio and I heard the milkman almost immediately after I put the telephone down, so I think it must have been a few minutes after ten.'

'Are you sure?'

'Yes I think I am. I remember the news and I'm quite certain that the milkman arrived almost immediately.'

'And can you remember whether the person you saw approached from the bottom of the street or the top?' Thomas asked.

'Oh he definitely approached from the bottom. I remember seeing him walk towards the gate and turn left into the path. I went back inside then.'

'You didn't see whether he went inside?' He probed.

'No I'm afraid I didn't.' Mrs. Stephens said sounding quite certain.

'Can you describe the person you saw, what he was wearing his age and height?'

'Not very well I'm afraid. My eyes are not that good you see and I only got a very brief look at him. I would have said he was about twenty five years old wearing a dark jacket, navy I think, and dark trousers. He was wearing one of those baseball caps that all young people seem to wear nowadays, I can't think why, they are dreadful things. Anyway he was wearing white shoes, trainers I think they're called.' Mrs. Stephens paused for a few seconds thinking, her hand to her mouth. 'Oh, and you asked about his height. I think he was about average height for a man.'

'Did you notice the colour of his hair?' Thomas asked.

Mrs. Stephens picked up her cup and took another sip of her tea. 'Dark I think, and quite long, below the neck.'

'Did you see anyone else around at that time?'

'No I'm afraid not.'

'What about Mr. Reed, did you happen to see him?'

'No and I'm sure I would have noticed if I had.'

'Did you know Mrs. Reed at all? Did you ever speak to her?'

'Not really officer; we would pass the time of day if we met in the street but nothing more than that.'

'Did you notice much activity around the house, people coming and going, that sort of thing?'

Mrs. Stephens looked apologetic. 'No I'm afraid I didn't.'

'Can you think of anything else that might help us; anything at all?' Thomas asked bringing the interview to a close.

Mrs. Stephens thought for a few seconds. 'No, nothing.' She smiled nervously. 'I'm sorry I haven't been much help, have I?' She said.

He stood up and smiled at her. 'On the contrary Mrs. Stephens, you've been a great help. Thank you for your time.' He said and handed her one of his cards. 'If you do happen to think of anything please call the number on the card.'

'Oh, yes, I will.' Mrs Stephens said and stood up from her chair to show them out.

Outside Thomas said to Grey 'Interesting; she is fairly certain of the time, a few minutes after ten, and she seemed fairly sure that she saw someone in his mid-twenties.'

'Yes,' DI Grey said 'but she also said her eyes were not that good, so she could be mistaken.'

'True' He said and sighed, 'where next?'

'Just up here' Grey said heading up the street and opening the gate of a house two doors up from Mrs. Stephens. Thomas followed her and stood behind her as she rang the front-door bell.

'I think you can do this one.' He said.

A tall good looking blonde woman in her late thirties dressed in a red blouse and charcoal slacks opened the door. Thomas and Grey introduced themselves and the woman showed them inside to a very modern lounge in white and smoked glass. No TV Thomas noticed, just a very expensive looking Alphason Symphony turntable and stereo system tucked in one corner and some abstract canvas prints on the walls; one Thomas recognised was a rolling swirl of energy called Chococream Tornado. Heavy full-length cream curtains hung either side of the window overlooking the rear garden. Compared to Mrs. Stephen's décor, this might have been from a different century. Thomas and Grey sat down on the white leather sofa and Miss Clare Trussler sat opposite them on a matching arm-chair.

'Sorry to trouble you again Miss. Trussler,' Grey began, 'we need to go over your earlier statement if you don't mind.' She said. *'Or even if you do.'* Thomas thought silently.

'No problem.' Trussler said.

'Ok, good; can you go over again how you came to see the person approach Mrs. Reed's house yesterday morning?'

'Yes, it was quite simple. Let's see, I had finished breakfast and was drawing my curtains when I noticed someone walk down the street and knock on the Reed's front door. That's all I know.' She said.

Thomas noticed that Trussler had not offered them a drink yet; he wasn't thirsty but he had hoped she might make the effort.

'Can you think back and try to pinpoint what time this was?' Grey asked.

'I'm certain now it was ten past ten. The reason I know is because I would have carried on looking up and down the street, I'm naturally nosey you see, but my mobile phone went off and I went to answer it; it was in the kitchen so I turned away from the window when I heard it. After your officer came to see me yesterday I checked the time of the call.'

Grey took a deep breath. This could be very significant information, so she pressed Miss Trussler. 'Are you absolutely sure of the time? Could you perhaps have delayed answering the phone?'

'I'm absolutely certain.' Clare Trussler said firmly. 'I didn't delay at all. As I said I stopped being nosey to answer it.' She laughed self consciously.

DI Grey smiled. 'OK, can you describe the person you saw?'

'I've been thinking about that too.' She said pensively, 'I think average height, say about five ten, dark jacket and trousers, light shoes, and a baseball cap; age about forty.'

'Are you sure about the age, could he have been younger?' Grey probed.

Thomas groaned inwardly. *'Don't lead her Grey, let her tell her story.'* He said to himself.

'Fairly sure; I did get quite a good look and as I said, I'm naturally nosey.'

'You say the shoes were light coloured. Could they have been trainers?' Grey asked. Thomas felt like giving her a swift kick on the shins.

'I don't think so; no I don't think they were. They looked like casual shoes to me.'

'Did you notice what colour hair the person had?'

'Fair and quite thick as I recall.'

'And did you see this person leave the house?'

'No I'm afraid I didn't; I was busy on the telephone for some time and to be honest didn't give it another thought at the time.'

'Did you see him enter the house?'

'No, as I said I went into the kitchen to answer the phone.'

'Did you notice anyone else in the street at the time?'

'No I didn't but I think I would have if anyone had been around at the time.'

'Did you know the Reeds?'

'Not well; I work most days and don't see much of my neighbours. Sometimes we would say hello if we passed each other in the street but that's about it.'

'You say you're naturally nosey; did you notice other people coming and going from their house?'

Clare Trussler gave Grey a knowing look. 'Oh yes, especially when Alan was out. She would turn up with any number of men.' She nodded to giver her information more emphasis.

'Can you describe them?'

'Not really although one I remember was a Rastafarian.'

'Would you recognise him if you saw him again?'

'Maybe but they all look alike don't you think?' Thomas decided to ignor the racial slur.

'Did you ever hear them arguing?'

'Oh yes, often, even from here. I've thought about telling them to keep the noise down on more than one occasion.'

'Could you make out what they were arguing about?'

'No not in detail.'

'Can you think of anything else that might help us?'

'No, I'm sorry; I can't; as I said I went into the kitchen at the back of the house so I wasn't looking in the street.'

'Well thanks anyway, you've been a great help. Here's my card; if you do think of anything else please give me a call.' Grey stood up and handed it to Miss Trussler. She examined it before showing Thomas and Grey out.

Outside in the street Thomas said. 'DI Grey, do try to keep your questions open, don't lead.'

Grey looked crestfallen. 'Yes sir, sorry sir.'

'Other than that, you did well.' He said smiling.

Grey's expression brightened immediately. 'Thank you sir.' She said.

'Let's go back to the station and go over what we've just heard. Hopefully there'll be a call from the M.E. and maybe some news from the CCTV boys.' He said as they were walking down Manfield Road on their way back to Grey's car.

Grey unlocked her Astra and buckled up. Thomas sat beside her and she switched on the ignition and indicated to pull out into the afternoon traffic trying hard to concentrate on her driving while inwardly fuming. She felt as though she was back at school with Thomas her teacher. She didn't take kindly to being treated like some first year pupil. She accepted that she could learn a lot from him, but sometimes he came across as just plain condescending and she didn't like that one bit.

And it wasn't as if she was a complete greenhorn; she'd been in the force for twenty years and had been promoted through the ranks on her own ability. Plus she had all the qualifications necessary to go further and unlike many she could think of, the drive and ambition to make sure she did.

The fact that Thomas had acted as though he was doing her a favour by letting her conduct the interview with Clare Trussler spoke volumes about his attitude towards her. Somehow she needed to get through to him that she was not some wet-behind-the-ears schoolgirl; she was a capable, experienced officer. OK, admittedly not experienced in murder enquiries, but quite capable of conducting what amounted to follow ups from house-to-house enquiries with little old ladies and bleached blonde yuppies, thank you very much!

A black VW Golf braked suddenly in front of her and she stamped on the brake causing the Astra to shudder to an abrupt juddering stop. Thomas shot forward until his seat-belt kicked in and he whiplashed back into his seat. 'Jesus Christ!' Grey cursed. Thomas gave her a mildly inquisitive look, raising one eyebrow. 'Sorry sir' she said her face red and temper at boiling point inside.

The journey to the station went without further incident and they made their way up to Thomas' office. 'Make yourself comfortable DI Grey.' He said, hanging up his jacket. He sat opposite her and began.

'So let's go through our new timeline shall we? What do you make of it now that we've talked to Mrs. Stephens and Miss Trussler?'

Grey took a moment to gather her thoughts then began. 'Well sir, Reed said he left the house at around ten. If the till receipt for the cigarettes and paper at Threshers belongs to him, then he was in there at seven minutes past. That would fit in with when he said he left the house because it takes about five minutes to walk from Reed's house to the shop. Mrs. Stephens said she saw someone in his mid-twenties knock on the Reed's door just after ten, and significantly, Clare Trussler seemed certain she saw someone in his forties knock on the door at ten past ten. She was certain of the exact time.'

Thomas was frowning as if in deep thought. 'She was wasn't she? So, if we assume for the moment that she was dead by ten twenty two when Alan Reed called the ambulance, and if, for the moment, we believe his story and he left her alive, went to Threshers, bought his paper and cigarettes, and walked straight back, then he would have arrived back home very shortly after ten past ten when Miss Trussler saw the second visitor arrive.'

'Let's say he would have arrived home at around ten fifteen. Again, if we believe him and Susan Reed was already dead when he arrived home, then that leaves only about a fifteen minute window for the murderer to have slit her throat and escaped. Of course there could have been two of them, both visitors, acting together; she might already have been dead when the second one arrived, or she might have let the second one in while the other one was still there and then they both killed her. Somehow I don't like that theory. No I think she was killed by one person. So it's either Reed, and I think he's favourite, or the first or second visitor.' He said.

Grey had a puzzled look on her face when she said. 'What troubles me is that Reed said he didn't pass anyone.

Mrs. Stephens said the first visitor, a young man in his twenties, approached the house from the bottom of the street. Assuming that this person left shortly afterwards, why didn't Reed pass him on his way back from the shop?'

'Maybe he left in the opposite direction.' He said shrugging his shoulders. 'Unlikely I grant you, but possible.'

They were both silent for a few minutes gathering their thoughts. Suddenly Thomas got up from his chair and said

'I'm going to see the M.E. Would you interview Reed again and find out exactly what he bought from Threshers? Was there a receipt in his belongings or does he know where it is? Question him again on whether he saw anybody on the way back from the shop. Then go to the college and try to track down some of Susan Reed's friends. We need to talk to them. I have a feeling this one still has a way to run.'

Grey suddenly felt needed and important again. Damn the man, one minute he's treating me like some school-kid, the next letting me almost lead the investigation. I can't fathom him. She was picking up the phone to call the Duty Sergeant as Thomas went out the door.

Chapter 7

Jane Edwards had an office in the Coroner's building along the Wellingborough Road close to the bottom of Manfield Road, about a mile from Campbell Square Station. Thomas decided to walk there. He wanted to clear his head and think and he did that best either when walking or sitting in the grounds of St.Andrew's.

When he stepped out into the mid-afternoon sunshine stray thoughts were buzzing around in his mind like lost bees searching for a nourishing flower. One concerned Alan Reed. Why was he so uncomfortable talking about his wife's friends and her cocaine habit, and was he really ashamed about not having a job? Surely there was more to it then embarrassment; he didn't strike Thomas as being very easily embarrassed. No, Thomas was convinced he was hiding something important to the investigation.

Another was the puzzling chronology. To believe Reed then one or more people killed his wife in the fifteen minutes between ten o' clock and ten fifteen. Two independent witnesses, both seemingly reliable in Thomas' judgement, saw two different people approach the Reed's house and knock on the door; the first, a young man in his twenties just after ten, the second a man in his forties at ten past ten. Nobody saw either one enter or leave. Reed had arrived back home at around ten fifteen and had called the ambulance at ten twenty two. When he had arrived his wife was dead and nobody else was in the house. It almost beggared belief.

It was easier to believe that the Reeds had argued and Alan had either picked up a knife or was already holding one, and cut his wife's throat. Then he'd disposed of the weapon on the way to Threshers. But against that theory was the method of killing. Most domestic murders are either strangulation or a frenzied attack from the front with a knife or blunt instrument. Edwards had said Susan Reed had been attacked from behind; there were no defence wounds. So she had been surprised by her killer. It had been a cowardly attack she had not been expecting. Not the action of an enraged husband.

Then again, to believe that Alan Reed had not killed his wife, Thomas had to believe that someone had either waited for him to go out or knocked on the door on the off-chance, was allowed in, and then attacked her. It just seemed so improbable. He shook his head; the only thing he knew for certain was that Susan Reed knew her killer.

Although coroners have been around since the twelfth century, nowadays they operate under the 1988 Coroners Act, carrying with it a statutory duty to investigate the circumstances of, amongst other things, violent deaths. In Thomas's experience most people thought the Coroner was attached to the local hospital or the police, but he knew that in fact it was a judicial post, responsible only to the Crown.

Nevertheless pathologists like Jane Edwards worked side by side with the Coroner so it made sense for her to keep an office close by. Thomas entered through the glass double doors fronting the very modern building and asked the receptionist to announce his arrival. While waiting he sat down on a red plastic chair and picked up a three month old copy of Today's Golfer. He was thumbing through it when the receptionist called him and accompanied him through a side door on the way to Jane Edwards' office.

Edwards was sitting behind her desk dressed in a white smock when he entered. She looked tired, her dark almost black hair needed brushing, and her face was drawn and pale. There were clouds under her eyes. A steaming cup of what looked like black coffee was untouched in front of her.

She leaned forward over her desk and stretched out a hand; Thomas shook it. 'Good to see you again.' She said amiably.

Thomas smiled. She could be attractive, he thought. She's young, perhaps mid-thirties, she has a good head of hair, not a bad figure, a pleasant enough face, and lovely deep brown eyes, but her vibrancy is being sucked out of her by the job. Government cuts meant long hours and not much pay and he imagined Jane Edwards carving up corpses and writing endless reports at all hours of the day and night. He noticed she was not wearing a ring. She's going to die an old maid unless she gets out fast, he decided.

Edwards lifted a manila folder off her desk and began to thumb through the papers inside. 'It's very much as I told you at the scene, little new I'm afraid. Death was from exsanguination resulting from the severed carotid and jugular. The cut was very clean and deep indicating it had been made by a sharp instrument, possibly a knife or scalpel. If it was a knife it was very sharp indeed, possibly a craft knife. Death would have occurred within a few minutes after she was slashed, and the larynx was severed so she couldn't have cried out. The direction of cut was left to right and from behind, indicating the assailant used his right hand to slash. The wound in the back was not fatal; it was fairly shallow and judging by the shape of it, it too could easily have been caused by a craft knife or something like it. Death occurred somewhere between ten and ten twenty.'

'Is it possible for you to be more precise about the time of death? In this case, it is particularly important.'

Edwards shook her head. 'Afraid not; as I'm sure you're aware DCI Thomas, trying to pinpoint time of death down to a few minutes is virtually impossible. I would say definitely no earlier than ten if that helps.'

It didn't much but he said 'Thanks' anyway.

'Nothing left in the wound that might be useful?'

Again Edwards shook her head. 'Nothing, I'm sorry.'

'Did you find any trace of cocaine abuse?' Thomas asked, knowing the answer already.

Edwards looked up from the folder and met his eyes. He could almost feel her wondering how he knew. 'As a matter of fact we did. There was swelling of the lining of the veins in the wrists and feet. Nasal membranes were also damaged and the septum was very weak. She had been a heavy user for some time, both intravenously and by intranasal snorting. Urine tests showed a trace, indicating she had probably shot up earlier in the day.'

'No sign of defence wounds?'

'None, again indicating the attack came from behind. The slash wound also bears that out. There was a tuft of hair missing from the back of her head, so it is possible her assailant grabbed her hair, pulled her head back, and slashed.' Edwards said.

Thomas remembered the hair he'd found in the hallway of Reed's house, and was glad he'd insisted that the SOCO had bagged it. He sighed dejectedly, feeling he was getting nowhere. 'Anything else?' he asked, more in hope than expectation.

'I mentioned at the scene that hair and the fibres went to forensics and no doubt they'll give you their report in due course. One thing that might help you; she had a rare blood type; AB negative. Less than one in a hundred have it. Other than that, nothing significant; I'll send you my full report later this evening.' Edwards said.

Thomas nodded. 'This type of crime, an attack from the rear, a cut throat, do you agree that it indicates that someone didn't want to fight; that it was a frenzied cowardly attack?'

Edwards shrugged. 'Could be Chief Inspector; it's difficult to reach inside the mind of a murderer but I do agree it indicates that possibility.'

Thomas nodded. 'Well anyway, thanks.' He said and headed for the door.

He walked briskly back to the station to find DI Grey waiting for him in his office.

'Reed said he bought The Sun and twenty Bensons but he didn't keep the receipt. That confirms what the check-out girl told us. He insists he saw nobody on his way back up the street, and repeated the names of Mrs. Reed's college friends he gave us earlier.' She said without preamble.

'OK, if we haven't come up with anything better by tomorrow we'll have to let him go I suppose. I'll call the CCTV team and you get over to the college; see if you can trace her friends.'

'Sir there were a few other names on the contact list on her mobile phone. Shall I try them too?'

Thomas gave her a withering look. 'Yes DI Grey; do that please.'

Grey blushed feeling ashamed she had actually let the question slip out. She hadn't meant to. 'Sir' she spluttered, hurrying out the door. *'Stupid, stupid, stupid bitch,'* she screamed inwardly.

As she walked to her car she wondered why she was trying so hard to impress Thomas. Ok, he was her boss and came from the MET, plus he'd had years of experience dealing with major crimes, especially murder, but around him she was acting like an overawed schoolgirl. Why was it she felt a wave of pride wash over her every time he gave her something to do? Was it because he was so quick to put her down, as he had a few minutes ago, and giving her something to do was a sign of approval? Was it because he might be her ticket to a DCI? By the time she reached her car she was no nearer finding an answer. All she had decided was that she must do better.

Chapter 8

Thomas enthusiastically supported the use of CCTV to help solve crimes. In his experience Police Forces that had deployed CCTV systems, had invariably been able to improve their detection of public order offences, theft, and burglary. It helped them to react quickly to developing situations, prevent incidents escalating, and it helped senior officers decide how to deploy manpower most efficiently, thus saving money without risking a fall in standards. Police funding was not high up in the thoughts of police men and women at constable level, but further up the ranks it became increasingly important. He had seen many a difficult operation pulled at the last minute and substituted with something easier with more guarantee of success when budgets were tight, and in his book anything that prevented that from happening was worthwhile.

So in many ways he couldn't understand why the public attitude towards CCTV was so mixed. He had shaken his head in bewilderment when he had read the 2005 Home Office survey that showed that people felt safer in areas where they knew CCTV had been deployed; they were fearful of becoming victims of physical violence, especially around town centres and some 'no go' areas, but they felt much safer if they knew that CCTV was being monitored by the Police. He empathised with people who held that view but he couldn't see why on the other hand one in six people found it overly intrusive. Civil liberty groups banged the big brother drum, and motorists in particular saw it as just another stealth tax. But he would ask how could people expect the police to monitor criminal activity if they didn't watch what was going on? And if motorists weren't breaking the law what did they have to fear?

There was a huge variety of systems in use; they were by no means all the same. In fact they varied enormously; some were analogue tape, some digital, some privately owned systems were incompatible with police software, and the playback quality of others was so poor as to render them useless. To be useful to the police the images captured needed to be clear enough to identify a vehicle number-plate, or a person's face. Other common problems he had encountered included images stored in systems failing to transfer clearly to a printer, inaccurate date and time prints, and private businesses failing to store their data efficiently or for long enough.

Despite all of that he was hopeful that CCTV might help solve the Reed murder. It might be useful when it came to identifying suspects, and proving or disproving alibis. Assuming for the moment that Alan Reed had not killed his wife, he guessed that whoever had killed her had approached Manfield Road from either Wellingborough Road at the bottom, or Wantage Road at the top, and he was hoping that CCTV had captured images of whoever had either driven or walked into Manfield Road at around the time of her death. Hopefully the images would be sharp enough to pick out a face or number plate. He also hoped it would help him prove, one way or another, whether Alan Reed had visited Threshers that morning.

Northampton had first introduced CCTV in 1989 to monitor car crime in car parks, but with money provided by the borough and county councils, deployment of CCTV had quickly expanded to cover the town centre, Greyfriars shopping centre and the bus station. Now there were almost five hundred cameras in everyday use and images from all of the publicly funded cameras were transmitted back to the County Control Room by fibre optic cable where trained operators could zoom in to any particular incident at the touch of a computer screen.

In 2001 the police had installed auBillatic number plate recognition (ANPR) software which amongst other things could alert the Police National Computer when a suspect vehicle was spotted allowing a response team to be despatched within seconds to apprehend the driver.

Thomas needed both the CCTV and ANPR systems to help him with the Reed enquiry. He had dialled the extension for the CCTV team working on the Reed enquiry, and was waiting for them to answer, fingers crossed that the CCTV images they were analysing would provide the breakthrough he felt he badly needed.

'BCC Safety, Mike Smith.' A voice answered. The CCTV team came under the Borough Council Community Safety department.

'Hi, this is DCI Thomas, Campbell Square. I'm following up on the CCTV evidence in the Reed case.'

Smith laughed ruefully. 'Yes well DCI Thomas, we're working through the images now, but I have to tell you it's going to be a slow and painful business.'

Thomas groaned inwardly. 'Oh, why's that?' He asked.

'Well, for a start, we've tracked a timeline from 9.50 a.m. through until 10.30 a.m. as you requested but there were over thirty vehicles a minute passing along the Wellingborough Road close to the bottom of Manfield Road, and just under thirty a minute passing along Wantage Road. So all in all, let's say sixty vehicles a minute over a forty minute period, that's two thousand four hundred vehicles.'

'For the moment, I'd like to concentrate only on those that turned into Manfield Road.' Thomas said, expecting that to reduce the numbers drastically.

'There's the problem', said Smith, 'we can't see whether they turned into Manfield Road or not; the system doesn't track them that far.'

'Oh Christ,' Thomas cursed out loud.

'The good news is' said Smith cheerfully, 'we will be able to give you a list of registered owners fairly quickly. We're feeding them into the National Database as we speak, so it shouldn't take much longer.'

'What about pedestrians?' Thomas asked, fearing already what Smith was going to say.

'Well, Wellingborough Road is very busy but Wantage Road not so busy. Again we can't see people turning into Manfield Road. There are about eight hundred images that we're downloading now from Wellingborough Road, and about fifty from Wantage Road. Unfortunately these will take a day or two to process and print, but I'll send you the file as soon as I can.'

'Can you see people going into and out of Threshers on the corner of Manfield Road?' Thomas asked.

'Afraid not.' Smith said.

'Damn.' Thomas cursed bitterly disappointed. 'Still thanks anyway; look forward to seeing the report when it's ready.'

Chapter 9

Sheila Grey steered her Astra into the Booth Lane College car park and headed for reception. Home to a thousand lecturers and thirteen thousand students, it was a modern looking building, constructed in the late nineteen sixties; all red brick and clear glass it sprawled over 21,000 square metres.

Grey showed her card to one of four receptionists and asked to see someone from Student Administration. After a short wait a tall mid-forties man with salt and pepper hair wearing pale corduroy trousers and a blue lumberjack shirt introduced himself.

'Hello,' he said offering his hand, 'I'm Chris Atherley, Student Administration.'

Grey couldn't help noticing his piercing blue eyes as he introduced himself; they gave her goose bumps. Under his shirt she imagined he would be all muscle. Flustered she shook his hand noticing it felt warm against her own. 'Detective Inspector Grey' she said and smiled. 'I wonder if you could spare me a few minutes.'

'Yes of course, would you like to come through?' Atherley said.

Grey followed him past reception into a long narrow corridor flanked by pale blue plastic vanity boards with glass tops. Watching him from behind she couldn't help but admire the way he walked, kind of languid and rhythmic.

Atherley led her into a corner of a huge open-plan office and offered her a chair. Grey sat down, noticing he wasn't wearing a ring, and he sat beside her. 'So, what can I do for you?' He asked, smiling.

Grey liked his smile. She pushed a stray piece of hair away from her forehead. 'We are investigating the murder of

Susan Reed. You might have seen last night's headlines in the Chronicle & Echo.' She said.

'Ah, yes, I did.'

'Well information has come to light that suggests she might have once been a student here.'

'Oh, right.' He said 'Well I can check that easily enough. In fact I'm fairly sure she was. I did read the article and the photograph in the paper looked vaguely familiar.' Atherley turned towards his computer and began tapping away on the keyboard. After only a few seconds he turned back towards Grey, beaming. 'There we are, Susan Reed, enrolled just over three years ago and left six months ago with a Diploma in Business Administration. Not great grades, I see; lived in Manfield Road when she left, next of kin Alan Reed.'

Grey said. 'Yes, that sounds like her. Can you tell me anything about her?' She asked.

'Only what I've just read out from the record I'm afraid.' Atherley said pensively. 'Her main lecturer was Colin Fullthorpe; maybe he could help you.'

'Do you know how I could contact him?'

'Oh yes, I'll give you his home telephone number or, if you prefer, I could get hold of his schedule and you could arrange to see him here.'

'Both if you don't mind.' Grey said flashing him her most brilliant smile.

In her eyes it seemed to work; Atherley beamed back. 'No problem at all.' He said and began tapping away again. After a few moments he got up out of his chair and walked over to a printer. He brought back two sheets of A4 containing the records of both Susan Reed and Colin Fullthorpe. He handed them over to her and smiled.

Grey looked apologetic. 'Sorry but there's more. I also need the records for Mandy Singleton, Vanessa Vokes, Bob or Robert Styles, and Louise Theroux.' She said. Styles and Theroux were names in the contact list on Susan Reed's mobile phone and Grey was guessing they had also been students at the college. The other two were also on her phone and Alan Reed had mentioned them when Thomas had interviewed him.

Atherley tapped away again for a few minutes and then printed out records for all four people. He brought them over and handed them to her. 'There you are.' He said smiling.

Grey said. 'Are any of these still at the college?'

'Actually,' He said, 'you can tell from the print outs.' He took one from her and leaned towards her, tapping the paper. She could smell his after shave, Hugo Boss, she thought. 'Here, you see. If this date field is blank then the student is still here, otherwise they left on the date inserted.'

Grey studied all four sheets; they all had dates inserted. 'Are the addresses the last known? What I mean is, are they ever updated once someone has enrolled?'

'They should be, but of course if the student fails to tell us they have moved, well then we wouldn't have a record.'

'Can you tell what they studied?'

'Yes, and again it's on the print out but I'll check for you anyway.' Atherley turned back to his computer. A few moments later he said. 'It looks like they were all in the same class.'

Grey had also been going over the papers looking for the right field. 'Yes,' she said 'so I see.'

'Is there anything else I can help you with DI Grey?' Atherley asked.

'Not just now, but many thanks, you've been a great help.' She said smiling and looking directly into his eyes. 'Here's my card in case you think of anything.'

Atherley took hold of it without taking his eyes off of her. 'Oh, thanks. It's been a pleasure.' He said.

He showed her out. They shook hands in reception, said their goodbyes and Grey headed back to her Astra, floating on air.

That evening Thomas convinced Alice to take a break from looking after Bill and go out for a meal. He thought she was looking tired and a couple of hours of relaxation talking about anything but Bill would do her good. At first she wouldn't hear of it, but after twenty minutes of negotiation he won her over and she agreed on the strict understanding they would be back home before ten. He changed into charcoal slacks and a cream shirt and Alice put on a simple knee length black dress she'd chosen from what M&S had described as their Muscat collection. He just stared in awe at her when she'd finished dressing. A quick shower, a comb through her hair, a touch of make-up, a simple dress, and even now, after all these years, she still took his breath away.

A neighbour who worked at Northampton General Hospital as a ward nurse had agreed to sit in with Bill and they set off at seven thirty for Overstone Manor where they could buy two meals for ten pounds and wash them down with a bottle of house red for an additional fiver.

Although he wanted to give Alice a break from her father he felt the need to at least broach the subject of what to do with him when his condition deteriorated and so driving on the way to Overstone he asked

'How's Bill been?'

Alice sighed. 'Not good today. I think his mood swings have been getting worse over the last couple of weeks, and he's definitely becoming more aggressive. His memory is in and out as well; this afternoon he went upstairs to go to the loo and couldn't find his way back. I was busy ironing and I didn't miss him for a few minutes, but when I did find him he was sitting on the bed crying. He had no idea where he was.'

'I've noticed his moods too, and if you say he's getting more aggressive that's worrying. Can you cope without help or shall we try to get some now?'

'I can manage for the moment. The real question is can you cope? He's my father not yours and it's not much fun for you.'

'Alice I've known Bill since I've known you and it hurts me to see him going downhill like this; if I could come up with a magic cure, I would, but his condition is a matter of fact; he's not going to recover from it and I've accepted that. But I am worried about you. You're the one who has had to sacrifice your career, and you're the one who is stuck with him alone in the house all day long. Yes I can cope because I'm out all day, but I don't think I could look after him day in day out like you do.'

Thomas knew he was treading on eggshells; it was obvious to both of them that soon Alice would not be able to handle Bill. Whether he became violent or not he would soon need twenty four hour nursing and that would be impossible for any one person no matter how much they cared. He had decided long ago that he would not allow Alice to be put in danger whatever happened; at the first sign of it he would make sure she wasn't left alone with him, but he knew that if he broached the subject of putting Bill into a home, she would react angrily. So he was relieved and more than a little surprised when she said

'Maybe we should start looking around for somewhere for him when he gets worse. I really don't think I could manage if he became violent. I don't think he would hurt me deliberately but I would hate to see him like that and have to restrain him myself. I think it would break my heart.'

'It's not certain that he will,' Thomas said, trying to keep her spirits up, but relieved that she'd voiced his greatest fear, 'but barring a miracle, he's not going to improve. It's a progressive disease and he will eventually need professional help day and night. I think at best he's simply going to become less and less capable of looking after himself.'

'He can't dress himself now.' Alice said hopelessly, pain in her voice.

'Well, we could perhaps hire some help to take the weight off of you.'

'No.' she said firmly. 'I don't want that; I'll take care of him for as long as I can.'

'I know you will,' He sighed, 'but we could maybe make some enquiries through the hospital; they must know of some good places.'

Alice said quietly. 'I suppose you're right; I'll ask when I'm next there.'

Overstone Manor was a large Mock-Tudor pub and restaurant built in the 1930's and fitted out with basic oak veneer tables and plastic chairs. Standing on the eastern edge of Overstone Great Park, home to caravaners and steam rallies, it was the kind of place where patrons chose their deserts from a fridge and sat wherever they could find a free table. If they chose the wrong one they could find themselves eating next to a bank of fruit machines and have their ears assaulted by mindless manic jingles, or by people drinking at the bar and telling the kind of raucous jokes people do when they're having a drink. Not exactly the place for an evening of intimate romance, Thomas reckoned, but the food was good and excellent value.

It was not very busy when they arrived and they quickly found a quiet table in a far corner, away from the bar and the fruit machines. Alice was sipping from a glass of cool Chablis and Thomas had a glass of Merlot in his hand, trying to unwind. Alice said. 'How's your day been?'

He let out a deep breath. 'Frustrating; it's a confusing case and I've got a feeling it's still got a way to go.'

'It sounds right up your street.' Alice said. 'You like a challenge,'

'That I do.' He admitted.

'Did you have time to read the paper?'

'No, was there something about the case?'

'Well yes there was,' Alice said, 'but I was meaning the article about that man who had defrauded Barclaycard out of two hundred thousand.'

Barclaycard's head office was in the town and it made the news quite often. Fraud wasn't the sort of thing that got Thomas' juices flowing but it was the sort of thing that would interest Alice, and he was quite happy to let her talk about it for a while just so long as it took her mind off of her father. 'No I didn't see it, but pray tell.' He said.

'It interested me because it was so simple the way he did it. He stole someone else's identity, managed to get Barclaycard to issue him with a dozen credit cards, all in different names, and went on a spending spree. Easy.' She said her face alive with excitement.

'However did he manage that? Surely they have something in place to stop that sort of thing.' He said, pleased to see Alice happy for a few moments at least.

'As I said, he stole identities.' The food arrived and Alice picked up a fork.

'I understood that but how did he manage to do it?'

'Ah well', she said pointing her fork at him, 'that turned out to be quite easy. He somehow got hold of their utility bills, perhaps he rifled through their bins, I don't know, but anyway he sent them into Barclaycard as proof of who he was when he applied for his cards.'

'But surely they would have had the genuine people's addresses on them?' Thomas asked, curious how he'd managed to get over that minor detail.

'Soon after he'd sent in his applications, he wrote in and told them he'd changed address. All of the cards went to his forwarding address, a newsagent I think it was.' Alice said.

'So are you telling me that Barclaycard accepted proof of identity in the form of a utility bill?' He asked incredulous.

'It seems that way.' Alice said, shrugging her shoulders.

'Amazing; and it didn't occur to them that they had issued a dozen cards to the same address in different names?'

'Well, if you think about it, that might not be as daft as it sounds. Imagine, for example, a block of flats. The block might be say number twenty in the street and all the post might be addressed to number twenty, but maybe the residents have a system of their own for distributing it when it gets there. In that case it wouldn't be unusual to see letters arriving for different people.'

Thomas took a bite of his steak. 'Good grief.' He murmured.

His air-raid ring tone went off and his phone vibrated in his pocket. Without thinking he lifted it out and put it to his ear. 'DCI Thomas' he said.

It was the nurse house sitting for Alice's father and she sounded upset. 'I'm sorry Mr. Thomas but I think you should come quickly. He's throwing things around the house and shouting at me. He doesn't know who I am. I'm scared; can you come now?' She cried.

'Yes of course, straight away. Keep talking to him, try to calm him down. We'll be there in ten minutes.' Thomas said. Alice had sensed trouble and was already lifting her jacket from the back of her chair.

'We need to go.' He said tightly, a mixture of anger, frustration and sadness whirling around in his stomach. He drove home as quickly as he could, Alice almost jumping out of the car before it ground to a halt in their drive. She ran to the front door and burst in, Thomas following quickly behind.

Bill was sitting in an easy chair sipping a cup of tea, the nurse standing by his side 'Oh Hi, Brian, Alice; have a good time?' He asked smiling.

Alice ran towards him and knelt down beside him. 'Dad' she said 'Are you alright?'

Bill shrugged his shoulders. 'Fine, thanks'

The nurse's eyes were red from crying and when Alice looked up at her she mouthed 'Sorry.'

Alice stood and took her arm. 'I'm the one who should be sorry. I really am, I had no idea it would turn out like this and I'm sorry to have put you through it.'

'Perhaps I shouldn't have panicked so quickly; shortly after I rang you he settled down and seemed to recognise me again. I made him a cup of tea and we've been chatting quite amiably for the last few minutes. Since he calmed down he's been as good as gold.'

'No, you did the right thing. He's never been this bad until now. Still, at least things have turned out alright; thank God you're not hurt. Listen, it was really good of you to come, why don't you go home and get some rest. I'll take it from here.' Alice said, leading her to the front door comforting her on the way.

Thomas could see broken glass and wet flowers scattered on the carpet where Bill had smashed a vase, and a glass panel in the lounge door had burst, a paperweight and splinters of glass on the carpet close by. He walked into the kitchen to find a dustpan and brush but stopped in his tracks when he saw the floor and worktops covered in smashed crockery, broken glass, saucepans and a frying pan. '*Bloody hell,*' he cursed in anger and frustration, '*this can't go on.*'

It took him over an hour to clean up and meanwhile Alice took Bill upstairs and undressed him ready for bed. Thomas had poured himself a large scotch by the time she joined him in the lounge.

'Can I get you one?' He asked, raising his glass.

'Yes, I think I need one.' Alice said flopping down into an easy chair. She sighed deeply. 'What are we going to do?'

'You can't be alone with him if he's going to do this sort of thing.' He said firmly, pouring her a large measure.

'I know, I know.' She said in resignation taking the scotch from him.

'I think we should arrange for someone to be here with you.'

'We can't afford that Brian; I'm not earning and day care will be horrendously expensive.'

He knew she was right; they could probably afford it for a few weeks, but not on a long term basis. Still, they had to do something, and fast.

'Let's get someone in and then see what options are open to us. Maybe the hospital staff can help.' He said encouragingly, but in his own mind he did not believe they would. He had little faith in the NHS.

'I'll call them in the morning.' Alice said.

Chapter 10

At nine the following morning DI Grey was in Thomas' office writing down all of the contact names and numbers from Susan Reed's mobile phone. She had already made a quick list but wanted to make sure she hadn't missed anyone. There was the usual 'mum' and 'Alan', plus the names Grey already had, Vanessa Vokes and Mandy Singleton whom Alan Reed had said had been friends of his wife at college, plus Bob Styles, and Louise Theroux, Colin Fullthorpe and someone called Leroy.

Colin Fullthorpe sounded familiar but she couldn't immediately place him until she suddenly remembered the name from her meeting with the gorgeous Mr. Chris Atherley yesterday. Grey smiled when she thought of him, God those eyes. She hoped he would ring so she would have an excuse to see him again.

Colin Fullthorpe had been Susan Reed's tutor at college. Now why would she have his telephone number stored in her mobile phone? Was that usual? Maybe it was but then maybe not. She'd never had the telephone number of any of her past teachers, but she had to admit to herself there had been one or two she'd have liked to have had. It would be interesting to find out why Reed had his and decided to call him first.

A male voice answered. 'Mr. Fullthorpe?' She asked.

'Yes, speaking.' Fullthorpe answered.

'I'm Detective Inspector Grey from Northampton Police; I'm investigating the death of Susan Reed. I believe she was a student of yours.'

'Susan Reed, dead? When? I didn't know; I'm very sorry to hear that.' Fullthorpe sounded completely taken aback by the news.

'I'm afraid so. She died on Monday; I need to see you and I wonder if you could spare me some time now.'

'But why are the Police involved? I'm sorry but I don't see how I could help you inspector; Mrs. Reed left college several months ago.'

'Yes I know sir, but it is important.'

'Oh well then, I suppose I could spare you a few minutes. Can you come to the college?'

'Yes no problem, I'll be there in fifteen minutes.' Grey said and hung up. She left Thomas a note saying where she would be if he needed her and headed out for her car. She drove out to the college again and parked very close to where she had the day before.

One of the receptionists showed her into Fullthorpe's room. It looked a bit like she had imagined it would. There was a teak desk scattered with sundry books and papers, a black leather faced chair and three filing cabinets. Fullthorpe was sitting behind the desk when she entered and he stood up and offered his hand.

Grey shook it and said 'Mr.Fullthorpe, I'm Detective Inspector Grey Northampton Police. We spoke on the phone.' Fullthorpe was about mid-forties, she guessed, slim, medium height, with quite long, slightly greying hair, and he was dressed in a plain blue shirt and denims. *Oldest swinger on the campus* was her immediate reaction.

Fullthorpe smiled and said, 'Please take a seat. What can I do for you?' He sat down as he finished speaking.

Grey sat opposite him. 'As I said on the telephone, I'm investigating the death of Susan Reed. According to college files she was one of your students. I'm hoping you can tell me about her; what she was like, who her friends were that kind of thing.'

Fullthorpe leaned back in his chair, rested his elbows on the arms, and steepled his hands together. 'I don't know a lot really; it was quite a long time ago. I think she joined my class about two years ago, maybe even earlier than that. I teach business administration. She was an average student as I recall, not brilliant but not dumb either. I think she scraped through in the end.'

'Do you know whether she had any friends at college?'

'Yes I remember she was quite a popular girl and I think she had many friends but probably Vanessa was closest to her, Vanessa Vokes that is. They always seemed to sit together anyway, and once or twice I saw them eating in the canteen together. Yes, I think they were quite close.'

'Anyone else come to mind?'

'Well as I said she had lots of friends; I think she was quite friendly with Robert Styles and I know she hung around some with Leroy James but I'm fairly certain that Vanessa was her closest friend.'

'Can you describe to me how things work at the college, between tutors and students, I mean?'

Fullthorpe looked a little taken aback by Grey's question but said. 'Students come to learn, we provide the means. There's very little more to it than that. I think our standards are quite high and certainly we achieve some of the best results in the country so we can't be that bad.' He smiled self-consciously. 'We insist on a certain standard, don't tolerate slackers and time wasters, but if somebody wants to learn then there's nowhere much better. Our support services are second to none.'

'By support you mean helping out students with problems, with their work for example? How would you help them, go the extra mile as it were?'

'In a variety of different ways; some get to a point where they lose confidence and feel as though they can't go on. In those cases we try to boost their egos, accentuate the positives as it were. If they get really stressed out then the college has a resident counsellor. Some reach a sticking point and we try to help them get through it. Others get bored and want to run before they can walk; those we try to rein in, get them to stick to the fundamentals.'

'How in detail do you help those who reach a sticking point?'

'Usually through out of hours support if asked.' Fullthorpe laughed ruefully. 'Most don't though unfortunately, they prefer to try to work things out for themselves.'

Grey nodded. 'I understand; can you remember if Susan Reed needed extra help?'

'Not that I can recall; why do you ask?'

'What was Susan's attendance record like?' Grey carried on, ignoring Fullthorpe's question.

'Not bad, but I recall she did spend quite a lot of time off sick towards the end of the course. Mind you that's not unusual; students can get nervous when exam time rolls around.' He smiled.

'Did she ever come to you with problems of a personal nature?'

'No she never did.' Fullthorpe said, eyeing Grey sharply. She sensed that he was becoming suspicious of where her questions might lead and was preparing to put up his defences. She wondered why. She was sure he was hiding something but unsure what. A major jump, but he did fit the description that Clare Trussler had given.

'Do you know of anyone who particularly disliked her?' Grey asked, deliberately scattering general questions amongst those pertinent to why Reed might have had his number in order to throw him off his guard. He was definitely not telling her everything.

'No, as I said she was a popular enough character as far as I could tell. I can't think of anybody who particularly disliked her.'

Grey decided to get to the point. 'When you provide out of hours support, is it here in the college or elsewhere?'

'Invariably here; anywhere else would be deemed inappropriate for obvious reasons.' Fullthorpe said.

'Why exactly?'

'Well fraternising with students is against college rules for one thing and if lecturers were to mix with students on a social basis, however innocent that might be, then they would be running a risk of getting the sack.'

'So you would never provide support anywhere other than on these premises; never at your house for example, or at a student's house?'

He began to look uncomfortable, obviously wondering why Grey was labouring this subject. 'No, never; the college has very specific rules against it as I've said.'

'Can you tell me where you were on Monday morning between ten and ten thirty?'

He suddenly appeared very flustered. 'Why; why should I tell you that?'

'Mr. Fullthorpe Susan Reed was murdered on Monday morning. Someone slit her throat; now please just answer the question.' Grey said; her voice hardening.

Fullthorpe shot up out of his chair. 'Murdered? What do you mean murdered? You didn't tell me she had been murdered.' He protested.

'Sadly I'm afraid it's true; she was killed on Monday morning sometime between ten and ten thirty.'

'And you think I had something to do with it?' He shouted.

Grey remained calm. 'Sit down Mr.Fullthorpe. Where were you between ten and ten thirty on Monday morning?' She persisted.

Fullthorpe sat down and tried to calm himself. He ran a hand back through his hair. He had begun to sweat, his upper lip and forehead glistening. 'I, I,m not sure,' he stuttered, 'I can't recall; I think I was at home.'

'Can anyone verify that?'

'Well, no I don't think so; I was alone I think. My wife was out playing golf.'

'Do you have a private mobile telephone?'

'What? Well yes. You called me on it.'

'It's not a college phone, one that you use for work?'

'No, it's my own private number.'

'Are you in the habit of giving students your private number?'

'No'. And then Fullthorpe suddenly understood where Grey's questions had been leading. 'How did you get it by the way?' he asked but already knew the answer and as the realisation sank in he began to blush and sweat began to run down his forehead and over his upper lip.

'It was stored in Susan Reed's mobile. Now why do you think that would be?' Grey asked sharply.

'I, I have no idea.' He stammered, clearly flustered, face bright red.

'So how do you think she came by it? You said yourself you don't give it out.'

Fullthorpe was trapped and sank back down into his chair. Grey noticed his hands were trembling, and his face was crimson, sweat running down both cheeks. He said. 'Inspector I have no idea.'

She decided not to press him for the time being. She was certain he knew more about Susan Reed than he was prepared to admit at the moment, but she had no evidence he had done anything criminal. Just because Susan Reed had stored his mobile number in her phone didn't mean that he'd killed her. She reasoned she might find something out about him when she spoke to Vanessa Vokes and Susan Reed's other classmates so decided she would wait until she knew more before challenging him again. *'Let him sweat on it.'* She smiled to herself.

She was walking back towards reception when she heard Chris Atherley call her name. Surprised, she turned around and saw him running towards her. She smiled and her heart leapt as he approached.

'Oh, hello again.' She said.

Atherley was mildly out of breath. 'You're here again. Come to see Fullthorpe?' He asked.

'Maybe.' She said evasively, not ready to share professional secrets with him despite finding him attractive. 'Have you thought of something else you think I should know?'

He looked embarrassed. 'Well, no actually.' He was looking at the floor as he spoke, both hands behind his back. 'I was wondering, well, if you wouldn't mind, well letting me buy you dinner one evening.'

Bingo! Grey smiled trying to keep calm and hide her excitement. 'That would be nice, yes, why not?'

Atherley beamed at her and Grey's heart missed a beat. 'Great, yes great, er when?'

'Tomorrow?' She suggested.

'Mm Tomorrow, yes, great. Wow, yes. Umm, I'll pick you up?'

Grey's heart went out to him. His shyness was new to her and she was all the more attracted to him for it. 'No, I'll meet you; how about at the Lumbertubs; eight o' clock?'

'OK, Tomorrow at eight then. Wow.'

Grey shook his hand, held it a little longer than she needed to and floated back to her car on cloud nine.

Chapter 11

'It might turn out to be a domestic sir, but at the moment we have nothing to hold him on.' Thomas was back at Campbell Square station giving Chief Superintendent Judd a progress report. 'Reed denies killing her and so far all we have against him is circumstantial evidence. CCTV has been next to useless and we're still waiting for forensics. The search team hasn't come up with any weapon yet and unless something crops up today, we will have to release him. We've-'

'Bloody expensive search team;' Judd interrupted with a growl, 'any idea how much longer they'll be out there?'

'A couple of days, I would think; there's a lot of ground to cover.' He explained.

Judd groaned. 'Oh Christ; look, the Chief is on my back, says he's getting fifty calls a day from Manfield Road residents whingeing about having the road closed. He calls me five times a day with the same bloody question. When will we be able to open the road?'

Thomas looked appropriately apologetic. 'Sorry Sir, hopefully they'll come up with something shortly.'

'What about the two witnesses?'

'Their statements are muddying the waters sir otherwise I'm sure I really would be treating it as a straightforward domestic. One says she saw someone just after ten knock on the Reed's door, the other saw someone at ten past ten also knock on the door. From the timing and descriptions, they sound like two different people. If we believe Alan Reed he was at Threshers and came back to find her dead. The till operator has a receipt for what he said he bought at seven minutes past ten. That means one or both of the two visitors probably killed her.'

Judd snorted. 'And her contacts, friends, enemies?'

'DI Grey is at the college now interviewing her tutor and we have the names of her classmates. Naturally we will interview each one and hopefully something will turn up. If her husband didn't do it Mrs. Reed let her killer in so we are working on the basis she knew him.'

Judd stood up. Thomas took it as a signal to leave. 'OK.' Judd said. 'Keep going. Let me know if you need anything and keep me informed. I'll try to keep the Chief cool for a few more days.'

'Thank you sir.' Thomas said and headed back to his office.

DI Grey had tried to call Vanessa Vokes from Thomas' office, and she was ringing off after speaking to her voicemail just as Thomas opened the door.

'Morning sir.' She said brightly.

'DI Grey;' Thomas nodded, 'how did you get on with the professor?'

Grey relayed the conversation she'd had with Colin Fullthorpe; voicing her suspicions that he was hiding something. 'He also fits the description given by Clare Trussler sir.' She finished.

Thomas said nothing for a few moments, thinking. Finally he summarised 'So, Susan Reed had his private number which he says he doesn't give out to students; he claims he was at home on Monday morning when she was killed but he has no alibi; and he fits the description given by Clare Trussler. Is that right?'

'Yes sir,' Grey confirmed, 'and he became very defensive when I questioned him about out-of-hours support for students. I'm sure he was hiding something sir.'

'I agree it sounds like he's hiding something. Was there something going on between the two of them do you think? That might have given him a reason to lie to you. Mind you, it's a college not a school and Reed was in her twenties.'

'Still taboo sir according to him; it's considered to be gross misconduct and can result in instant dismissal. If he had been having it off with her and he wanted to end it, but she threatened to tell the governors, he would have been staring down the barrel at the end of his career and public disgrace might well have followed. That could have been enough of a motive to kill her plus it would explain why she let him in; she obviously knew him.'

'Mmm, yes could be, plus it might have given Alan Reed a motive if he'd found out. Mind you it's all speculation. Have you spoken to any of her friends?'

'Not yet sir, I'm trying to get hold of one of them now.'

'OK.' Thomas said, 'Carry on. By the way the Chief is getting fidgety about how long the search is taking, any news?'

'Nothing yet sir, but I'll get an update later today.'

'One last thing, leave me the list of Susan Reed's contacts; you work from the top and I'll start at the bottom. Also I'm expecting a list of registered owners from the CCTV team so hopefully we'll find a match with someone she knew.'

Grey copied her list gave it to Thomas and left to make more calls using the contact numbers on Susan Reed's mobile.

Thomas had a habit in major cases of listing on a marker board all of what he considered to be important facts. It somehow helped him organise his thoughts. He reached into a desk drawer and pulled out a black marker pen. A dual sided board stood on a metal frame in one corner of his office, and he picked up Grey's list, walked up to the board and began writing.

- 10.00 + Reed says he left the house
- 10.00 + Mrs. Stephens sees 20-30 year old male knock on door
- 10.10 Miss Trussler sees mid 40's male knock on door
- 10.22 Alan Reed calls ambulance

- 10.00 – 10.30 Susan Reed murdered

- Susan Reed admitted her killer into her home assuming not already dead

- Susan Reed's mobile phone contacts;
    o Vanessa Vokes – college friend according to Alan Reed 00441604445501
    o Mandy Singleton- college friend according to Alan Reed 00441604643305
    o Colin Fullthorpe – tutor – why the mobile number?- 00447880636755
    o Bob Styles – contact – 00441604845667
    o Louise Theroux – contact – 00440273944327
    o Leroy – contact- 00447880614378

One of the things that seemed unusual to Thomas was that all the contact numbers included the international dialling code for the UK. Normally, he thought, you would only need that if you were travelling abroad, yet Alan Reed had said that Susan Reed had not worked and he couldn't hold down a steady job. Holidays abroad would probably be beyond their means, so why the international dialling codes? He made a mental note to ask Reed before he released him.

He pulled up a chair in front of the board and sat staring at it for several minutes. Was one of these people the killer? She almost certainly knew her killer; after all she had let him in assuming she hadn't already been murdered, and these were all in her list of contacts. Alan Reed was the obvious suspect but they had no evidence against him without forensics or a weapon. Forensics would take a few more days yet and so far the team searching for the weapon had come up with nothing.

Susan Reed had Fullthorpe's private mobile phone number yet Fullthorpe had told Grey that he did not give it out to students and hadn't given it to her. So why did she have it and how had she got it? The obvious answer was that Fullthorpe had given it to her. Had they been lovers? If they had been, did Fullthorpe kill her to keep her quiet? Or, again assuming they had been lovers, had Alan Reed found out and killed her in a jealous rage? Reed had definitely reacted when he had quizzed him about his wife's nights out with her friends. Had he seen her out with Fullthorpe and killed her out of jealousy? Was he planning to kill Fullthorpe too?

He felt as though they were making progress; they had lots of possibilities already but they were lacking hard evidence. He remembered his maxim; let evidence lead. He decided to have one final talk with Alan Reed and called the Duty Sergeant to ask him to take him to an interview room.

Reed was waiting with his solicitor when Thomas arrived. His body language gave Thomas the impression that he was feeling angry and intended to give him a hard time. No doubt he was feeling hard done by following the grillings he'd given him over the last couple of days, and now he had his solicitor with him thought that he could turn the tables. Thomas switched on the tapes and began. 'Alan, did you and Susan ever go on holidays abroad?' He asked.

Reed shook his head in bewilderment, as if he couldn't believe he had to tolerate listening to some of the stupid questions Thomas was asking him. 'What has that got to do with the price of fish?' He asked and Reed's solicitor also quickly protested. 'Really DCI Thomas, does this have any relevance to your enquiry?'

Thomas said calmly 'It might have; could you answer the question Alan?'

'No, we never considered it.' He said sulking, leaning back in his chair both hands in his pockets.

'And did Susan ever go abroad on her own or with her friends?'

'No, of course she didn't; at least definitely not since I've known her.'

'Why of course?' Thomas probed.

'She had no money. I told you.' Reed said glowering at Thomas.

'Did Susan ever mention a Colin Fullthorpe?' Thomas asked, changing the line of his questioning, and immediately noticed a momentary change of expression on Reed's face.

Reed quickly recovered but still looked uncomfortable. 'He was her teacher at college I think.'

'Did you ever meet him socially?'

Reed averted his eyes and sounded evasive when he replied. 'No, why should I have met him? He was no friend of mine.' To Thomas his whole demeanour had become defensive but he couldn't fathom why. Was it because he suspected his wife had been seeing Fullthorpe?

'Did Susan ever meet him socially?' Thomas probed further.

'No! What are you trying to get at?' He shouted, glaring at Thomas.

'Really DCI Thomas, is this necessary? My client's wife has been murdered. Please show some sensitivity.' Reed's solicitor protested.

'Please answer the question Mr. Reed.' Thomas said his voice hardening.

Reed sprawled back in his chair, his expression hostile. 'I already did answer it. I said no.'

'But she did go out often with her friends, so how do you know she hadn't told you she was seeing them when in fact she was seeing Fullthorpe?' Thomas continued, trying to get Reed to reach flash-point; that way he might say something he could use.

'Why the hell should she have done that? I told you she went out with Vanessa and Mandy. I would have known if she had been lying to me, I could always tell when she lied.'

'Did you ever see them together, turn up unexpectedly?'

'No, why should I spy on her like that? I had no reason to suspect she was doing anything behind my back. '

'So she could have told you she was seeing Vanessa and Mandy when actually she was out with Fullthorpe.' Thomas reasoned.

'She could have but she wasn't; Susan wasn't like that and I told you I would have known if she had lied to me. She was a terrible liar; she would blush and stutter over the least little white lie.' Reed sounded definite.

'Do you know when your wife acquired her mobile phone?' Thomas asked quietly.

Reed glared at Thomas 'Are we back onto general knowledge with no relevance to anything? What kind of question is that? Why don't you ask me how long the Milky Way is?'

'Well, do you know when she got it?' Thomas persisted.

'Yes I know, I bought it for her when we got engaged, so two years or so ago.'

'Thank you Alan, that will be all for now. If you see the Duty Sergeant he will sign you out.'

Reed looked incredulous. 'Do you mean I can go?'

'For the moment, yes you can.' Thomas said.

'What do you mean for the moment?' Reed shouted. His face contorted in rage and he leapt out of his chair and tried to scramble over the desk separating him and Thomas. 'You bastard, I've told you I didn't kill her, so why are you trying to treat me like I murdered her? Why are you persecuting me?'

Thomas ignored him and his solicitor stepped in quickly and grabbed Reed's arm. 'Alan, this is not the way. Come on, let's go. Let me take you home.' He said.

Reed shrugged his arm free and glared at Thomas. 'I'll have you for this Thomas! You're not fit to be a copper.' He bawled.

'Come on Alan, let's go.' His solicitor said, and Reed backed out of the door his hate-filled eyes never leaving Thomas.

Thomas didn't blame Reed for his outburst, it was understandable, innocent or guilty, and it wasn't the first time someone had been close to attacking him in an interview room; neither he imagined, would it be the last.

He returned to his office and called Sheila Grey. 'Where are you now?' He asked.

'I'm on my way to see Vanessa Vokes at her flat in Westone; she finally answered her phone.' Grey said using her hands free as she drove the Astra.

'Ok, I've released Reed for the moment pending results of the search and forensics. I'll begin working my way up your list.' He said. 'We'll meet first thing Tomorrow morning in my office unless anything urgent turns up.'

'Ok sir.' Grey said surprised and disappointed that Thomas had let Reed go; she reasoned he could have held him for a few more hours and something might still have turned up that would have incriminated him, after all the uniforms were still searching Manfield Road. Plus if he knew Fullthorpe had been having an affair with his wife he was a potential danger to him. On the other hand it was possible that this case might be more than a simple domestic. True Reed seemed nailed on for the murder, but since the two witnesses had given their statements, and having spoken to Fullthorpe, there might still be more to it than met the eye.

Chapter 12

She parked the Astra directly outside Vanessa Vokes' block of flats and walked to the entrance. Built in the early twentieth century it had once been a four storey shoe factory, but had been converted into luxury apartments a couple of years earlier. From the outside she could see that the old red bricks had been re-rendered and the once metal framed windows had been replaced with white plastic double glazed units. The original slate roof had been replaced with modern roof tiles in rustic red, and the entrance was security controlled by CCTV and key pad activated locks. The access door, at least ten feet high, was flanked either side by reinforced smoke grey glass panels.

These were some of the most expensive apartments in town and Vanessa Vokes had said on the phone that she owned a penthouse suite, so Grey assumed hers would be something special. She pressed the bell and waited. After a few seconds a female voice answered and Grey introduced herself. She heard the door click and pushed it open, walking into a huge atrium with a solitary glass lift that connected all four floors. She entered the lift and pressed number four. It was a fast ride and Grey's stomach hit the floor for a second as it took off but in no time at all it had reached the fourth floor and she looked around for apartment 4B. It turned out to be the last on the left and when she reached it she rang the bell.

Vanessa Vokes opened her door and Grey introduced herself, showing Vokes her warrant card. Vokes took a long time studying it, Grey thought, but finally satisfied, she smiled and invited Grey in.

The first thing that Grey noticed was how big and high the lounge was. Being on the top floor the ceilings took on the shape of the gabled roof, creating impressive height, and this particular apartment obviously ran the whole width of the building; the lounge alone must have been forty feet wide, she estimated, and almost as long. She was awestruck. The roof beams looked like solid oak, and Vokes had invested in two enormous crystal chandeliers, each with a dozen branches containing four scalloped cups of white candles. Gold beading and droplets weaved between each branch and the centre-piece was a suspended clear crystal ball that hung like a tear drop from the base. Discreet wall-lighting, three high quality black leather sofas, a thick beige carpet that Grey bounced on as she walked, expensive looking prints on the walls, and a stainless steel DVD and stereo, all combined to create a comfortable elegant room.

Grey sighed, envious. Compared to her little one bed, this was paradise. Vanessa Vokes was obviously not short of money. Mind you she wouldn't have wanted her heating bills.

Vokes offered her tea or coffee and Grey chose coffee. Vokes disappeared into the kitchen for a few minutes and returned with a silver tray on which she carried two bone china cups and saucers, a matching milk jug and a sugar bowl. *'Well, what did you expect, a mug of Nescafe?'* Grey asked herself.

Vokes put the tray down on a mahogany side table and Grey helped herself to two sugars and some milk. Vokes, she noticed, took hers black, no sugar.

Vanessa Vokes was medium height with thick auburn hair cut just below the neck line. Her deep brown eyes held a warmth and kindness that suggested inner peace, while full red lips, proud breasts and shapely legs promised sophistication and passion in equal measure. She was dressed in a Chloe silk day dress in watercress that Grey guessed must have cost all of a thousand pounds. Envious, she felt like scratching her eyes out.

'It's good of you to see me at such short notice.' She began.

'Not at all inspector,' Vokes replied with a smile. 'I'm only too willing to help.' She spoke in a soft voice with perfect diction.

Grey continued. 'As I said on the telephone I'm investigating the death of Susan Reed who died on Monday morning. Your name was in her mobile phone list of contacts.'

'Yes, I read about it in the Chronicle & Echo. What a terrible business. We were good friends; from different backgrounds, but good friends nevertheless.' Vokes explained sadness in her voice.

Grey took a big gulp of coffee. 'How do you mean, from different backgrounds?' She asked, hoping Vokes would open up about herself.

'Well, education for a start. I am a Roedean girl whereas I think Susan went to a local comprehensive, plus as you might already have guessed inspector, I haven't yet had time to make enough money from work to afford all this.' Vokes spread her arms wide and took in the whole room. 'No, as much as it is my ambition to make my own way in life, my father has kindly provided the money for this place. Susan, on the other hand was always short of money.'

'Your family is wealthy?'

Vokes frowned as if it pained her to talk about money. 'Comfortable; my family has been in securities for generations and my father is Chairman of Vokes-Bradbury.'

'Vokes-Bradbury the stock brokers?' Grey knew the name. It was one of the biggest.

'Yes, it's been in my family for years.'

'So why choose Northampton; why not somewhere like London?'

'Oh I suppose it's the usual story. I want to make my own living, survive on my own talent not my father's. I could work for him if I wanted to, have a comfortable life I suppose, he would certainly prefer it if I did, but as I said I prefer to try on my own.' She sighed. 'Of course he wouldn't dream of letting me rent a place. No he insisted he buy this flat, and I must confess, I'm rather glad he did. I suppose my independent streak only runs so deep.' She smiled self-consciously.

'Why not university; surely you could have chosen any number of more high profile places than Northampton College?'

Vokes nodded her agreement. 'I suppose I could have, but I liked the look of their BA course and if I'm honest I haven't regretted it for a single day. It was the main reason for moving to Northampton and it's fairly easy to commute back to London when I need to. Now, well there are other reasons why I'm happy to stay here.' She said turning to look at a photograph of herself and a smiling young man dressed in full ski gear standing proudly on top of a snow capped mountain.

Grey drained her cup. 'Can you tell me how you met Susan Reed?' She asked, trying to steer Vokes around to the purpose of her visit.

'We met at the college about three years ago; we enrolled more or less at the same time. Sue was on the same course as I. We were both a little lost in such a big and strange place and we helped one another get acclimatised. We hit it off right away.'

'What was your impression of her?' Grey probed.

Vokes took a deep breath, a rather sad one Grey thought. 'When we first met she was fine. She was good looking, popular with the boys as you can imagine, friendly, happy most of the time, and fairly bright. But later, after her marriage broke up, she became mixed up in many ways, emotionally, financially, academically, just about every way; nevertheless despite all of her problems she maintained her wicked sense of humour. We had some marvellous times together.'

'Did she talk to you about her problems?'

'Yes she was quite open most of the time, although she could be very secretive when it suited her.' Vokes went on. 'I think she opened up to me because in some ways she felt she could trust me. It's not in my nature to gossip and I think she knew she could count on me to keep things to myself. And I never judged her whatever she did; I took her as she was.'

'Did she talk to you about her marriage?'

Vokes laughed in derision. 'She did, and frankly it was a disaster from the start. Alan was completely wrong for her. I warned her but she didn't listen to me. They met not long after she joined the course. I think to understand why she married him you need to understand the kind of woman she was. You see Sue loved excitement and Alan provided that for her at the beginning, but more than anything, she needed to be looked after. She needed a strong man, one she could lean on. She was by no means independent; she lacked confidence.'

She continued. 'At the beginning Alan was all laughs and fun, and I think she agreed to marry him in the belief that their life together would be like that forever after; she thought that he was strong, but I must admit from the first my view of him was completely different. In my opinion he was a weak man with a certain boyish charm who had asked her to marry him because he saw her as a meal ticket. He didn't have a steady job when they met and she was after all studying for a qualification that could eventually get her quite a lucrative job. How wrong they both were! They had totally misjudged one another; she thought she could rely on him, and he thought he could rely on her; both were sadly mistaken.'

'Did you know Alan Reed well? You say you thought you were able to work out what type of character his is.' Grey enquired.

'Not really; I met him a couple of times when they first began seeing each other, but not after that. Nevertheless I pride myself on being a pretty good judge of character and I think I weighed him up fairly quickly. As it turned out, unfortunately I was right.' Vokes said with a deep sad sigh.

'So what happened? ' Grey asked.

'Well, as I said, at first everything was fun and exciting, but then Alan lost his job. Now to his credit he found another one quite quickly but then, shortly afterwards, he lost that one too. Thereafter he seemed to be in and out of work every few weeks. I think she quickly realised he wasn't the rock she had thought she could lean on, and of course once the initial excitement began to wear off there was very little left. They had only been married six months and already the marriage was virtually dead.'

'How did Susan take it?'

'She was a wreck; you see her parents weren't very supportive and Alan had a remarkable gift for making her believe it was all her fault. It wasn't of course, and to be fair, neither was it entirely his, they just weren't suited. As I said she needed someone she could rely on and suddenly she had nobody. She was lost and frightened and she clung very closely to Mandy and I, that's Mandy Singleton by the way, Sue's other close friend. They did try to shore up the marriage but it was a complete sham and they both knew it. Then she met Leroy.'

Grey didn't want to stop Vanessa Vokes in full flow; for someone who was a self professed non-gossip she could certainly talk, but she needed to interrupt briefly. 'Leroy?'

'Yes,' Vokes continued, 'Leroy James, a very bad piece of work; he homed in on Sue's vulnerability like a Cruise Missile, and she, poor girl, was helpless to resist. He charmed her with his silky sweet smile and Rastafarian dreadlocks, plus he was a keep fit fanatic and had what Sue used to call 'a hard body'. Oh yes, she fell for him alright.' Vokes shuddered as if trying to blot out some horrible picture from her mind. 'And of course it wasn't long before he had her hooked on cocaine.'

Grey's expression turned to one of surprise. 'Cocaine; was he a dealer?'

Vokes shrugged her shoulders. 'I'm not sure whether he is what you in the police would call a dealer inspector, but he certainly introduced her to cocaine. Pretty soon she didn't know what day of the week it was; she was either high on it, miserable as sin in need of it, or whittling about Alan or Leroy. She was a hopeless case.'

'Do you think she was sleeping with Leroy James?' Grey asked. If she was and Reed had found out, then that might have given him a motive to kill her.

'Oh definitely, in fact she made no secret of it; she talked quite openly to both Mandy and I about sleeping with him, sometimes in gruesome detail unfortunately. She was completely bowled over by him. As a matter of fact, even after their relationship ended she still slept with him in return for cocaine when she couldn't afford to buy it. She told us that too.'

'He didn't give it to her for free?'

Vokes laughed knowingly. 'Good heavens no; it was all business to James. I suspect he probably gave her just enough to get her hooked then began to demand payment for it.'

'Sounds like a real charmer this Leroy James.' Grey opined.

'Absolutely; anyway she was in such a state after James dropped her that Mandy and I tried very hard to persuade her to see a counsellor; the college has one, a woman called Anne Goodchild. Fortunately I think even though she wasn't thinking straight by any means she realised she did need help, and to our great relief, she agreed.'

'Did it do her any good; was she able to help her?'

'I think so, certainly she became happier, but the drugs were dragging her down all the time. Nevertheless for a short while she appeared to be in better spirits and she was able to settle down again and concentrate on the course. But the craving for drugs was eating away at her and she was constantly short of money and desperate for her fix; at that time she went through long periods of very black depression when she couldn't see a way out. Then she made friends with Robert Styles; he fell for her in a really big way, more I think than she fell for him; but she was on the rebound from James and Alan was still making her life a misery and perhaps she hoped that Styles would support her addiction or in some way help her wean off of the cocaine. In any event they started seeing one another, and for a while she seemed a lot happier.' Vokes explained.

'Did she sleep with Robert Styles too?'

'Oh yes, of course but the trouble was he was as financially challenged shall we say as Alan was, and although I'm sure he was deeply in love with her, she soon tired of him and tried to end it. I think once she discovered he couldn't fund her drugs then she lost interest in him. But Robert wouldn't leave her alone, wouldn't take no for an answer; he would telephone her at all hours of the day and night, in class, at home when Alan was with her, and once she told me he called at her house when Alan was at home.' Vokes put her hand to her mouth as if horrified.

'Did Alan know she was sleeping with Leroy James and Robert Styles?' Grey asked, clear motives for Reed to have killed his wife forming in her mind.

'I doubt it. I don't think she had told him because, at least in the early days after she had met James, it was one of the things she got herself wound up about; Alan finding out that is.'

'Why did she care if they'd split up?'

'They still lived together even though the marriage was dead; perhaps they had a joint mortgage, I don't know. Lack of money tied them together I suppose. They had nowhere to run. They were trapped together.'

'But surely Alan must have suspected something was going on? He must have suspected she didn't love him.'

'Oh I think she still loved him in her own way; she never once spoke about leaving him even when she was head over heels in love with James. I think somehow she was in love with both James and Alan, but of course in entirely different ways. But she couldn't go crying to Alan after James ditched her and so she used Styles as a stick to lean on, but Alan was always there in the background like a good faithful dog, never questioning, poor man.'

'So to summarise what you've told me so far, Susan married Alan but the marriage wasn't successful, then she met Leroy James, became his lover and he introduced her to cocaine. She became an addict, the relationship with James cooled down but she still slept with him in exchange for drugs, and then on the rebound she had an affair with Robert Styles. That ended but Styles wouldn't accept it, and as far as you're aware, Alan Reed had no knowledge of any of this. Is that a fair summary?' Grey asked.

Vokes smiled. 'You have been paying attention inspector. Yes that's about it.'

'Do you think Alan Reed knew of his wife's drug dependency?'

'Oh yes, they argued about it all the time. She would demand money from him, you see, especially when she was desperate. The arguments became very bitter as her dependency as you put it increased. Alan was hard up most of the time and I think despite their difficulties, it genuinely hurt him to see her health deteriorate as her addiction took hold. She told me he had begged her to seek help, but of course she never did.' Vokes said firmly.

'Was Alan ever violent towards her to the best of your knowledge?'

Vokes looked aghast. 'Good Lord no; for all he is Alan Reed is not a wife-beater. No, oh my no; she would complain he was verbally cruel, but then I can imagine so was she, but never violent.' Vokes shook her head as if to emphasise her point.

Grey was trying to collect her thoughts; Vokes was providing so much information it was difficult to assimilate it all. She thought of one question she hadn't asked. 'You said James had dropped her, as you put it; so he ended their relationship?'

'Oh definitely, no question he ended it. Sue was still besotted with him, couldn't get enough of him, but he was never really interested in her. I think when they met he saw her as his next customer, and I'm sure seducing her into bed was just part of his sales pitch. Once she was hooked on cocaine, then he lost interest; he knew he had her.'

'And you say she was heartbroken?'

'Absolutely, she loved him no question about it.'

'It wasn't just the cocaine she found attractive?' Grey probed further.

'No; that helped of course but came later; no, she loved him; in her eyes he had strength and power and he excited her. Everything she wanted I suppose. She didn't seem to care that he was morally cruel.' Vokes said wistfully.

'What did Mandy think about all this? I assume she knew too.'

Vokes laughed ruefully. 'Oh Mandy, my God! She was outraged, disgusted I suppose you could call it, although of course she never showed it. Dear Mandy, she never said a word, not of encouragement nor in judgement, but of course she was horrified deep down. Mandy you see is the niece of Father Christopher Charles, parish priest of St.Gregory The Great, and daughter of the equally devout Mrs. Linda Singleton, his sister; both good Catholics and of course Mandy is too.'

'So Mandy didn't approve?'

'Good heavens no, but Mandy never says Boo! To a goose so she never told Sue how she felt. Mandy would simply listen to her stories and fume inwardly; you could almost see the steam coming out of her ears when Sue was in full cry.' Vokes laughed at the memory.

'How can you be sure; did Mandy confide in you about how she felt?' Grey asked.

Vokes' expression grew sour for a split second then recovered quickly. 'Well, no, but I know Mandy.' She reassured herself.

'Do you know Louise Theroux?' Grey asked; Theroux had been another name in Susan Reed's contact list.

'No I don't although I have heard of her. I never met her; but I do know that Sue once shared a flat with her when she first enrolled at college; somewhere in Abington I think. Louise dropped out after a couple of months and went home I believe.'

'Do you have any idea where she is now?'

'No, I'm afraid I don't inspector.'

'What did you think of your tutor, Mr. Fullthorpe?'

Vokes pulled a face. 'Letch, there's no doubt about it, like a rutting stag in season. Don't know how he gets away with it.'

'Does he make it that obvious or is this your famous intuition working?' Grey asked smiling.

'Oh no, everybody knows it's true; the word is he has been spotted out with students quite often.'

'Why hasn't anyone reported him?' Grey queried, incredulous.

'Well I don't suppose he drags them out against their will and they are all old enough to make up their own minds. Still, it is against the rules and I think a few have complained about harassment but I imagine so far he's always been able to come up with a plausible explanation. Clearly nothing has stuck because he's still teaching.'

'So there's no real proof, just rumour?' Grey challenged.

'Oh it is true inspector, take my word for it,' Vokes declared.

'Do you think Susan might have had an affair with him?' Grey asked finally.

Vokes sighed and lowered her head. 'I was hoping you wouldn't ask inspector.'

Grey interrupted. 'Miss Vokes, this is a murder enquiry. If you know anything it is important you tell me. I understand this might be difficult for you, but if we are to catch Susan's killer, we need to know everything about her.'

Vokes conceded sadly, 'Yes, I do understand. It's just that, well I don't want you to think of Sue as some sort of easy lay, she wasn't like that at all. She only got involved with all these men because she was not herself; she was very vulnerable.'

'So she did have an affair with Fullthorpe?' Grey pressed.

'Yes I'm afraid she did, after she had finished with Robert, she started seeing Fullthorpe.'

'And she slept with him?'

Vokes was at pains to defend her friend and spoke quickly. 'Yes but it's important to understand inspector that by the time Fullthorpe laid his clammy paws on her she was already a drug addict and an emotional wreck. She had no idea what she was doing. She could barely function without cocaine and she had been falling behind with her studies. I think Fullthorpe sensed it and offered to help with only one thing on his mind - getting her into his bed. In the state she was in she would have latched on to anybody she thought could somehow help her. She was easy prey to someone like Fullthorpe and well you can imagine what happened.' Vokes let out a deep breath. 'It's not fair she should be thought of in this way; Sue was a lovely kind person.' She cried voice shaking with emotion.

'Was she still seeing him in the weeks immediately before she died?' Grey delved deeper, but tenderly.

'Yes, yes I think she was.' Vokes looked close to tears but Grey was fairly certain she would never allow herself to cry in public; she imagined it wasn't the sort of thing Roedean girls did. Gossip or not, she realised, Vanessa Vokes was genuinely very upset over her friend's death.

'To your knowledge did she have any enemies?'

'None that I'm aware of; she was very popular.'

Grey gathered her thoughts, trying to work out if there was anything she had missed but decided she had taken in all she could for one day.

'I hope you don't mind but I have to ask you this. Can you tell me where you were on Monday morning between ten and ten thirty?'

Vokes seemed distant when she answered. 'Oh yes inspector, I was in class; you see I have enrolled for another course. I have thirty or so witnesses.'

Grey smiled. 'Thanks, you've been very helpful.'

'I just hope you find the killer quickly inspector; you're welcome anytime of course and please don't hesitate if you think of something else.' Vokes said rising from her chair and showing Grey to the door.

As the lift carried her down to the ground floor, Grey took a deep breath. Vanessa Vokes had been exhausting.

Chapter 13

On reaching her car she decided to call Thomas; the information she had learned from Vokes would be useful to him when he talked to either Robert Styles or Leroy James. Thomas answered and once she'd given him a brief summary he asked her to meet him at Campbell Square.

The drive from Vokes' apartment took about fifteen minutes and she found him in his office re-reading the M.E.'s report. 'Take a seat.' He said without looking up. 'I'll just be a minute.'

Grey sat on the chair facing him feeling like a schoolgirl waiting for the Headmistress. She had been bursting to tell him in detail what she had discovered from Vanessa Vokes when she entered his office and had expected him to be as enthusiastic, but now, as she sat watching him thumb through the M.E.'s report, not even acknowledging her presence, she felt all the adrenalin and motivation drain out of her. She really couldn't make him out; one minute he was praising her, the next indifferent.

'Sorry to have kept you.' He said finally, and smiled. 'So, you've managed to put some meat on the bones of our case. Well done. I think I got the gist of what you managed to gather from Vanessa Vokes, but perhaps you could summarise it for me again.'

Grey quickly put her irritation behind her and took a deep breath while she ordered her thoughts. 'It seems as though Susan Reed was very mixed up. According to Vokes she should never have married Alan Reed; she needed someone to rely on but he couldn't hold down a job, plus Vokes says he only married her for a meal ticket. So not long after they married it all started to go sour and she picked up with Leroy James, a Rastafarian cocaine pusher who, again according to Vokes, only befriended her so he could get her hooked. Once she was hooked he lost interest and demanded payment for the coke.'

'He didn't give it to her free, even when they were seeing one another?' Thomas interrupted.

'Not once she was hooked sir.'

'I wonder what on earth a drug dealer was doing at college; surely he could have thought of better places to ply his trade. I'd have though he would have chosen somewhere less public and less expensive; it costs money to take a college course. Still, I suppose it gave him quite a large and wide potential market.' He shook his head in bafflement.

'She was besotted with James but as I said he lost interest in her once she was hooked and then she met Robert Styles on the rebound. Styles fell for her in a big way but she quickly tired of him. Trouble was he wouldn't leave her alone; he'd telephone her at all hours and sometimes call at her house when Alan Reed was there with her.'

Thomas raised his eyebrows and looked at her sharply. 'Oh really?'

'Yes sir, but according to Vokes Alan Reed never knew of any of his wife's affairs.' Grey explained.

'Maybe he didn't show it DI Grey, but it's asking a lot to believe a husband wouldn't notice something awry when a man knocks on the door asking to see his wife. He must have known something was going on.' Thomas argued.

'Yes sir', Grey agreed. 'Anyway she was an emotional wreck and getting more hooked on cocaine. She couldn't always afford her fixes from James and, according to Vokes, often slept with him when she couldn't pay him. Her college grades suffered too and that was when Colin Fullthorpe offered to help by providing one on one coaching; shortly afterwards she was sleeping with him too. Vokes says Fullthorpe is a serial letch and probably made a play for her because he could see she was in a mess, easy prey so to speak. So for the last few months of her life she was sleeping with at least two men plus her husband, Colin Fullthorpe and Leroy James.'

'And before that Robert Styles; it sounds like she bounced from one man to another looking for somebody to help her, yet she'd ditched Styles the one man prepared to help her if only she'd have let him.' He sighed. 'Difficult to fathom what goes on inside the mind of someone like that; there's no logic to it; she was a mess.' Thomas added.

'One other thing sir, Vokes and her other friend Mandy Singleton, managed to persuade her to seek some counselling at the college. According to Vokes, the college has a resident counsellor by the name of Anne Goodchild. Susan Reed went to see her and, again according to Vokes, she managed to help her for a while.'

'What do you suggest as our next move?' Thomas asked.

Grey saw his question as a test, whether Thomas meant it as one or not. She thought for a moment, asking herself. *What is the right thing to do? What would I do if it were up to me?* and when she'd made up her mind offered. 'We only have Vokes' word for this entire story sir. Some of it could be quite damming for any one of the people on our list, so I think we should try to corroborate her statement.'

Thomas smiled, seemingly in satisfaction. 'So do I; I suggest you take Mandy Singleton and I'll take Anne Goodchild.'

'Sir.' Grey agreed, the feeling of immense pride that she had pleased him washing over her once again.

Chapter 14

That evening Thomas had finished dinner at home with Alice and Bill and he was relaxing in an easy chair in the lounge, eyes half closed, glass of Merlot by his right hand, listening to the Intermezzo from Mascagni's Cavalleria Rusticana, one of his favourite operatic pieces.

Thomas was a student of opera and this one, he recalled, had been written in 1890 based on a short story by Giovanni Verga. At its first performance in the Teatro Costanzi, Rome, there had been forty curtain calls and it was still Mascagni's most popular opera to this day. He had written sixteen in all, but to Thomas' ears, none compared to the Rusticana.

The story was one of love betrayed, adultery, seduction and murder. Not dissimilar to the Reed case, he observed as the soaring crescendo ended. Suddenly he felt a tap on his knee and opened his eyes in surprise.

Bill was having one of his better days. Alice had said he'd been no trouble at all; he'd been happy, alert, and had even helped her around the house. Thomas was relieved; he had been worried that neither he nor Alice had been able to find any help and she had been alone in the house with him all day. He had insisted she call him at the first sign of trouble.

Bill had pulled up a chair next to him and was leaning towards him, a big grin on his face. He said 'Listen to this one. A small child was sitting on his Grandma's knee one day and said. 'Grandma, will you do your frog impression please?"

Grandma said. 'Frog impression? I can't do frog impressions, whoever gave you that idea?'

The young boy said 'Dad did; he said when you croak we can all go to Disney.' Bill roared with laughter, tears rolling down his cheeks.

Thomas laughed too, but deep down he was very worried about Alice's safety and determined to try to find her some help as soon as he could. The trouble was that he could not afford private care for long and he wasn't at all sure whether he could claim NHS care. The diagnosis was clear enough; Bill's doctor had said he was in the early middle stages of Alzheimer's, but according to the people at the NHS he had spoken to there were no clear guidelines as to who was eligible and who wasn't.

As far as he was concerned the situation was perfectly clear; Alice needed help, but whether the NHS agreed was another matter. He had looked at all the web sites on the subject and it had simply depressed him. There were no clear guidelines and he had groaned in disbelief when he had discovered that in 1999 someone had felt the need to take the Government to court because her local NHS Trust had refused to pay for her care. She had won, but what had followed was a bewildering number of interpretations as to what constituted eligibility and what didn't.

Worse, in 2001 the Government had moved the goal posts and introduce what it called 'free nursing care for all' which he had quickly discovered meant anything but. In his eyes, what it really meant was that the NHS would pay a small contribution to the overall cost of care, but again there was an eligibility test, and different NHS Trusts were free to put their own interpretation on the rules. The post-code lottery had continued until 2006 when a Mrs. Grogan had appealed to the High Court against the interpretation Bexley Care Trust had put on her eligibility. She had won her case and the judge had criticised the Department of Health saying they should have issued much clearer guidelines to the NHS. He wondered why then, if the guidelines were supposed to be so clear, he couldn't understand them, and what was worse, neither could the staff at Northampton General Hospital.

Alice entered with a glass of Chablis in her hand. Thomas raised his glass to her and said. 'Bill's just told me a joke; don't worry it's a clean one. Come on Bill, tell Alice your little boy joke.'

Bill looked completely blank and Thomas' heart sank

Chapter 15

He called Anne Goodchild as soon as he began work the next morning and she agreed to see him straight away. She lived in Great Brington, a picture postcard village six miles west of Northampton. Part of the Spencer estate, it had passed down from William the Conqueror through his son William Peverel until the Spencer's had acquired it at the beginning of the sixteenth century. It was a one church one pub place, God and sinners present in equal measure.

Thomas had listened to Radio 2 as he drove towards Great Brington, not willing to risk ending his five song string from the shuffle until the case became clearer. He turned into Anne Goodchild's drive, a long winding gravel track flanked by high leylandii hedging and well cared for borders that led him to an impeccably kept lawn of football-pitch proportions and an imposing eighteenth century manor House.

It was a warm sunny day and Anne Goodchild was sitting in a pine garden chair looking cool in a lemon cotton dress, coffee and biscuits on a table next to her. A spare cup and coffee pot, milk and sugar were waiting for Thomas and she rose to greet him. 'Chief Inspector Thomas?' Goodchild asked.

'Yes, you must be Anne Goodchild.' He replied.

They shook hands and she led him to the garden chairs. 'I hope you don't mind chief inspector, but it is such a lovely day. I thought we would sit outside. Please help yourself to coffee.' She suggested.

'No not at all, this is a magnificent place.' Thomas commented looking around at the gardens. 'Have you lived here long?' He asked pouring himself a cup of coffee.

'Over twenty years; my husband bought the house not long after we married. We've never dreamed of living anywhere else, even though Billy spends much of his time in the City; business you know.' She explained.

'Yes, well I can understand why you wouldn't want to move away from here. You have so much ground and such a marvellous setting.' He said admiringly,

'Twenty acres plus some adjoining fields at the back; it really is beautiful but tremendously difficult to keep up and expensive of course.' Anne Goodchild had the kind of plum mouthed diction that wouldn't have been out of place at the local Hunt, he thought. Tall and blonde, with elegant features, she looked very toned and fit for someone her age; he put her early to mid forties. She looked upper class from head to toe.

He took a sip of coffee and asked. 'Could I ask what your husband does?'

Goodchild smiled and held an expression that reminded Thomas of a patient aunt humouring a favourite nephew. 'Billy owns Laceys the supermarket chain. It's a public company now of course, he's Chairman; he founded it when he was nineteen. Billy left school at fifteen and began working for a local green-grocer. At seventeen he bought him out and the rest as they say is history.'

Thomas fanned away an irritating wasp and decided to get to the point. 'As I said on the telephone I'm investigating the death of Susan Reed.'

'Poor girl.' Goodchild interrupted. 'It's been all over the papers of course. What an awful thing to have happened.'

'Indeed. As I understand it you met her at college; can you tell me what you knew of her?'

Goodchild's brows furrowed in thought. 'Well she came to see me at college; I do some part time charity work, counselling the students you see. I trained in psychology in my twenties and I've been involved in counselling for many years, mostly with MIND and CAB, but I knew someone on the college board of governors and a few years ago she invited me to help them out. I think Susan came to see me about two years ago; she was stressed about college, her marriage and life in general as I recall.'

'Drugs?' He probed.

'Yes, I'm afraid so, cocaine I think.' Goodchild allowed.

'Were you able to help her?'

'I think so, at least for a while, but her drug addiction was ruining her. When I first saw her she was almost suicidal, life was weighing her down; she couldn't see any way forward and the drugs made her dark moods even blacker. Her mother and father had all but disowned her; they had warned her against marrying so young and when it started to go wrong it was more a case of 'we told you so' than lending a sympathetic ear. She had very few close friends to lean on, and her husband was dismissive of her; he blamed her entirely for the failure of their marriage. So she felt guilty and frustrated at the same time. I tried my best to encourage her to look on the bright side, told her she was young and intelligent and in time things would turn for the better, and for a while I really think she did improve, but in the end the drugs took a hold and she stopped coming to see me.' She explained sadness in her voice.

'Did she go into detail about her worries?' Thomas enquired.

'She had not been long married, less than a year I recall, but when it hadn't worked out she'd been disillusioned; her husband was in and out of work and they were short of money. When she had married him she had expected life to be a never ending adventure, all excitement and thrills. It was naïve of her perhaps but she was very young and that was how she saw it. So when reality set in she didn't know how to deal with it, her dreams had gone and all she could see was misery and poverty in front of her. When her husband turned against her and blamed her for just about everything she was devastated; her self esteem hit rock bottom. Then Leroy James began to hang around her and she allowed herself to fall for him. Again she was very naïve and she told me that he had introduced her to cocaine. I would imagine she willingly experimented with it; she would have relished anything that gave her a few hours of blessed relief from her abject misery. It was very sad I'm sure. Regrettably by the time I saw her, she was already hooked and James had more or less dropped her, but she totally relied on him to supply her and I think she lowered herself when she couldn't pay him.'

'Lowered' was an interesting word for what she'd done Thomas thought, but it was probably as strong as Anne Goodchild would use in the circumstances.

'You mean you believe she prostituted herself in order to buy drugs from him?'

She looked hurt as though the blunt way he'd put it had affronted her, but she nodded in agreement. 'I think it amounted to that. From what she told me James had lost interest in her but wasn't averse to bedding her when she couldn't pay him. I think at first she still loved him and couldn't fully understand why he wouldn't help her when she couldn't pay, but eventually I'm sure she came to realise what he was really about and of course when she did, that made her feel even worse. No woman likes to think of herself as a prostitute chief inspector.'

Thomas nodded in understanding. 'Did she ever mention Vanessa Vokes and Mandy Singleton?' He was interested to know whether Goodchild could confirm Susan Reed's friendship with them.

Goodchild laughed, surprising Thomas. 'Dear Mandy, she's my God-daughter you know. Yes Mandy and Vanessa were her closest friends at college I believe. Susan told me the pair of them had persuaded her to come and see me.'

'Mandy Singleton is your God-daughter?'

For a split second something passed over Anne Goodchild's face but Thomas couldn't decipher what it meant and let is go. Goodchild said 'Yes, I've known her mother Linda for well over twenty years; we were at Oxford together. She lives at the vicarage next door to St.Gregory's church. Linda is the sister of Chris Charles, Father Chris Charles that is, priest of St. Gregory's in Northampton.'

'Well I never.' Thomas exclaimed, amazed. *Six degrees and all that.* 'So Mandy and Vanessa were good friends with Susan Reed.' He repeated.

'Yes,' Goodchild confirmed.

'Can you tell me how many times you saw her, over what period?'

Goodchild put her finger to her lips. 'Now let me see, I think only about three or four times over I would say, a two month period. As I said the drugs had begun to take over and I think she lost interest in the advice I was giving her.'

'Which was?'

Goodchild sighed. 'That she was young, bright, with her whole life in front of her, and that she should try to think positively about herself. Plus of course a standard lecture on the dangers of drug addiction. I advised her to seek professional help over that although I'm a firm believer in self help Chief Inspector. I believe we all have choices in life, including whether to be miserable and depressed or happy and carefree. I always try to instil those maxims in the students; it helps them build self confidence. Most people like to be in control of their own destiny but it's not always easy to make yourself believe that you are.'

'In your time counselling students, have you ever heard complaints about Colin Fullthorpe?' He asked.

Goodchild was clearly taken aback; she looked quite shocked that Thomas should ask such a question. 'Why do you ask Chief Inspector?'

'It is relevant to the case Mrs. Goodchild.' He assured her.

Godchild nodded. 'I see; I'm afraid Colin has a weakness for the girls Chief Inspector - of any age.' She gave Thomas a knowing look, 'and sometimes he allows it to get the better of him. Yes, a few of the girls have admitted feeling harassed by him.'

'Did you report him to the board?' Thomas asked.

For the first time since he'd arrived Anne Goodchild lost her composure; she appeared flustered and suddenly uncomfortable. 'No chief inspector I did not. Firstly everything the students tell me is in strict confidence, and secondly it would have been their word against his.' She explained in justification for her inaction.

'Perhaps if there had been only one complaint, but more than one would have aroused suspicions surely?' He argued.

She sighed. 'Yes I know and I have often wondered whether I did the right thing. On balance perhaps I didn't.' She conceded.

Just then a silver Jaguar XF crackled down the drive towards the house, much too quickly by Thomas' reckoning, and skidded to a halt a few feet away from where Thomas and Goodchild were sitting. Anne Goodchild stood up and walked towards the car as a short overweight man in an ill fitting grey suit climbed out. 'Billy.' Anne Goodchild greeted him with a kiss on the cheek.

'Hello babe.' Billy said, 'who's the nigger?'

Thomas overheard but did not react. 'Billy this is chief inspector Thomas; he's here about the murder of a student at the college, Susan Reed.' She explained as they both approached where Thomas was sitting.

Thomas stood up. Billy Goodchild did not introduce himself or give Thomas a chance to, instead he said in a harsh voice. 'So why are you bothering my wife; shouldn't you be somewhere else looking for a murderer, or do you just enjoy sitting on my deck drinking my coffee?'

Thomas felt his stomach tighten but said calmly 'And you are?'

'Billy Goodchild; and who are you? Force needed to fill their quota of commonwealth brothers when they hired you, did it?'

'Billy, really!' Anne Goodchild exclaimed sternly.

Billy Goodchild ignored her. His eyes were on Thomas.

Thomas returned the stare. 'DCI Thomas; I'm investigating the murder of Susan Reed. Can you tell me where you were between ten and ten thirty on Monday morning?' He asked, temper boiling up inside.

'Yes.' Billy Goodchild said.

'Well?' Thomas persisted.

'Call Arthur.' Goodchild ordered, looking at his wife.

'Billy, I don't think...' Anne Goodchild interrupted.

'Call him, now!' Billy Goodchild cut in, repeating his order.

'Tell him to come to Campbell Square station;' Thomas advised, eyes drilling into Billy Goodchild, 'that's where we'll be.' He imagined that Arthur must be Billy's solicitor.

Billy Goodchild suddenly looked flustered. 'Now just a minute.'

Thomas remained outwardly calm but inside he was molten. 'I think you should come with me now sir.'

'Alright, alright, I'm sorry. I was in London all day on Monday.' Goodchild said quickly.

'Can you prove that?'

'Of course I can, I was in meetings with some of my biggest suppliers, Captains of Industry you might say.' He responded proudly.

'No doubt Arthur will be able to give me their names; I'll look forward to receiving them. Shall we say this afternoon? I'd hate to have to come back for you.' Thomas said coldly 'and of course we will have to check them all out individually and in great detail. That will mean interviews, visits to police stations, that sort of thing.'

Billy Goodchild was incandescent. 'I'll be writing to the Chief Constable about you Thomas, make no bones about it.' He bawled, shaking his fist and pointing at him.

Thomas was already making his way to his car. 'Thank you for your help Mrs. Goodchild.' He said and waved goodbye.

As Thomas' car disappeared from view Anne Goodchild turned on her husband.

'Really Billy, was that absolutely necessary?' She demanded bitterly.

'Oh shut up.' Billy ordered. 'What do you think you were doing letting a nigger cop come here without Arthur being around?'

'He simply wanted some background information; I'd been counselling the poor girl who was murdered that's all.' Anne Goodchild protested.

'Counselling pah!' Billy spat disdainfully. 'Waste of bloody time. Next time he asks to see you, make bloody sure Arthur is here with you. Christ, nigger cops on my decking! What next?'

'Do you have to be so uncouth and racially abusive? He's a policeman for God's sake. Why do you want to make an enemy of him?' Anne Goodchild protested.

'Bloody low level goon, that's what he is. He should have called.'

'He did call for Pete's sake!' She cried turning red with rage. 'He called and asked when I could see him. I agreed to see him straight away; he didn't just turn up at the front door.'

'You should have called me or Arthur; it was stupid of you to see him on your own.'

'He came to ask me a few simple questions about Susan Reed and her friends, nothing more.' She explained. She was trying to keep herself under control, reason with Billy Goodchild, but she knew from bitter experience that when Billy was in this kind of mood, there was no reasoning with him.

Billy moved very close to his wife so that his face almost touched hers. 'We never, and I mean never, speak to goons without representation. Am I clear?' He said firmly.

Anne Goodchild said coldly. 'Oh yes, Billy, very clear.' and stormed into the house.

Billy Goodchild spat onto his well manicured lawn and followed her.

Chapter 16

DI Sheila Grey rang the front doorbell of the vicarage at St.Gregory's and waited. She was looking forward to her date that night with Chris Atherley and trying to decide what to wear. Her stomach tingled with excitement at the thought of seeing him again but she was brought back to the moment when the door was opened by a mid-forties woman with greying mousey hair wearing a petal print smock and a white freshwater pearl necklace. She smiled and said. 'Hello, can I help you?'

Grey held up her warrant card. 'I'm Detective Inspector Grey, Northampton Police, I wonder if I could see Mandy Singleton.'

The woman took a step back, suddenly turning pale and looking full of concern. 'Mandy, why; is she in some kind of trouble?'

Grey replied reassuringly. 'No, but we think she might be able to help us with our enquiries.'

The woman put a hand to her mouth as if unable to decide what to do or say. Finally she said. 'Come in inspector I'll fetch my brother.'

Grey entered the spacious but sparse hallway and the woman directed her into a small ante-room where she sat and waited. A few moments later a tall priest in dog collar and purple clerical shirt entered with the woman close behind him. He smiled and offered Grey his hand which she shook.

'I'm Chris Charles and this is my sister Linda inspector. Now what can we do for you?'

'I'm investigating the murder of Susan Reed and I believe Mandy Singleton might be able to help with our enquiries.' Grey explained.

Father Singleton looked shell-shocked. 'Murder, but what could Mandy possibly know about a murder?' he asked, incredulous.

'I believe she knew the victim.' Grey said, not offering any further clarification.

A wave of relief and understanding swept across Chris Charles' face. 'Oh, now I think I see inspector. Mandy was at college and she perhaps knew this poor woman there?'

'Is Mandy here sir?' Grey asked becoming impatient.

'Yes, of course inspector. Linda, dear, could you possibly ask Mandy to join us?'

Mrs. Singleton left to find her daughter and Father Charles said. 'Can we offer you some tea or coffee inspector?'

'No, I'm fine thanks. Father, I really need to see Mandy alone if you don't mind.' She said apologetically but firmly.

A shadow passed across Charles's face but his smile quickly returned. 'Yes, yes of course inspector. I'll introduce you and then make my exit as it were.' He said looking uncertain whether this was the right thing to do.

'Thanks.' Grey replied.

A few moments later Linda Singleton returned with a tall thin short-haired brunette with very pale skin and deep brown eyes dressed in blue jeans and navy blouse. To Grey she looked very shy and nervous, almost timid. From the college records Grey knew she was twenty one. 'This is my daughter Mandy.' Linda Singleton said in introduction.

Grey rose to greet her. 'Inspector Grey.' She said.

Mandy Singleton smiled. 'Hello, mum says you want to talk to me about Sue.' She said.

Chris Charles coughed. 'Um, well, if you need anything inspector then please shout.' He said and ushered his sister out of the room.

Grey and Mandy sat down. 'I'm hoping you can tell me about your friendship with Susan Reed while you were at college.' Grey began.

'Friendship, what do you mean inspector?' Mandy asked eyes wide open.

Grey thought it was a strange reaction to the simple question but explained anyway. 'Well, as I understand it you were both in the same class, and I'm hoping you can tell me something about how she was when you last saw her, her state of mind, other friends, that sort of thing.'

Mandy became expressionless, almost guarded Grey thought, but put it down to shyness. 'Yes, we were in the same class. I was her friend.' Mandy admitted.

'Can you tell me when you saw her last?'

'The last time I saw her to speak to was about six weeks ago; we went out for a coffee with Vanessa.'

'In your opinion was she happy?' Grey felt that unlike Vanessa Vokes, Mandy Singleton might be less than forthcoming in her replies. Perhaps it was because she was naturally shy; whatever the reason Grey could tell that she was going to be hard work.

'Not really.' Mandy said.

Grey noticed that Mandy constantly stared at her; she was watching her with the same detached curiosity that people have when they stare at exhibits in a zoo, she decided. 'Do you know why?' She asked.

'She had been arguing with Alan, and I think she needed a fix.' She said flatly.

'A fix of cocaine?' Grey offered forgetting Thomas' warning about leading witnesses.

'Yes.'

'Do you know what she had been arguing about with Alan?'

Mandy shrugged her shoulders and began picking her nails. 'Money I suppose, that's what they usually argued over; she needed a fix but neither of them could afford it.'

Grey decided Mandy Singleton was a curious character. Shy, definitely; terse, yes; but also somehow hypnotic, very still and predatory, the way a hungry heron is when it stands on the river bank waiting to spear a passing fish.

'Can you tell me about the time you knew her at college?'

There was that shrug of the shoulders again. 'In what way; sorry I don't understand what you mean?' Mandy didn't seem to realise that she was giving Grey the impression that she was being deliberately obtuse; Grey was becoming impatient with her but bit her tongue. 'Tell me about the people she knew, her problems if she had any.'

'Well there was Vanessa Vokes; she was her best friend I think.'

'Anybody else you can think of?'

'Leroy James;' Mandy almost spat his name out, as if she'd swallowed something she shouldn't have. 'She went with him for a while but it didn't last long. She told us, that's Vanessa and I, that he'd introduced her to drugs.'

'Was her drug habit bad?'

'Not at first but it got much worse; I think she was an addict in the last six months or so. Leroy had finished with her though and she couldn't always afford to pay him.'

'Do you know if Leroy James had been her lover?'

Another look of distaste formed on Mandy's face. 'Yes he had been while she was at college; still was sometimes when she was desperate. She made no secret of it; in fact when she first met him she took great pleasure in describing sex between them in all the gory details. It made Vanessa and I feel quite sick.'

'She slept with him for drugs?' Grey asked.

'Yes sometimes.'

'Do you know whether her husband knew of this?'

'Who knows?' Mandy shrugged. To Grey it seemed as though Mandy Singleton was bored with her questioning, which was strange considering her close friend had just been murdered. And she hadn't yet expressed any regret or sadness at her friend's death. Grey expected her to want to help, to show some emotion, but instead she was saying only what she thought she needed to and no more.

'Were you aware of any other lovers she had?'

'Robert Styles and Colin Fullthorpe.' Mandy said expressionless.

'Can you tell me when she met Styles?'

Mandy shrugged yet again. Grey decided it was something she did when she felt under pressure. 'After James dropped her; Styles was infatuated with her, but I think she only went with him because she was heartbroken about James and needed someone to lean on. It didn't last very long.'

'What happened, can you tell me?' Grey enquired.

Mandy smiled. 'She dropped him.'

Grey thought it was a strange attitude to take, almost as if Mandy had been pleased when it had ended. 'And how did he take it?'

'Not well; he pestered her for months afterwards, stupid man.' Mandy said disdainfully.

There it was again; that unexpected tone; off-handed, couldn't care less. Time and again her answers seemed to hide an attitude of mind Grey couldn't quite put her finger on, but which she knew subconsciously was inappropriate.

'Do you think he could have killed her?'

Again Mandy shrugged 'Who knows; he might. I didn't know him well enough to form an opinion.'

'You said you believed Colin Fullthorpe was her lover; how do you know?'

'Because she told me and because I saw them together.'

'You saw them?' Grey echoed knowing this could be significant information.

'Yes, canoodling in The Fox & Hounds in Great Brington one evening about a month ago. I was there with Anne Goodchild, my Godmother. I don't think they saw us.'

'What do you mean by canoodling?' Grey had not

heard that word for years; it sounded quite quaint.

Mandy blushed. 'They were, you know, kissing. It was disgusting.' She said.

'Kissing in full view of the people in the pub?' Grey pushed. She needed to be absolutely clear about what Mandy had seen.

She shrugged again; now Grey wasn't so sure what it meant; did it mean she didn't know or didn't care or was under pressure? Mandy was very difficult to read no matter how hard she tried. 'There weren't many people there; it's usually a very quiet pub during the week and they probably felt safe. I'm not sure they were aware we could see them; they were in a small cubicle so maybe they thought nobody could, but I could.'

'You could see them clearly?'

'Oh yes, and so could Anne.' Mandy insisted.

'And you say she told you as well?' Grey asked, her heart thumping with the significance of having some corroborated evidence at last.

'Yes. She had been doing badly at college and she told me Fullthorpe had offered to help her with some private lessons. After a while, well as I said, they began to well, you know.' She left the inference to Grey's imagination.

'Do you think she was still seeing Fullthorpe before she died?'

Again Mandy shrugged. 'I suppose so; she didn't say it had finished.'

'Would you be prepared to sign a statement to the effect you saw Susan with Fullthorpe when you were with your Godmother?' Grey asked fingers crossed.

'Yes, why not?' Mandy said, shrugging again.

'Do you think you could remember the exact date?'

'It will be in my diary.' She said.

'Do you know of anyone who might have wanted to kill Susan? Did she have any enemies?'

'No.' Mandy said but silently Grey begged to differ; she'd definitely had at least one.

'I have to ask you Mandy; can you tell me where you were on Monday morning between ten and ten thirty?'

'Yes, at Mass.' Mandy said flatly.

On her way out Grey waited while Mandy consulted her diary and gave her the exact date when she and Anne Goodchild had seen Susan Reed with Fullthorpe. Grey was excited when she telephoned Thomas from her car with the news. Mandy Singleton, the very strange Mandy Singleton in Grey's opinion, had provided them with their first corroborated information that Colin Fullthorpe had been having an affair with Susan Reed and she was almost breathless when she told Thomas.

Thomas' response seemed surprisingly flat, as if he was preoccupied with something else, 'Are you alright sir?' She asked, concerned and deflated at once.

Thomas said distantly, 'Yes fine; I suppose you'd better pull him in.'

Chapter 17

Grey wondered what was wrong with Thomas but quickly put it out of her mind and, heart racing called for back up to meet her at the college from where she would invite Mr. Colin Fullthorpe, full time college lecturer and part-time seducer of young students in flagrant breach of his code of conduct, to accompany her to the station to help with her enquiries. Grey believed she was on the verge of breaking the case.

In her mind she imagined two scenarios. The first was that Alan Reed had somehow found out about his wife's affair with Fullthorpe and killed her in a fit of rage. The second was that Fullthorpe had been the man Clare Trussler had seen knocking on the Reed's door at ten past ten on Monday morning. Fullthorpe had knocked, Reed had let him in, and he had killed her because she had threatened to spill the beans about their affair. Either way, with a witness statement from Mandy Singleton she could confront Fullthorpe with what she knew about his relationship with Susan Reed and see where it led her. If she could crack the case it might be the stepping stone to a DCI.

Thomas was silently fuming at the racial abuse he'd suffered at the hands of Billy Goodchild, that pompous racist fat little ass. How could a man like that possibly run a public company? Who on earth would have dealings with such a pathetic creature? Thomas laughed in derision; the little bonehead couldn't have been more that five feet six inches short and probably had a prick the size of a peanut. Judging by his thick gut, he probably hadn't seen it in a while either. Lord alone knew what Anne Goodchild ever saw in such a dull schmuck; but then thinking about it there were probably several million things she saw in him. Thomas smacked his thigh hard. Brian you're getting bitter, don't lower yourself to his level.

Anne Goodchild interested him; she was obviously upper class born and bred. She hadn't fine-tuned that perfect diction at a city centre comprehensive, and neither had she developed her ramrod straight posture slouched in chairs from an early age. No, she had been brought up in an environment where good speech, deportment, and demeanour were as, if not more important than brains. And she made the most of what she had. Not a great beauty, but tall, athletic, and well toned, with elegance to match, she cut an attractive figure. He guessed she was old money and he wondered whether years ago her family had fallen on hard times. Why else would she attach herself to a loud-mouthed racist like Billy? He wondered whether she and Billy boy were still having sex after twenty years together; did she have a lover, did he?

She had been very quick to tell him that the work she did for the college was pro bono; it was the sort of thing he imagined she would do. She didn't need to make a living; she probably employed gardeners to keep the grounds trim and cleaners for the house, so how would a woman like that spend her day? Charity work would satisfy two fundamentals; fill up her time and appeal to her upper-class sense of responsibility to the less well heeled. Perhaps, he cautioned himself, you're being too hard on her because Billy rattled your cage, but then again perhaps not.

She had confirmed most of what Vokes had told Grey but like Vokes had offered no concrete proof that he could use in court if it came to it. Everything was hearsay; Susan Reed had told them both she had been seeing Leroy James and Robert Styles and Colin Fullthorpe, but only Mandy Singleton had actually said she had seen her with any one of them. He imagined the interviews he might have with James or Styles. Question, 'Were you Susan Reed's lover?' Answer

'No'. 'Well she told her friends you were lovers.' 'She's dead, prove it.' Very useful, not, he thought ruefully.

Interesting that Anne Goodchild turned out to be Mandy Singleton's Godmother; small world indeed.

He was still waiting for the list of owners from the CCTV team and he had been promised some forensic results by late Tomorrow. Until then he knew he would have to rely on confessions which in his experience were rare breeds indeed in murder cases.

He decided to update his board with the information he now had following the interviews with Vanessa Vokes, Ann Goodchild, and Mandy Singleton.

- 10.00 + Reed says he left the house
- 10.00 + Mrs. Stephens sees 20-30 year old male knock on door
- 10.10 Miss Trussler sees mid forties male knock on door
- 10.22 Alan Reed calls ambulance
- 10.00 – 10.30 Susan read murdered

- Susan Reed admitted her killer into her home or was already dead

- Susan Reed's mobile phone contacts;

  o Vanessa Vokes – college friend according to Alan Reed 00441604445501
    - Said Susan Reed had lovers, Leroy James, Robert Styles, Colin Fullthorpe.
    - Confirmed she was friend of Susan Reed
  o Mandy Singleton- college friend according to Alan Reed 00441604643305

- Said Susan Reed had lovers, Leroy James, Robert Styles, Colin Fullthorpe,
            - Confirmed she was friends with Susan Reed
            - Said saw Susan Reed with Colin Fullthorpe
            - Anne Goodchild's Goddaughter
    - Colin Fullthorpe – tutor – why the mobile number?- 00447880636755
        - Seen by Mandy Singleton with Susan Reed
        - According to VV and MS was Susan Reed's lover
        - Denied relationship with Susan Reed when interviewed by Grey
    - Bob Styles – contact – 00441604845667
        - According to VV and MS and AG was Susan Reed's lover
    - Louise Theroux – contact – 00440273944327
    - Leroy – contact- 00447880614378
        - Leroy James?
        - If so according to VV and MS and AG was Susan Reed's lover and supplier of drugs
- Anne Goodchild
    - Susan Reed's counsellor at college
    - Said Susan Reed had told her she had had affairs with Leroy James and Robert Styles,
    - Said she had received complaints of harassment about Fullthorpe from students
    - Is Mandy Singleton's God mother
- Billy Goodchild
    - Husband of Anne

He felt encouraged; his board was filling up nicely, meaning in his experience at least, that they were making progress. But, he admitted to himself sadly, they really only had three pieces of concrete information; Susan Reed had been murdered, she knew her killer, and Colin Fullthorpe had lied when he'd told Grey he had not been seeing her.

Chapter 18

Not long after Grey had left the vicarage, Linda Singleton called her friend Anne Goodchild. She just had to tell her the exciting yet appalling news that the police had called at the vicarage to interview Mandy of all people.

Linda had not known what reaction she had expected from her very best friend when she'd called, but she had not expected her to burst into tears. Full of concern, Linda asked. 'Whatever is wrong my dear?'

Anne Goodchild sobbed into the phone. 'Oh Linda it was just so awful, just awful.'

Linda had no idea what Anne was talking about. 'What was so awful dear, tell me, what?'

'Billy, he was just so rude, so appallingly rude.'

'Billy, he's home?'

'He was but he's gone back to London now.' Anne Goodchild cried.

Linda decided her friend needed support. 'Do you want me to come over?'

'Oh could you, would you mind awfully?'

Linda could hear her friend crying and said. 'Of course not my dear; I'll be there as soon as Chris finishes Mass.'

Replacing the receiver, Linda Singleton felt flat, deflated. She had been so excited after the police had left and couldn't wait to tell Anne all the details, but Anne was in no mood to listen. The poor dear sounded so upset. Billy again, she sighed to herself, what has he done this time?

Colin Fullthorpe was brought into the interview room in mid afternoon after Grey and the uniformed officers had interrupted one of his lectures in full view of his startled students. Before then she had advised the Principal what was going to happen but had given him no details why. Grey had had no compunction in hauling him out; Fullthorpe had lied to her when he'd said there was nothing between him and Susan Reed. Mandy Singleton had said she was prepared to testify that she had seen him with Susan Reed in the Fox & Hounds in Great Brington while she had been having a drink there one evening with her Godmother Anne Goodchild.

Thomas was already waiting when Grey arrived and she sat down beside him. Fullthorpe sat opposite looking frightened and nervous. His hands were shaking as he rested them on the desk.

'Mr. Fullthorpe, do you remember the conversation we had yesterday in your office?' Grey asked.

Fullthorpe could not meet her eyes. 'Yes of course I remember.' He said quietly.

'Do you still maintain that you have no idea how Susan Reed came by your mobile telephone number?'

'Yes, I have no idea. There was no reason why she should have it and I certainly didn't give it to her.'

'So you still maintain that you don't know why she had it?' Grey went on.

'Yes there's no reason that I can think of.' Fullthorpe said.

'Do you know the Fox & Hounds public house in Great Brington?' Grey asked quietly.

Fullthorpe suddenly raised his eyes to meet hers. 'Why would I?'

'Do you know it Mr. Fullthorpe?'

'I, I don't know; I don't think so.' He answered sounding unsure, a sign that Grey interpreted as confirmation that Mandy Singleton had told her the truth and Fullthorpe was wondering how much she knew.

'Did you go to the Fox & Hounds with Susan Reed six weeks ago?' She asked, her eyes drilling into his.

Fullthorpe blushed, something Grey noticed he had done in his office when she'd asked him about the phone number. 'No, I told you, I don't see students outside the college.'

'So why do you think witnesses say they saw you with Susan Reed in the Fox & Hounds?' Grey pressed.

'I have no idea.' Fullthorpe said, but Grey could see his hands were shaking and his lips had begun to quiver; in Grey's eyes he was on the edge and she needed to push him just a little harder.

'Why do you think witnesses would lie about something like that? They would have no reason to.'

'I have no idea and since I don't know who your so called witnesses are, I couldn't comment on whether they would have a reason to. Over the years I've made many enemies in my job.' He said challengingly.

'So let's see; according to you, you never give out your mobile number and yet she had it. How can you explain that?'

'I have no idea; the only explanation is that someone I know had given it to her.' Fullthorpe said again.

'Why would she even want it unless she was going to telephone you?' Grey asked.

'I have no idea.'

'Do you mind if we look at your phone now? We would prefer it if you agreed but of course we could obtain a warrant.'

'No of course not.' He said and then immediately realised he had been stupid to have lied to her. His phone would have a record of calls made and received and so would Susan Reed's phone. Grey already knew they had called one another and she had simply been testing him to see if he had been hiding something. Not knowing which way to turn, he put his elbows on the desk and held his head in his hands. Grey sensed that he had at last realised he had been a fool and so she decided to let silence hang in the air.

After about half a minute he said. 'Alright I admit it; she did have my number and I had hers.'

'Why did you have each other's number?' Grey pressed on.

'Because she was having problems with her work and I had agreed to help her. That's all.' He maintained.

'But didn't you tell me earlier that you never give out your mobile number to students?'

'Yes but Susan was an exception.' He said.

'Oh, why was Susan so exceptional?'

'I felt sorry for her. I knew she had been having some personal problems and I thought I could help her.' He explained.

'Did you feel so sorry for her that you took her to the Fox & Hounds?' Grey persisted.

'It was only for a drink.' Fullthorpe admitted.

'But witnesses say they saw you kissing one another.'

Fullthorpe became agitated and shouted 'They're lying!'

'Why would they lie? Why would more than one person lie?'

'I have no idea.' He said again.

'Aren't you lying? Isn't it true that you were having an affair with Susan Reed?'

'No!' He cried, his voice faltering.

'Mr. Fullthorpe Susan Reed had your mobile number which you say you don't give out to students, and you have hers. Independent witnesses, that means separate unconnected witnesses, say they saw you both at the Fox & Hounds and that you were acting like lovers. You've already proved to me that you're a liar, so who do you think I should believe; you or them?' Grey demanded.

Fullthorpe had turned crimson; his hands were shaking and his lips quivering. 'It was a mistake; a terrible mistake.' He admitted, 'She was having difficulty with the program and asked me to help. I agreed. At first everything was normal, we met only in my office and talked only about the course but she seemed very upset and when she asked if she could have my number so that she could call me when she felt desperate, stupidly I agreed. Then she called me one night and asked to meet me. I felt sorry for her and so I agreed. We talked about her problems and she seemed very grateful for my help. Soon afterwards we began to meet regularly and our conversations became more intimate; we became very fond of one another. She was a very attractive young woman and I was flattered that she took an interest in me. I knew it was wrong and I tried to end it but she was insistent and I couldn't bring myself to hurt her. We became very close. It was stupid of me but I couldn't help myself.'

'You were lovers?'

'Yes.' Fullthorpe admitted.

'Why did you lie to me when I asked you about this earlier?'

'Isn't it obvious?' Fullthorpe cried. 'I told you it's against college rules; if the Board found out it would lead to disciplinary action for gross misconduct. I would face instant dismissal and possibly loss of pension rights. I've been a lecturer for fifteen years DI Grey. Why would I risk losing all that I've worked for?'

'But you had already risked all that when you started your affair with Susan Reed. This is a murder investigation and frankly we are not concerned with your misdemeanours with students, but we do take very seriously attempts to obstruct our investigation. Obstructing the police with their enquiries is a very serious offence. Did you seriously think we wouldn't find out?' Grey said flatly. 'When was the last time you saw her?'

'I don't know, about a week ago I think.'

'You didn't see her on Monday morning?'

Fullthorpe looked aghast, suddenly and terrifyingly aware of the enormity of what he could be facing. 'You can't possibly think I had something to do with her death?' he cried.

'Why not; you were lovers; did something go wrong? You said yourself you had a lot to lose if the College Board found out. Did she threaten to spill the beans?'

'No of course not!' He protested.

'Did she demand money from you to keep quiet?'

'Of course not; don't be ridiculous; she wouldn't have even considered doing something like that; we were very fond of one another.'

'Where were you on Monday morning between ten and ten thirty?'

'I told you, I was at home.' Fullthorpe sobbed. He sounded completely broken; his face was so red he looked like he was about to explode and snot was beginning to run down his nose and over his upper lip making Grey gag. She passed him a tissue and to her relief he blew into it straight away.

'But you also told me you hadn't been seeing Susan Reed, so why should I believe you now?' She pressed.

'You have to believe me, I was at home. I didn't kill her.'

'Do you own a car?'

Fullthorpe was taken aback at the question but quickly recovered. 'Yes, a black Focus.' He said.

'Are you aware there are CCTV cameras on the roads adjoining Manfield Road both top and bottom?'

'No, I didn't know that.' Fullthorpe admitted, recovering his composure a little.

'When we analyse the tapes will we see your car on Monday morning? Don't lie to us again.' Grey left the threat unspoken but fully intended to charge him with obstructing enquiries if he lied again.

'No, inspector, you won't. I have told you the truth; I was at home.' He said firmly.

Thomas had been listening without interruption but he felt that now was the time to move on. He stood up and said. 'We'll take a break for a minute or two.'

'No wait' Fullthorpe pleaded. 'Inspector will it be necessary for you to inform the college about all this?'

Grey gave him a scornful look. 'I have no idea but I'm sure they'll want to know why we felt it necessary to arrest you in the middle of a lecture.'

Fullthorpe looked aghast. 'You told them what you were going to do?'

'Of course; what did you expect? You could have saved yourself a lot of bother if you had told us the truth in the first place. As things are I suspect you'll have a lot of explaining to do.'

Fullthorpe opened his mouth as if to say something else but closed it again, took a deep breath and put his head in his hands.

Thomas and Grey walked out of the interview room into the corridor. 'Well done.' Thomas said encouragingly. 'Arrest him on suspicion, get a warrant and search his house and his office.'

Grey felt so proud she almost burst. 'Yes sir', she said fighting to keep the excitement out of her voice.

'Ok get to it then. I'm going to see Judd and tell him we're making some progress, but I won't go overboard in case this turns out to be a damp squid.'

'Thank you sir.' Grey said and Thomas gave her a curious look. She wasn't sure how to interpret it but a small voice inside her told her to be careful. Taking a deep breath and reminding herself to maintain her professionalism, she went back in to see Fullthorpe.

As Thomas walked back to his office he was having mixed feelings about giving Grey her head by allowing her to lead the interview. He had thought it would be good experience for her and he wanted to see how she would handle it, but he had a feeling that she thought she had already got her man. He hoped he was misjudging her. In his view she had the making of a good investigator, but it was important she did not close her mind to other possibilities. The arrest of Fullthorpe was a logical next step in the course of the investigation but probably not the final one; they would have to release him in a day or two unless they found the weapon or blood on his clothes, and that meant the investigation would continue and other suspects would almost certainly emerge before they uncovered the truth.

The case had many aspects he didn't understand, some fundamental such as the identity of the two mystery visitors at Reed's house between ten and ten past ten on Monday morning; others more oblique, such as why Susan Reed had recorded international dialling codes on her mobile when she hadn't travelled abroad. To Thomas mysteries such as these carried equal weight and he was determined to solve them.

Chapter 19

That evening in Great Brington Anne Goodchild sat on her plush handmade sofa sipping a glass of chilled Dom Perignon in the company of her friend Linda Singleton. Linda had driven over from the vicarage of St.Gregory The Great in Park Avenue with two purposes. The first to comfort her best friend who had sounded so upset when she had called earlier, and the second to impart the exciting news of the visit from the police that afternoon.

'So what has Billy been up to now?' Linda asked tiredly as she sipped her iced water. Linda was strictly tea-total and did not approve of Anne drinking alcohol but tolerated it because, well, Anne was Anne.

Goodchild sipped her champagne before she answered. 'A Detective Chief Inspector Thomas called to see me today; he wanted to know whether I knew Susan Reed, you know that young woman who was murdered on Monday.'

Linda clapped her hands. 'Oh my dear; what a coincidence! That was precisely what I wanted to talk to you about on the telephone.' She said excitedly.

Ignoring Linda, Goodchild continued. 'He wanted to know whether I had met her, which of course I had because I had been counselling her. Anyway, we had been chatting quite amiably for a few minutes when Billy screeched to a halt in his new Jaguar. I wish he wouldn't drive so fast.'

'You know Anne dear, a most charming policewoman came to see us, or should I say, more particularly, came to see Mandy. Detective Inspector Grey I think her name was, yes Detective Inspector Grey.'

Anne seemed not to hear. 'Anyway Billy jumped out of the car and was just so awful to the poor policeman; he was hurling racial abuse at him of all things. The poor man was as black as the ace of spades but of course he couldn't help that and Billy had no right. He called him a nigger. He was so disgusting.'

Linda went on. 'Well of course dear Christopher was apoplectic, poor man; he didn't know which way to turn. Anyway eventually it became clear that she simply wanted to know if Mandy knew this poor soul and could give her any information that might help the police 'with their enquiries' I think they call it, so he relaxed a little.'

'I thought for a moment that Billy was going to get himself arrested for murder. The policeman more or less accused Billy of it. Of course that was preposterous but Billy brought it on himself by being so appallingly rude.' Anne continued, sipping her champagne between breaths.

Linda drained her glass. 'Anyway it turned out that Mandy had known this girl and was able to provide the police with what she was sure was a crucial piece of information; she remembered she had seen her canoodling of all things with her tutor at college in the Fox & Hounds while out one evening with you. Imagine that my dear; canoodling in public!'

Linda looked up, startled, when Anne Goodchild dropped her glass. 'My dear, are you alright? You look very pale all of a sudden.' Linda said hurrying over to help her friend.

Anne Goodchild quickly recovered. 'Yes, yes I'm fine;' she said, 'Oh how clumsy of me.'

'It's Billy; really my dear he should not put you through all this; his insensitivity is doing you no good at all. Where is he now?'

'He said he had to return to London.' Anne Goodchild said sadly.

'Did you believe him?' Linda probed.

Anne Goodchild stood up from the sofa and walked to the table where she refilled her glass. Linda couldn't help herself. 'Really my dear, do you need that?'

Anne Goodchild ignored her and took a sip from her glass. 'I don't know what to believe. He says he's going to meetings and I'm sure sometimes he's telling the truth, but often he comes home stinking of cheap women and whisky.'

'Are you sure dear? Billy is a good man at heart.' Linda reasoned unable to see ill in any man.

'Why he wants to lower himself with these harlots I don't know.' Anne Goodchild sighed with frustration. 'We had a perfectly good marriage.'

'Do you still, well you know?' Linda asked gently.

'No of course not! Good Lord Linda do you think I would go near him knowing he's been with these, these strumpets? They might have given him gonorrhoea or herpes or even AIDS God forbid.'

'My dear please don't blaspheme.' Linda cautioned.

'Oh I'm sorry; he's changed such a lot Linda; he used to be kind and considerate towards me; alright I give you that he's always been brash but that was part of his charm. Now he treats me like dirt and I'm sure he has lost respect for me. Why else would he prefer to spend his time with these whores?'

'Perhaps you're mistaken my dear; have you tried to talk to him?'

Goodchild refilled her glass despite another disapproving glance from Singleton. 'Oh there's no mistake Linda, believe me, the stench of cheap perfume is singular and lingers for days. It makes me feel sick. Oh no there's absolutely no mistake. Yes I've tried to talk to him but you know what he's like; if he's not on the telephone talking to Arthur or his accountant then he has his head buried in one report or another. He's not interested in talking to me; he hasn't got the time.'

'Is there anything I can do to help my dear; perhaps if I asked Christopher to talk to him?' Linda offered.

Goodchild shook her head. 'No, no, but thanks anyway. It's something we have to work out for ourselves. Perhaps it's just a phase he's going through.'

'I shall pray for you both, as will Christopher.' Linda announced.

Chapter 20

'**Name** the actors who played the Magnificent Seven in the 1960 film of the same name' The quizmaster at the Lumbertubs asked.

Grey groaned but Atherley was busy scribbling down the answers. 'Yul Brynner, Robert Vaughn, James Coburn, Charles Bronson, Steve McQueen, Horst Buchholz, and Brad Dexter.' He spoke the names of each one as he wrote them down.

'Brad Dexter?' Grey asked incredulous. 'Who's he?

'He played Harry Luck but Harry's luck ran out when he was shot trying to save Yul Brynner.'

'Who wrote the film score?' Was the quizmaster's follow up question.

Atherley put his pencil to his lips, looking pensive. 'Hmm, I can't remember whether it was Elmer Bernstein or John Williams.' Atherley admitted.

'Definitely Elmer Bernstein, John Williams would have been in nappies.' Grey helped out.

Grey and Atherley were both drinking pints of John Smith's Smooth Bitter. Grey liked a man who drank a proper drink; men who drank wine or alcho-pops were not really men at all in her book. She was having a whale of a time with Atherley, completely at her ease and mentally wilting under the gaze of his wonderful deep blue eyes. Now and then they would accidentally touch hands and once or twice he had leaned towards her and she had thought he was going to kiss her, but then he had turned away and concentrated on the quiz.

Atherley asked 'Are you enjoying yourself? I feel, um, well, as if I should have perhaps treated you to, well, you know, something more um, exclusive, more intimate.'

Grey loved the way he suddenly became shy when he asked her something personal. She wanted to take him in her arms and tell him everything was just fine and she would have been quite happy sharing a bag of chips with him. Instead she smiled and put a hand on his knee.

'This is great, really. Sorry I'm not very good at the quiz.' She said, suddenly conscious her hand was on his knee.

Atherley beamed and Grey felt her heart melt. 'Oh, well then, that's just perfect.' He said and kissed her on the cheek.

Grey blushed, amazed that a man could still make her feel this way. *'You'd better slow down girl'* she told herself and pulled her hand away, concentrating again on the quiz.

'And finally, who did Yul Brynner marry on the set of the Magnificent Seven?' The quizmaster asked to the collective groans of the audience. Instantly Atherley grinned and began scribbling. Grey raised her eyes to the heavens. *Good grief, the crap some people store in their memory boxes!*

Chapter 21

The following morning the search of Manfield Road ended without a weapon or anything incriminating being found with the exception of a few used condoms in back gardens and a World War 11 Enfield No2 Mark1 revolver found buried in a shallow grave under a headstone marked. 'In Loving memory of Joey, faithful friend died 1992.' There was no trace of any dog or budgerigar.

Thomas related the good and bad news to Judd; good that Manfield Road could be re-opened, bad that the search had proved fruitless. Judd seemed pleased about the good and unconcerned about the bad. 'Thank God for that' he said, sounding relieved, 'perhaps now the Chief will get off my back for a while.'

'Let's hope so sir, but it brings us no nearer finding the murderer.' Thomas reminded him.

'Yes, well,' Judd said accurately. 'It eliminates one avenue of the enquiry.'

Thomas tried not to laugh outwardly at Judd's unintended pun. 'Yes sir.'

'By the way, the Chief has received a complaint from a Billy Goodchild; he says you were harassing his wife yesterday. His big shot lawyer's on the case. The Chief says Goodchild's some big-wig businessman; always trouble that type. Have you met him?'

Thomas swore silently. 'Briefly sir; he turned up when I interviewed his wife yesterday but it was a standard enquiry; I was gathering background information on the victim and possible suspects.'

'Oh well, no doubt we'll know more about what his gripe is once his lawyer sends in the details. Meanwhile keep at it; progress report my office Tomorrow at nine.'

'Sir.' Thomas agreed and rang off. *So, Billy boy wants to cause trouble. I wonder why? Does he just not like the colour of my skin or is there something deeper?*

He knew that Grey was busily writing up her report on her meeting with Mandy Singleton, and he had spent last evening likewise on his meeting with Anne Goodchild. He called the CCTV team and was told the list of registered owners would be with him later that morning. Forensics, he'd been promised, would have something later that day. Before then he decided he had time to pay a visit to Leroy James, alleged lover of Susan Reed and alleged drug pusher.

He drove towards Salisbury Street in the Semilong district of town with his shuffle playing Dolly Parton's Jolene. He had grinned when it had begun because it continued his musical title string; Jolene was Comfortably Numb with The Emperor having been to the Freaker's Ball on Telegraph Road, On the Moon. He had a feeling in his water this might be the big one.

He knew some of Semilong's more recent history. At the outbreak of WW11 it had been a well-to-do area, many of the then modern red bricked houses had boasted long gardens and ornamental cast iron gates and railings. Unfortunately the iron had been seized by the military to make much needed armaments, and it was only after the war that residents had discovered to their dismay that their beloved gates and railings had been made from pig iron and had been of no use whatsoever to the war effort. Unsurprisingly the government of the time had not offered to compensate them in any way.

Many of the streets had been named after famous historical figures such as Gordon, Stanley, and Salisbury, and much of the local industry had been converted from shoe-making to the manufacture of radar parts and armaments, whereas before the war over forty percent of it had been involved in making shoes.

Semilong had constructed its own air raid point in Adelaide Street and back gardens had been littered with Anderson Shelters. As it turned out they had been unnecessary; the Luftwaffe had only dropped two bombs on Northampton throughout the war, neither of them on the Semilong district. Indeed the worst damage Northampton had suffered had been when a Stirling Bomber had crashed in Gold Street, killing all of its crew when their parachutes had failed to open.

Semilong's main recreation ground, The Racecourse, an eighteenth century track much favoured by the Prince of Wales and Edward V11, had been turned over to the Army and they had promptly built barracks on it. Earlier, before 1818, it had been used for public executions

So Thomas was sad that an area so rich in history, so typical of districts in towns throughout the country, was now a haven for drugs and prostitution. Over the years the area had become tired and neglected and was a magnet for the poor. Immigrant refugees from Idi Amin's Uganda, Eastern block escapees taking advantage of their EU membership, West Indians and displaced English from the London overspill had flooded the area. Prostitution was rife, particularly around Spring Lane and Grafton Street, and gangs and drug pushers roamed the ill-lit back alleys and narrow streets. Considered an attractive design feature in the late nineteenth and early twentieth centuries, these dark passageways were perfect for street-walkers and illicit drug dealers to ply their trade without much fear of being disturbed. Thomas was aware that the Police had arrested over one hundred prostitutes in the past six months and sent warning letters to over four hundred kerb-crawlers. Gangs fuelled on cheap alcohol and crack congregated around Burleigh Road and Paddy's meadow, intimidating residents and mugging the unwary.

Salisbury Street was one of several running off of St.Andrew's Road, the main link road that ran north to south along the western edge of the district. As Thomas turned into it he could see houses with rotting window frames and paint peeling from front doors. Empty beer cans, discarded chip paper, Styrofoam cups and cigarette ends littered the gutters and an old mattress and three rusting supermarket trolleys had been dumped on waste ground at the far end of the street.

Thomas parked outside Leroy James' house where a plain clothed officer was already waiting for him, his blue unmarked Astra parked further up the street. He nodded to him as he walked towards the front door and rapped the lion's head brass knocker. A few seconds later a tall Rastafarian with dreadlocks, naked from the waist up, opened the door, an angry look on his face.

Thomas showed him his warrant card. 'Leroy James?'

'Wha chew want man?'

'Are you Leroy James?' Thomas asked again.

'Yeah, wha chew want wi mi?'

'I'm Detective Chief Inspector Thomas Northampton Police; I'm investigating the murder of Susan Reed; can we come in?'

James suddenly looked wary. 'You wanna fit mi up man?'

Thomas said patiently. 'Nobody's going to fit you up Leroy but I need to talk to you. Now we can either do it here or at Campbell Square; your choice.'

James opened the door wider and Thomas and the constable followed him inside to a small dark sitting room. Two well-worn easy chairs flanked the window overlooking the back yard, and a scratched and burnt dark coffee table stood in the centre of the room, a burning cigarette resting on the edge of it. The curtains were drawn, the only light in the room coming from a ceiling lamp; there was no lampshade. Stubbed out cigarettes littered the bare floor-boards together with small strips of aluminium foil, used matches and screwed up newspaper. James pulled a red sweatshirt over his head and stubbed out the cigarette.

'Take a chair man.' He offered and Thomas sat on the one facing the door; James sat opposite; the constable stood by the door arms behind his back. Thomas estimated James was about six two; age about twenty five and very fit; he reeked of stale smoke as did the room.

'I'm sure you've read that Susan Reed was murdered on Monday morning.' Thomas began. 'I have reason to believe you knew her.'

'Yeah man, I see her at college.'

'Can you tell me about her, about your relationship with her?'

James lit another cigarette, pointed the packet at Thomas but Thomas shook his head.

'Mi meet her at college, She like mi buddy.' James leered. Thomas was not great at Jamaican slang but he understood it to mean she liked having sex with him. James had wasted no time in boasting about his sexual prowess and Thomas took an instant dislike to him.

'How did you meet her?'

James shrugged. 'At college man; she ready; she have trouble with her man so Mi take make a move. She like mi buddy an everything jus fine.'

'You were her lover?'

'Yeah.' James said grinning.

'Did you ever supply her with drugs?'

James' grin disappeared instantly and he became agitated. He stubbed out his cigarette, stood up and began pacing around the room.

'Why you ask mi that man? Mi do nothing to this woman. You mi brother, you shouldna ask mi questions like this.'

Thomas corrected him calmly. 'I'm not your brother Leroy. Now you have a choice; you can either answer my questions here and now, or you can answer them later at the station. Meanwhile I'll arrange for a search warrant and have this place taken apart piece by piece. I'm investigating a murder and I haven't got time to waste; it's not a good idea for you to try to mess me around.'

James stopped pacing and sat down again. He reached for another cigarette and lit it, inhaling a deep lungful of smoke. 'Wha chew want from mi man? Why you bother mi like this?' He asked as if in pain.

'Did you supply her with drugs?'

'A lidl man, jus one time.'

'You supplied her with cocaine?'

'Yeah.'

'Did she ask you for it?'

'No man, we were just rompin an smokin spliffs, then we take a line man, truss mi.'

'Who did you buy your cocaine from?' Thomas demanded to know.

'Looky mi no bad man, Mr. Thomas, no.' James said evasively.

Thomas decided he could ask him again later who his supplier was and changed the direction of his questioning. 'How long did you know her?'

'No long; she need money man but mi no bupps.'

'Bupps?' Thomas asked bewildered.

'Sugar daddy man! Mi no bupps, she gotta work for her money. Mi no bupps.' James repeated.

'Why did money come into your conversations if you were only 'taking a line' as you put it? Did you demand money from her?'

'She want more man. After we finish, she want more.' James suddenly became agitated again, saying sharply. 'Look man this ain't right. You shouldna be asking me these questions.'

'She wanted more cocaine?'

'Yeah man but she don't have no money.'

'So you weren't prepared to give it to her for free?'

James looked at Thomas as though he'd just landed from some far away planet. 'No man; we'd finished. If she want more she need money. Mi no get it for free.'

'She needed money to buy drugs from you?' Thomas pressed.

'No man, no.' James protested. At that moment someone knocked on the front door and James grunted and strode out of the room. Thomas heard some low murmuring before James returned a few moments later. 'So why did she need money?' He continued.

James looked confused and wiped his brow. 'Mi dunno man; she need di money.'

'When was the last time you saw her?'

'Mi dunno man, weeks ago.' James said evasively.

'Are you sure?' Thomas pressed.

James looked irritated. 'No man, mi dunno, mi dunno. This ain't right man; you shouldna bother mi like this.' He repeated as if in pain.

'Where were you on Monday morning between ten and half past?'

Someone knocked the front door again and James cursed in frustration as he hurried to answer it. Thomas heard more murmuring and then James returned. Thomas repeated his question.

'Mi dunno man, maybe mi here.'

'Can anyone vouch for where you were?'

James seemed to be in pain again, his voice tight as a drum. 'No man, mi dunno.'

Thomas stood abruptly. 'Ok Leroy that's enough; you're coming with me to the station. I'm arresting you on suspicion of murdering Susan Reed.' Thomas said his patience exhausted.

James was shouting 'Dis is a fuckery, a fuckery man. Mi no bad man' and struggling as the constable cuffed him and dragged him towards his car. Thomas waited until the constable had driven off before he called Grey to tell her what he'd done and instructed her to organise a team to search the house. He had decided early in the interview with James what action he was going to take. The aluminium strips on the floor and James' admission that he'd supplied Susan Reed with drugs was enough to charge him, and he had guessed that the visitors had been James' customers.

He reasoned James would tell him nothing about the case while he felt safe in his own home, but suspected things would be different when he was facing prosecution for dealing in cocaine; it carried a maximum life sentence. That would be more than enough to frighten a small time dealer like Leroy James. If he had been conducting a cocaine operation from this house, then even if the search team found nothing to incriminate him in the murder of Susan Reed they would surely find his stash of drugs.

The constable would book Leroy James in and Thomas would wait for the results of the search of his house before talking to him again.

Chapter 22

He decided to take a slow drive back to his office where he hoped the CCTV results would be waiting for him and was listening to Jeremy Vine on the radio on his way back to the station, not willing to risk the shuffle. He turned into St.Andrew's Road. At the south end stood Castle Station, so named after the eleventh century Norman Castle where Thomas Becket had once been imprisoned after he had fallen out with Henry 11. Henry111 had defeated Simon De Montford there in 1264, and Henry V1 was briefly imprisoned in the dungeons in 1460 during the War of the Roses. With that sort of history Thomas wondered idly why they hadn't named it 'King Henry's Road'. All remains of the castle had been demolished or buried long ago on the orders of Charles 11 after the town had supported Parliament in the Civil War against his father. Now a dull grey-bricked railway station stands on the site.

At the north end towards which Thomas was driving, stood Kingsthorpe Hollow, a stopping point on the route of the old horse drawn tram system that had run from the town centre northwards towards Kingsthorpe on the northern edge of the town. He turned right past the imposing arches of the Barratt Shoe Factory designed by Alexander Ellis Anderson and constructed in 1913. A student of local history, Thomas had learned that Northampton could trace its shoe-making origins as far back as the ninth century; the town was surrounded by forests and agricultural land where oak trees flourished and animals could easily breed. Oak bark was used exclusively to tan leather skins in those days and so the growth of the industry in the town was inevitable. King Alfred had ordered boots from local cobblers for his whole army in

890AD and a succession of Kings and Queens had given local tradesmen the honour of making their shoes ever since.

Thomas turned left at the top of Primrose Hill into St. George's Avenue with the Racecourse on his right and the University on his left. He followed the old race-track around two right turns before heading back along the Kettering Road that ran parallel with the old home straight, and as he drove over the Mounts on the approach to Campbell Square Station he passed by the only art-deco swimming baths in England which had been built on the site of the eastern edge of the old prison in 1936.

He parked his car and ran up the steps to his office. Slightly out of breath when he arrived he threw his jacket onto the nearest chair and picked up a manila envelope left on his desk by the CCTV team.

They had handily organised the names of the registered keepers in alphabetical order but there were over two thousand names in all and he groaned inwardly when he felt how thick and heavy the report was. Quickly he began to scan down the list, looking for a match with those on his board. He was about two thirds of the way down and beginning to feel disheartened when a name suddenly caught his eye and his finger stopped. Robert Styles was there, his car recorded being parked in Wellingborough Road about a hundred yards from the south end of Manfield Road at 09.56 a.m. on Monday morning; description of person leaving the car and heading in the direction of Manfield Road, white male, baseball cap, dark jacket and trousers, light shoes, age mid twenties.

Thomas tapped the paper with his fingers, 'Gotcha' He whispered to himself. The description fit the one given by Mrs. Stephens so in all probability Styles had been the first caller after Alan Reed had left the house. He would be able to obtain zoomed-in close ups of the images later if he needed them, and he thought he might.

Quickly checking that the addresses from DVLA and the college matched and having confirmed they did, Thomas called a DC and asked him to bring Styles into the station straight away. Then he phoned DI Grey and asked her to join him.

While he was waiting for Grey he received a telephone call from the senior officer in charge of the team that had searched Colin Fullthorpe's house. He told him that Fullthorpe's wife had been inconsolable, unable to take in what was happening when they had turned over the house and gardens; they had found no weapon, and no bloody clothes. If it was any consolation they had uncovered letters and notes in a wall-safe in the garage suggesting that Colin Fullthorpe had been no stranger to secret liaisons with his students; it looked like he'd been at it for years and he'd kept the correspondence as trophies. The team had bagged his clothes for forensics just in case.

Thomas thanked him, put down the receiver and pondered what to do with Fullthorpe. Whilst seducing his students was against college rules and would certainly result in him losing his job, it wasn't a criminal offence. All the students were over the age of consent and there had been no suggestion of attempted rape. He couldn't charge him with breaking college rules so without a weapon or forensics he had nothing to hold him on and he knew he would not receive any forensics from his clothes for a few days yet. He'd have to release him before then. True he had lied to Grey about his relationship with Susan Reed but he had had good reason to; his career and perhaps more hung on the college remaining ignorant of his relationship with her. He would have reasoned, probably correctly, that if the Police found out the college would surely follow. He certainly had motive and he had no alibi but on balance Thomas decided he would have to let him go.

He wondered how Grey would take it, suspecting as he did that she had pinned her hopes on Fullthorpe being Susan Reed's killer. Maybe he was maybe he wasn't; either way Thomas could do nothing without evidence.

He walked over to his board and updated it with what he knew about Fullthorpe and now Styles. As he was writing he reminded himself that Billy Goodchild had not yet provided the list of alibis he had promised and pondered whether he should ring him or wait given that Goodchild had already complained to the Chief about his conduct. As groundless as Thomas knew it was, mud had a habit of sticking and the last thing he wanted was for the Chief to form the wrong impression of him. He decided to wait a day. When he had finished writing he stared at the board for a few minutes, thinking, testing theories and ideas that sprang to mind.

His list of facts was getting longer; Susan Reed had been murdered, she knew her killer, Colin Fullthorpe had been her lover as had Leroy James who had also been her supplier of cocaine, and now Robert Styles' car and someone resembling the person Mrs. Stephens had seen, presumably Styles, had been picked up by CCTV in the vicinity of Manfield Road. But, he asked himself wearily, was he any nearer to finding Susan Reed's killer? In all honesty, he had no idea.

Chapter 23

Sheila Grey was feeling warm and tingly after her night out with Atherley; they had won the pub quiz, much to her astonishment, Yul Brynner marrying Doris Kleiner on the set of The Magnificent Seven had been the clincher, and then sat and talked until almost closing time. Atherley had made her laugh and when she had gazed into his deep blue eyes she had felt herself go weak at the knees. He had insisted they share a taxi and they'd kissed when it had arrived at her door. As it drove off to take Atherley home, she felt suddenly lost but he had promised to call her soon to arrange another date and she couldn't wait.

She had finished typing up her report from her meeting with Mandy Singleton and carried it into Thomas' office where she found him sitting in front of his marker-board in deep thought. He waved to acknowledge her as she entered but remained pondering and she sat silently waiting for him to break out of his reverie. After a few uncomfortable minutes he stood up and walked to the chair behind his desk. Sitting down again he said 'We're going to have to let Fullthorpe go.'

Grey felt the heat rushing to her face; Fullthorpe was top of her list for killing Susan Reed. 'Why sir, he has admitted having an affair with her and he has an excellent motive for killing her? He needed her to keep quiet about their affair and if she had been threatening him…' She argued

'We have no evidence to hold him.' Thomas interrupted. 'We've found nothing in his house; no weapon, no bloodstained clothes, his car is not on the CCTV list; we have nothing that places him at the scene.'

'But he has no alibi sir, and what about Clare Trussler's evidence; she saw someone resembling Fullthorpe knock on the door at ten past ten?' She protested.

'Yes but she's vague about the description. I'm sorry but unless forensics find something then we have nothing on him.'

Grey wanted to carry on but zipped her mouth because she didn't want to antagonise Thomas to the point where they had a stand up row. She thought he was wrong and too hasty, as in her view he had been when he had released Alan Reed. Nevertheless she had to accept that as things stood he was technically right; they had no direct evidence against Fullthorpe, everything was circumstantial, but it didn't stop her believing he was the killer. He was sly, deceitful, and had a lot to lose; definitely the likely killer.

'Uniform are bringing Robert Styles in and we need as much background as we can get so I'd like you to carry on working on the contact list.' Thomas continued.

Grey felt every ounce of confidence drain out of her. 'Don't you want me in on the interview with Styles sir?' She asked lamely.

'Not at this stage.' Thomas said ignoring Grey's obvious disappointment, 'Is this the report of your meeting with Mandy Singleton?' He asked picking up the manila folder from his desk.

Grey was livid at being sidelined like this; she had done nothing wrong! 'Yes sir' she managed to say using every ounce of her self-control to prevent herself from screaming at him.

'Good; here's mine on my meeting with Anne Goodchild;' he said handing her a folder, 'read it and look for inconsistencies with what you know from talking to Vanessa Vokes and Mandy Singleton. I'll do the same. There might be something in there that doesn't fit.'

Grey took the folder from him and left the office, silently cursing him for releasing her number one suspect, excluding her from interviewing Robert Styles, now his prime suspect, and putting her on clerical duty cross-checking bloody statements! And all this after telling her she'd made a good job of interviewing Fullthorpe.

In her anger she decided that Thomas was a two-faced trophy hunter; all smiles and well-dones, but when it came down to it, he wasn't going to allow her to get anywhere near anybody he suspected might have committed the crime. Now that he was going to release Fullthorpe, even if they eventually proved that he had killed Susan Reed, he could claim all the credit when solid evidence came to light. As for Styles, CCTV had probably put him at the scene and Thomas had made damn sure that she was going to be nowhere near him if he coughed, whereas he would be right there interviewing him. He wanted the glory all to himself.

Back at her office she called the number on the contact list for Louise Theroux but a voice said 'the number you have dialled has not been recognised on this network.' She dialled it again more carefully and got the same answer. Sighing in frustration she gave up and began reading Thomas' report of his meeting with Anne Goodchild.

Thomas wanted to make sure he had all he knew about Styles clear in his mind before interviewing him so he re-read Grey's notes from her conversation with Vanessa Vokes and tried to recall whether Fullthorpe had mentioned him; he didn't think he had.

Vokes had said that Susan Reed had met Robert Styles at college on the re-bound from Leroy James. He had fallen for her in a big way, but she had quickly tired of him. Nevertheless Styles had not given up and he had called her on the telephone and turned up at her front door, even when Alan Reed had been in the house. Anne Goodchild had said very much the same thing.

So was Robert Styles Susan Reed's murderer? He had motive; unrequited love; he had opportunity; CCTV had captured him, at least Thomas assumed it must have been him parking his car and heading towards Reed's house just before ten on Monday morning. Did he have the means? Thomas decided he would have to arrange a search of his house and car for the weapon and have his clothes taken in for forensics to examine. He picked up the telephone and asked DI Grey to organise it straight away.

So now, Thomas summarised in his mind, we have three searches with results pending and two completed. The search of Reed's house has produced nothing and neither has Manfield Road; Fullthorpe's house likewise so far; uniforms are still turning over James' house, and very shortly they will be doing the same at Styles'. We desperately need the weapon or at least some physical evidence tying one of the suspects to the murder, unless of course Robert Styles coughs.

A call came in from the Duty Desk and Thomas headed down to Interview Room1 where Styles was waiting accompanied by a duty constable. He looked pale and frightened. He was dressed in blue jeans and a navy sweatshirt, and had a day's stubble on his face. His hair, shoulder-length, dark brown and untidy hadn't been combed. Thomas switched on the tapes and introduced himself. 'For the purpose of the record Mr. Styles can you state your full name?'

'Robert John Styles.'

'Thanks. Now you have read about the murder of Susan Reed in the newspapers?'

'Yes.' Styles replied. Thomas noticed his hands were shaking.

'And therefore no doubt you would have read our appeal for people who had information to come forward. It has been printed with every article. Did you see that appeal?'

'No.'

'No? And yet you say you have been reading the newspaper reports. Are you sure?'

'I didn't see any appeal; I was only interested in reading about the murder.' Styles insisted.

'And have you heard the appeal on the radio?'

'No,'

'If you had read it or heard it, you would have come forward wouldn't you?' Thomas went on.

'I have no information that would help you so why would I?'

'Did you know her?'

'Yes, from college.'

'Can you tell me where you were between ten and ten thirty on Monday morning?' Thomas asked. Styles was looking at the floor, both his hands clenched together on the desk as if in prayer. Thomas wasn't sure but he looked as though he was trembling.

'At home I think.'

'You think or you're sure?' Thomas pressed.

'Fairly sure.' Styles said quietly.

'Can anyone confirm that?'

'No I was alone.'

'Do you own a car?'

'Yes, a black Clio.'

'Can you remember the registration number?'

'Sure KR07 YUB.'

Thomas took a photo from the CCTV image from his pocket and placed it on the desk. The photo showed the time-stamp 09:57 and date April 16 2007. In the centre of the photo was an image of a black Clio registration number KR07 YUB. Part of the picture, the part that Thomas now knew showed Robert Styles, had been blacked out.

Styles groaned and put his head in his hands. 'Is this your car Mr. Styles?'

'It is.' He said, peering from between his hands.

'This picture was taken by CCTV along the Wellingborough Road last Monday morning. Can you explain how your car came to be there?'

Styles sat back and took a deep breath. 'I'd been out the night before, had a few drinks, I left it there and walked home.'

'Very sensible,' Thomas allowed, and then picked another photo from his pocket, this one with the image of Robert Styles locking his car clearly visible. He skimmed it across the desk towards Styles like a dealer in a casino. The trump card, Thomas reckoned; he didn't think Styles would have a 'get out of jail' card.

Styles just stared at it, uncomprehending for several seconds and Thomas allowed time for the meaning of the photograph to sink into his brain before he asked. 'Can you explain how you are in this photograph in Wellingborough Road at 09:57 on Monday morning when you told me a moment ago that you were at home?'

'There must be some mistake.' Styles argued.

Thomas raised his voice slightly. 'Oh no mistake Mr. Styles I can assure you. We even have the moving images showing you driving up to this spot, parking your car, getting out and walking towards Manfield Road. No, the mistake is yours isn't it?'

'I told you I was at home.' Styles insisted.

Thomas sighed theatrically and said in a scathing tone. 'So when we take statements from all the other car owners who were captured in the picture they're all going to say it's a mistake are they? Get real Mr. Styles; you were in Wellingborough Road on Monday morning now weren't you?'

Styles thought for several seconds. He seemed to be holding his breath, his cheeks were puffed out and he was tapping his forehead with his clenched fists. Finally he exhaled and admitted. 'Alright I admit it, I was there.'

'And can you tell us why you were there?' Thomas probed quietly.

'I went to see Susan. I wanted to see her, tell her how much I loved her. Make her understand how I felt, how I could help her, but she refused, she wouldn't let me in. I knocked on her door and she asked who was there but when I told her it was me she wouldn't open it. I said I needed to see her but she shouted 'Go Away'. I pleaded with her but she told me to 'F off'. Styles spoke in a calm voice but Thomas could see his hands were shaking and a lump had formed in his neck, it was beating very fast in rhythm with his heart. 'I waited perhaps a minute or two, pleading with her, but she didn't answer and so eventually I gave up and left.' Styles continued.

'You went back to your car?' Thomas asked, knowing that his car hadn't been moved by ten thirty when the CCTV team had cut-off their analysis.

'No I wandered around for a while, my head spinning. I couldn't understand why she had rejected me.'

'Did you go back, try again?'

'No I walked around for a while then headed over to the Racecourse trying to get my head straight, telling myself it was useless and I should give her up, but I loved her and as hard as I tried to make myself see sense nothing was working so in the end I went into the White Elephant and got drunk.' Styles explained.

'Did you meet anybody you knew in the White Elephant?'

'No, it's not my local. I just sat in a corner feeling sorry for myself and getting quietly drunk.'

'How did you get home?'

'Taxi.'

'Can you remember the name of the taxi company?'

'No but the barman ordered it so maybe he'll remember.' Styles offered.

'Any idea what time you arrived home?' Thomas asked.

'I don't know, maybe two or two-thirty. My mum will know; she was at home when I got back.'

Thomas was surprised. 'You live with your mother?'

Styles looked taken-aback that Thomas had asked. 'Yes and my father.' He replied meeting Thomas' eyes for the first time since the interview had begun.

Somehow Thomas had never imagined that Styles would still be living with his parents; he'd pictured him as having his own flat, or at least a room where he and Reed could have found some privacy. He wondered how they had conducted their affair; was it in his car or in her house? His parents would be upset to say the least when the search team knocked on the door. 'So you went to see Susan Reed at around ten o' clock on Monday morning and you didn't think to come in and tell us?'

'No, I thought it might get me into trouble.'

'Why would you think that if you've got nothing to hide?'

'I would have thought that was obvious; she was killed on Monday morning. I went to see her on Monday morning. I would have been a prime suspect.'

Thomas decided to change direction. 'Tell me about when you met her, your relationship with her.'

Styles leaned back in his chair and fidgeted around, trying to get comfortable. 'We were at college together studying Business Administration. I knew she was married but I fancied her from the start and tried to chat her up. At first she wasn't interested, but I knew she had been having marital problems because Vanessa Vokes had told me so I kept on trying. But then I found out she had started to see that jerk Leroy James. He's a cold hearted drug pushing black bastard.' Styles scowled bitterly then suddenly put both hands to his mouth when he realised what he'd said. 'Oh sorry, no offence.'

Thomas let out a long weary breath. 'Carry on.' He said.

'We often sat together in the canteen and sometimes over the lunch break and we got on really well; she told me about her marriage and the problems she had been having with Alan, her husband, but she didn't mention Leroy James at first. I asked her out lots of times but she always refused. She was a moody type; some days she would be on edge, other days hyper-excited, but I didn't understand why until Vanessa told me she had been taking cocaine. James had got her hooked. Then one day she burst into tears and I put my arm around her and asked her what was wrong. She admitted she had been seeing James and that he had dumped her. I think she had fallen in love with him. Anyway we talked for a long time and eventually I offered to give her a lift home. We went for a drink. My mum and Dad were away and I took her home. We talked some more and eventually we made love and then began seeing one another regularly, usually at my house when my parents were out at work or in the car, sometimes but not often at her house.'

'For sex you mean?' Thomas asked.

'Not just sex; we talked a lot and had some fun.'

'Did she ever admit to taking drugs?'

'Not at first, but it was obvious what was wrong with her; she could be distant and sometimes she would shake. It was quite scary. I would ask her what was wrong and for a long time she would say 'nothing', but eventually she admitted it.'

'To your knowledge did Alan Reed ever find out about your affair?'

'I'm fairly sure he knew; we were in bed one afternoon at her house; we had been drinking and we both fell asleep after making love. We woke up in a panic after we heard him unlock the front door. We scrambled about getting dressed and made an excuse that I'd been helping her with her homework but I'm sure he didn't believe us. He must have heard us getting dressed. He didn't say anything at the time, didn't accuse us of anything, but he made it fairly obvious by his expression that he knew what had been happening. I wouldn't have denied it if he had confronted us.' Styles declared firmly.

'Do you think she would have denied it?'

Styles sank back into his chair. 'Probably; I don't think she wanted him to know and in any case she didn't really want me she wanted James.' He said resignedly.

'Can you remember when this was?' Thomas asked knowing the date might be important.

'A couple of months ago I think, the day after my birthday, February 11th.'

'Do you think Alan knew she had been seeing James?'

'Oh absolutely he knew. She told me James would demand money from him when she couldn't pay him for her drugs. He was a greedy bastard, wanted paying twice. He would make her sleep with him for a fix then pester Alan for payment. James had no qualms about it; it was just good business practice for him. Sue told me she had told him that she'd been sleeping with James. So yeah, he knew.' Styles said bitterly as if bad memories were coming back to haunt him.

'Did she ever speak to you about Colin Fullthorpe?' Thomas asked.

'Fullthorpe, no why should she?'

'He was your tutor at college wasn't he? It would be natural for you both to talk about him.'

Styles shrugged his shoulders. 'Not that I can recall.'

'What about extra lessons, outside college hours, I mean; did she ever mention anything about having extra lessons with Fullthorpe?' Thomas pressed.

'No.' And then Styles suddenly seemed to realise why Thomas was asking him about Fullthorpe. 'Are you saying that Fullthorpe was trying it on with Sue? Is that what you're saying?' They weren't really questions the way Styles was spitting them out, they were accusations.

'Was he, to your knowledge?' Thomas persisted.

'No! That bastard; if he was.'

Thomas interrupted, changing the subject. 'Did you kill her Robert?' He asked gently.

'Me? Kill her? Of course not, I loved her.' He exclaimed.

'Did you go to her house on Monday morning and slit her throat, stab her in the back?'

Blood flooded into Styles' face and his eyes were wide in horror. 'No, she wouldn't answer the door, I didn't see her.' He maintained.

'Did you argue with her; did she tell you she didn't want to see you again, turn her back on you, and in a fit of rage, did you cut her Robert?'

Styles looked ready to explode, his face was crimson his neck bulging, the pulse throbbing like a volcano about to erupt. 'No, I didn't kill her; I swear; I didn't see her; she wouldn't let me in.'

'But you went to her house to see her, didn't you; you went to reason with her, tell her how much you loved her?' Thomas pressed on.

'Yes, I did love her; I needed to see her.'

'But she refused to see you, told you to 'F off' you said. Here's what I think; you pleaded with her and she let you in; but then she turned her back on you, told you she loved Leroy James, told you that you were nothing to her, and you saw the red mist, saw the red mist and cut her throat.'

'No!' Styles cried looking defiantly at Thomas. 'I didn't kill her.'

Thomas waited for a minute until Styles had calmed down. Styles looked up and met Thomas' eyes wondering what was coming next. Suddenly Thomas shrugged and said. 'Oh well, no doubt after we've searched your house we might find the murder weapon or some clothes with blood on them, and then we'll know whether you've been telling the truth.'

Styles looked aghast. 'Search, what are you talking about? You can't do that.' He protested.

Thomas shrugged again. 'It's being done as we speak.' He told him nonchalantly.

'My Mum and Dad, you can't; it'll kill them. They know nothing about this.' Styles pleaded.

'Then you could have saved them a lot of hassle and heartache by coming forward at the start.'

Styles sank back into the chair again. 'Sod you then; I didn't kill her.' He said finally.

Thomas had the constable lead Styles back to the cells for the night and went back to his office hoping for some news from forensics, but when he arrived there was nothing from them so he went over in his mind what Styles had told him.

Styles had said that Alan Reed knew his wife had been sleeping with Leroy James because she had admitted it to him. Reed had said he didn't know.

Styles had also said that Leroy James had demanded money from Alan Reed in payment for drugs he'd supplied her, but Reed had denied knowing the name of her supplier.

Finally Styles had said that he was certain Alan Reed knew he and Reed's wife had been lovers because he had almost discovered them in bed together; but Reed had denied knowing his wife had a lover.

All were good enough reasons for Reed to have murdered his wife. One scenario Thomas could think of was that Styles *had* been telling the truth; he *had* gone to the house and she *had* turned him away but Reed had seen him leaving as he was making his way back from Threshers. Knowing she had been sleeping with him, Reed had worked himself up into a rage and did her in. That would fit with the timeline and the way she had been killed. An attack from the rear, her throat cut; both possibly suggested rage and the stab in the back added weight to that theory. The problem was still the weapon; where was it?

Then something else occurred to Thomas that filled him with dread. Based on what Styles had told him about trudging off disconsolately onto the Racecourse after being turned away from Susan Reed's door, he would have to ask Judd for more bodies to search that whole area for the weapon. Murderers often told half-truths and it was possible that Styles had cut her and then disposed of the weapon on the Racecourse. Knowing how much he'd already spent on search parties and the pressure coming down from the Chief concerning budgets he knew it wouldn't make him the most popular DCI in the county. *'God help me.'* He pleaded silently.

Chapter 24

When Thomas arrived home that evening Bill didn't recognise him; in fact he was sitting in his favourite chair looking at the TV oblivious to what was going on around him. Alice had tried speaking to him but he had ignored her too and when Thomas had said 'Evening Bill' he had not even acknowledged him. He wondered where Bill's mind went when he switched off like this. Was he remembering something from his past, did he imagine he was somewhere else at a different time? Could he recall people; did he think they were here with him? How long would he be like this, days, weeks, forever? Would he ever recognise the two of them again? It was impossible to tell.

Thomas poured himself a drink and kissed Alice then made himself a quick sandwich before retiring to his study to read Grey's report on her interview with Mandy Singleton. Judging from her notes Singleton had been brought up in a strict Catholic household, her uncle a priest, her mother a very devout Catholic. Grey had described her nature as enigmatic and Thomas wondered what she had meant by that. Her reaction to Grey's questions had been terse and sometimes she had appeared apathetic to sensitive questions when Grey had expected her to show some horror or at least sadness over her friend's murder. Grey had written in her notes that she had been perplexed by her demeanour and that somehow she had felt uncomfortable with her. Thomas was trying to work out what to make of it all and was considering calling her when he heard a muffled scream from the back of the house.

He jumped out of his chair and ran into the kitchen. Alice was lying unconscious on the floor and Bill was standing over her with a heavy saucepan in his hand. Heart in his mouth Thomas knelt down beside her and put two fingers to her throat, checking for a pulse; he found one quickly and breathed a sigh of relief. As he rolled her into the recovery position he could see Bill out of the corner of his eye approaching him with the saucepan raised. Quickly he stood and took it from him. Bill did not resist but looked frightened. 'For God's sake Bill, it's me Brian, and this is Alice your daughter; can't you see?' Thomas asked in temper and frustration

Bill shook his head and said threateningly. 'I don't know either of you; what are you doing in my house?'

'We live here and so do you.' He shouted.

'You don't live here; I've never set eyes on you before.' Bill shouted. 'I've lived here on my own for years.'

Thomas ignored him and, careful not to let him out of his sight, dialled 999 for an ambulance. After he had put the phone down he sat Bill down on a kitchen stool and waited. The paramedics arrived ten minutes later by when Alice had regained a groggy consciousness. They checked her over and then carefully put her into a wheelchair, pushing her to the ambulance before driving her to Northampton General Hospital.

Thomas waited patiently in casualty with Bill while they checked Alice over and after about an hour a nurse told him he could see her but she would be kept in overnight as a precaution. He left Bill with the nurse and was shown towards one of the casualty cubicles where Alice was tucked up in a bed. She had a huge lump on the back of her head where Bill had hit her with the saucepan. Thomas smiled and leaned over to kiss her. He took her hand in his and said. 'The saucepan's out for the count, how are you?'

Alice smiled back but it was obvious to him that she hadn't a clue what he was talking about. 'Hey you.' She said and began to cry.

Thomas kissed her tears. 'What happened?' He asked gently.

'I don't know; one minute I was putting some washing in the machine, the next I heard somebody, turned round, thought I saw Dad, went to stand up, then wham; I passed out'

'Bill whacked you with a saucepan; he thought you were a burglar.'

'What?' Alice cried in disbelief.

Thomas nodded his head. 'Afraid so; I heard a crash and you screamed. He was standing over you with the saucepan in his hand when I rushed into the kitchen; you'd passed out. Bill must have heard you, went to see who was there, and thought you were an intruder. He didn't recognise me either.'

Alice was incredulous. 'Dad didn't recognise me?'

'No; Alice he could have killed you.'

She squeezed his hand. 'He wouldn't do that. I know it.'

Thomas squeezed back. 'We'll talk in the morning; right now you need to rest.' He kissed her again. 'I love you.' He whispered.

'You too.' Alice said.

Thomas waited until Alice had fallen asleep and then went back into the waiting area where Bill was pacing around like an expectant father. He saw Thomas and rushed towards him. 'Brian, Alice, tell me is she alright? The nurse told me she had been taken ill, some sort of accident; is she alright?'

Thomas took his father in law's arm and led him out of the hospital towards his car. 'Yes Bill she's fine. Just a minor accident that's all. They're going to keep her in overnight under observation but she'll be home Tomorrow all being well.' He said choking on his words and unable to hide his tears as emotion welled up inside him. He had no idea how to deal with this.

Chapter 25

Grey was back in Thomas' office bright and early. She wanted to speak to him about what she felt might be inconsistencies in Anne Goodchild's statement. She waited for a quarter of an hour and when he didn't turn up tried him on his mobile. He didn't answer so she decided to knuckle down and try to trace Louise Theroux.

The number in Susan Reed's mobile had not been recognised by any network and the college only had the address of the flat Theroux had shared with her when they'd first enrolled. Grey decided to pay it a visit; there could be a forwarding address for mail or the current tenants might know where she was.

Thomas had managed to convince the hospital that they needed to provide full time care for Bill, at least for the next few days until he could organise something more permanent, so he had taken him there and dropped him off on his way to work. He paid a very brief visit to Alice while he was there. Apart from a very blue and yellow egg-sized bump on her head, she seemed fine and the hospital staff assured him she had spent a peaceful night. Surprisingly she hadn't argued with him when he'd told her that the hospital was keeping Bill for a few days.

He left her to keep his appointment with Judd in Judd's office and brought him up to date with the enquiry. He told him about Fullthorpe and James and Styles and the inconsistencies Style's statement had uncovered in Alan Reed's. He hadn't yet plucked up the courage to ask him to authorise a search party to trawl the Racecourse for a weapon.

Judd had listened patiently before summarising; 'So, Fullthorpe had been her lover, but you have no evidence against him; James had been her lover and you have no evidence against him either, although it sounds like you might well be able to do him for dealing, and Styles had been her lover too. She was a busy girl wasn't she? Evidence against Styles, the CCTV and the statement from Mrs. Stephens, plus his own admission he was at the scene around the time of death. Alan Reed has lied to you if you believe what Styles has told you, but you have nothing concrete against him either. You need the weapon or forensics.'

'Yes sir; I was hoping to get the forensics report yesterday but it didn't arrive. I'll chase them this morning.'

'Pain in the arse I know, but have you thought about searching the Racecourse?' Judd asked.

Thank you Lord' Thomas said silently. 'Yes sir, I was about to ask you for approval.'

Judd nodded his head and said firmly. 'I think it's vital, given what Styles has told you.'

'I do too; thank you sir.'

'Now about this Goodchild complaint; the Chief wants a full report on exactly what happened between you two. Billy Goodchild has some powerful friends, so it's probably best if you stay away from him and his wife for a while. With a bit of luck it will all blow over.'

Thomas groaned inwardly. 'I need to see Anne Goodchild again sir; there are problems with her statement, and Billy Goodchild promised to send me the names of his alibis for last Monday; they haven't arrived.'

Judd gave him a stern look. 'Why do you need an alibi from him; is he a suspect?'

Thomas had to admit he wasn't.

Judd gave him a sharp look. 'Sounds like the pair of you had a pissing contest to me. Temper can be very dangerous Chief Inspector; curb it. You have nothing on Billy so drop it unless something turns up against him. Send Grey to talk to his wife.' He ordered.

'Sir.' Thomas acceded, hurt by the ticking off but knowing Judd was right. He stood up to leave.

As he did Judd said. 'I have a feeling there's more to this one than we're seeing Brian.'

Thomas said 'Maybe sir; we could certainly do with a break.' and headed towards the door. On his way to his office he called Grey but she didn't answer her mobile so he left a message. On his desk when he reached his office was the report from the team that had searched Leroy James' house the night before.

Thomas sat down and read it carefully; the summary told him they had found no blood stained clothes, and no weapon, but they had found a kilo of cocaine under a floorboard in his bedroom, plus forty two hits wrapped and ready for sale. 'Well well!' Thomas exclaimed aloud, delighted that his hunch had been proven right. Now, with the threat of a long prison term hanging over him, James might be more willing to talk than he had been the day before. He picked up the phone and asked the Duty Sergeant to fetch James from his cell and bring him into one of the Interview Rooms.

James was waiting for him with a uniformed constable when Thomas arrived. He looked tired but relaxed. He sat back in the chair with one hand in his pocket, the other by his side. Thomas went through the normal cautions, leaned against the back wall with one hand in his pocket and then ploughed straight in.

'Did you ever meet Alan Reed Leroy?'

James shook his head. 'No man, why you hold mi here?'

'Did you ever sell drugs to Susan Reed?'

'No man, we share a line that's all.'

'Did you ever have sex with Susan Reed in return for drugs?'

James leered. 'No man, but she like mi buddy.'

'Leroy, are you aware of the penalties for supplying cocaine, including passing some to your friends without payment?'

James stopped smiling and suddenly looked worried. 'No man, mi no dealer.'

'The maximum sentence is life imprisonment Leroy; life.' Thomas repeated firmly.

'Me no dealer;' James protested. 'We only shoot a line man, one time.'

'Officers searching your house last night found a kilo of cocaine Leroy, and over forty portions ready for sale. I think even you would agree that's a little more than one line; that's dealer quantity. How did it get there?'

'Mi dunno man; maybe you plant it. You try to fit mi up.' James said; sweat beginning to run down his forehead.

'Leroy, you're looking at a life sentence; nobody is going to believe somebody planted that cocaine in your house. Admit it Leroy, you're a dealer.'

'No man; you plant that stuff in mi room; mi no dealer; no way man.' James insisted.

Thomas paused for a few seconds, allowing time for James to realise his mistake. In the moment James had incriminated himself, Thomas had realised instantly that he was dealing with someone who was not that bright. And suddenly he had a picture in his mind of what James really was; a small time dealer who got by through a natural charm with women and use of his powerful physique with men. 'I didn't mention exactly where we found it Leroy.' He said quietly.

'Shit.' James cursed, shaking his head and eyeing the carpet. 'Wha chew want man? Mi help you, you help mi OK?' He asked, clearly disappointed with himself.

'I want the truth Leroy; I want to know everything about your relationship with Susan and Alan Reed. I want to know where you were on Monday morning, and I want you to stop this fooling around; it's wasting my time.' Thomas decided to stand up straight to his full height; he wanted James to feel inferior while he had him on the back foot. Pushing away from the wall he said, 'Let's start with how you met.'

'Wi meet at college man; she in my class.'

'Why did you enrol at college Leroy?' Thomas couldn't understand why someone like James would bother studying Business Administration.

'Mi businessman, mi goin places.' James explained proudly.

'Carry on.' Thomas said encouragingly.

'She have problems wi her man Alan; mi move in and give her what she need. She like mi buddy an everything alright for a while, but then mi grow tired. She want the coke but have no money. Mi businessman, mi no bupps.'

'So you dropped her?' Thomas asked.

'Yeah but she come back for more; she need the coke but she have no money.'

'Did you have sex with her in return for coke?'

'No way man; mi have sex wi her, but mi need payment. Mi businessman.' Thomas repeated and seemed offended that Thomas could suggest such a thing.

'So, if you had finished with her, why did you have sex with her?'

'She like mi buddy.'

'Did you offer her cocaine in return for sex?' Thomas asked. 'And remember Leroy, I need the truth. It will not help you if you lie to me.'

James shrugged. 'Maybe she think that, but mi always need money.'

'You led her to believe you would give her coke in return for sex?'

'Maybe she think that.'

'Let me put it another way, after you had grown tired of her did you ever have sex with her after you'd given her cocaine?'

'Maybe not.' James admitted

'You say you always expected payment, so did you then ask Alan Reed for payment?'

James looked sullen and answered reluctantly. 'Sometime man. I no give my stash away, mi need payment. She no pay, he pay. Mi businessman.'

Thomas stared down at Leroy with an expression of incredulous repugnance. 'So let me get this straight Leroy; firstly you form a relationship with Susan Reed in order to get her hooked on cocaine, then you dump her, then when she comes to you for a fix you supply her in return for sex, but afterwards you demand payment from her husband. Is that right?'

James stared at the floor. 'Maybe that how it look but mi businessman, mi need cash.'

'What was Alan Reed's reaction when you demanded payment?'

'He angry man! He attack mi,' James laughed derisively. 'but he a weak man, mi strong, very strong. Mi say he must pay.'

'And did he?'

'Sometime man, but he always owe mi.'

'Did you ever assault Alan Reed when he couldn't pay you? Did you beat him up?'

James looked at the floor. 'No man, except when he get angry and attack me. Afterwards he pay me sometime.'

'Did Alan Reed know you were having sex with his wife?'

James sneered. 'Sure man, he know.'

'How did he know?' Thomas probed.

'He see us one time. She clean mi in the hallway an' he walk in.' James laughed at the memory.

Thomas took a few seconds trying to interpret what James had told him. 'She was giving you oral sex and he interrupted you?'

'Yeah man. He go crazy but he a weak man; mi strong, very strong; he easy to control. He try to fight mi but mi too strong.'

Thomas took a deep breath. 'Does Susan Reed still owe you money?'

'No man. She pay mi.'

'Susan Reed paid you?' Thomas asked, leaning over the desk towards him, completely taken aback by James's answer. 'When?'

'Two weeks ago man. She knock on mi door and pay mi.'

'How much did she pay you Leroy?'

James fidgeted uncomfortably in the chair. 'Over a grand man, cash.' He admitted grudgingly.

Thomas sucked in air. This was a new development. He leaned on the desk, both arms outstretched, balancing him. 'She gave you a thousand pounds in cash, two weeks ago?'

'Yeah man, she pay mi. She make mi happy man. She clean me too.' James added unnecessarily in Thomas' book.

'Did she say where she got this money from?'

'No man but she say everything alright from now on. No more worry about money.'

'When was the last time you saw her?'

'A week ago, she need more coke.' James said.

'And she paid you?'

'Yeah man, no problem; she give mi cash.'

'Did you ever supply Alan Reed with cocaine?'

James laughed disdainfully. 'No man, he no user.'

'Where were you on Monday morning Leroy?' Thomas asked ready to end the interview. He would quiz James about his supplier later.

'In bed man, wi mi lady.'

'Does she have a name?'

'Sure man, she be Susan.'

'Very convenient I'm sure.' Thomas said. 'I'm assuming Susan will confirm this?'

James nodded emphatically. 'Oh yeah, mi sure. You let mi go now? Mi tell you truth.' James asked a questioning look on his face.

Thomas looked down on him and said sternly. 'Oh no Leroy, I'm afraid not. You will be charged with supplying drugs and possession of drugs. I don't think we'll be letting you go for a very long time.'

James shot up from his chair wagging a finger at Thomas. 'But you lead mi to believe you let mi go if I tell you truth.' He protested.

The constable stirred in the corner but Thomas waved him away. He leaned forward so that his face was only inches away from James' nose. He could feel James' breath on his cheeks when he spoke and he could smell the stench of stale smoke. 'Can't think what gave you that idea Leroy; I don't negotiate, I'm no businessman.' Thomas said quietly and walked out.

Chapter 26

Grey was on her way back from the flat in St.Edmunds Road that Susan Reed and Louise Theroux had shared when they had first enrolled at college. She had spoken to the current tenants but they had never heard of Theroux and there was no forwarding address. Frustrated she decided to try Chris Atherley again at the college. He might be able to throw some light on where she was, plus he hadn't called her and if nothing else it would be a good excuse to see him again.

She'd been waiting for him in the reception area for a few minutes when he opened the side door and strode towards her, his face beaming. He moved in close to kiss her but Grey backed away.

'Business.' She whispered giving him a mildly reproachful look.

'I've missed you.' He whispered, blushing.

'You haven't called.' Grey chided smiling.

Atherley looked flustered. 'No, well, you see, I didn't want to appear, well, you know, too keen, but I, well I am, keen that is.' He said.

Grey's heart went out to him; she loved his shyness. 'So why not tonight?' She asked teasingly.

Atherley beamed again. 'Oh well, marvellous. Yes, marvellous.' He said. 'Eight o' clock?'

'Yes, same place.' Grey said excited. 'Now I'm hoping you can help me.' She continued, pulling herself together.

'Oh, yes, anything. What can I do?'

'Well for a start you can take me to your office.'

'Oh, yes of course.' He said and she followed him along the familiar plastic and glass lined corridor to where his computer was already switched on, and papers were randomly strewn over his desk like pieces of a jigsaw.

'I can't find Louise Theroux and I need to. Do you have any other address for her?' Grey asked.

Atherley frowned. 'I doubt it; we only record the last known address. I can search for an emergency contact though, that might help.' He offered hopefully.

'Yes please.' Grey said encouragingly

Atherley tapped away at his keyboard for a few seconds before cursing. 'Bugger; the person named as the emergency contact is Susan Reed, same address as the one you already have. I honestly don't think there'll be anything else on file, but I can ask around if you like.' He suggested.

'What about physical records, like application forms and medical records?'

He shook his head. 'We don't keep them once they've been entered onto the database. In any case the application forms are mirrored on the computer; they don't contain any more information than what we record on the system.'

Grey sighed. 'Is there nothing you can think of that might help me find her?' She asked wondering where to go from here.

'Not from the system, but I'm sure somebody here must know where she is, or at least have some idea. Would you like me to ask around?'

Grey could see no harm in it so said 'Yes please.'

She said goodbye to Atherley and decided she might save a lot of time by returning to the office where she could at least trawl through local computerised electoral roles and the Registrar's database; she would also contact the telephone companies, credit card companies, and utility companies. Theroux must be on some list somewhere. She was walking back to her car when her mobile went off. 'DI Grey.' She answered.

Thomas was on the line. 'Can you come back to the office? We need to discuss our reports and there have been a few developments.'

'Will do sir.' She said still mulling over in her mind how she was going to go about tracing Louise Theroux.

While he waited for Grey, Thomas updated his board.

- 10.00 + Reed says he left the house
  - LJ says Reed knew he had been sleeping with his wife
  - LJ says Reed paid him for his wife's cocaine
  - RS says Reed knew he had been sleeping with his wife
- 10.00 + Mrs. Stephens sees 20-30 year old male knock on door – probably Styles
- 10.10 Miss Trussler sees mid forties male knock on door
- 10.22 Alan Reed calls ambulance
- 10.00 – 10.30 Susan read murdered

- Susan Reed admitted her killer into her home or was already dead

  - LJ says SR paid him £1,000 cash two weeks before she died

- Susan Reed's mobile phone contacts;

  - Vanessa Vokes – college friend according to Alan Reed 00441604445501
    - Said Susan Reed had lovers, Leroy James, Robert Styles, Colin Fullthorpe.
    - Confirmed she was friend of Susan Reed

- Mandy Singleton- college friend according to Alan Reed 00441604643305
  - Said Susan Reed had lovers, Leroy James, Robert Styles, Colin Fullthorpe,
  - Confirmed she was friends with Susan Reed
  - Said saw Susan Reed with Colin Fullthorpe
  - Goddaughter of Anne Goodchild
  - Enigmatic demeanour
- Colin Fullthorpe – tutor –mobile number?- 00447880636755
  - Seen by Mandy Singleton with Susan Reed
  - According to VV and MS was Susan Reed's lover
  - Denied relationship with Susan Reed when interviewed by Grey but now admits it on second interview.
- Bob Styles – contact – 00441604845667
  - Admits being Susan Reed's lover when interviewed
  - Was probably the man Mrs. Stephens saw
  - CCTV puts him close to scene at 09:57a.m.
- Louise Theroux – contact – 00440273944327
- Leroy James – contact- 00447880614378
  - Admits was SR's lover
  - Admits supplying her with cocaine
  - Says AR knew about his affair with his wife.
  - Says AR paid him for his wife's drugs
- Anne Goodchild

- Susan Reed's counsellor at college
- Said Susan Reed had told her she had had affairs with Leroy James and Robert Styles,
- Said she had received complaints of harassment about Fullthorpe from students
- Is Mandy Singleton's God mother
- Statement inconsistent with Mandy Singleton's
  - Billy Goodchild
    - Husband of Anne
    - Promised alibis not yet provided.

For the first time since the investigation had begun Thomas was beginning to feel that he and Grey were getting somewhere. True they had very little concrete evidence other than the CCTV images, but they were building quite a strong circumstantial case against Alan Reed. If James and Styles had been speaking the truth, and in Thomas' judgement they had been, he had lied when he had said he hadn't known his wife had been unfaithful; James had said he'd actually caught them at it in the hallway. So he certainly had motive, and he had opportunity. If only they could find a damn weapon, without it he doubted he had enough to go to the CPS with. The weapon was a real problem if Reed had committed the crime. They had already searched the house and surrounding area and found nothing, yet if Styles was to be believed then Susan Reed was alive when he had called. That meant that Alan Reed must have murdered her after he returned from Threshers. So where had he hidden the weapon? Maybe they wouldn't need it and forensics would provide the answer.

Styles too had motive and opportunity; they could place him in the vicinity and he had admitted going to the house. He had been in love with Susan Reed but she had forsaken him. But again without the weapon or forensics he couldn't charge him.

Fullthorpe could have killed her to save his career. Although there had been no trace of his car on the CCTV he did not have an alibi for Monday morning. Perhaps she had been blackmailing him; after all she had come into money in the last two weeks. That gave him motive, but opportunity was inconclusive and again no weapon or forensics. Nevertheless Thomas made a mental note to have his bank account checked for recent large cash withdrawals.

Vokes had said she had been in a class at college and Singleton had been in church. Both of their alibis had stacked up.

Leroy James had said Susan Reed had paid him £1,000 in cash two weeks before she died, and then had paid him cash again a week later. He really didn't seem to have much of a motive for killing her and he had an alibi, which left him precisely nowhere without forensics or a weapon.

Where had she found that kind of money? Until she had suddenly turned up at James' door two weeks ago she had been paying for drugs with sex. Then without warning she had handed over a thousand pounds or more. She hadn't worked, neither had Alan Reed, and by all accounts Alan Reed was still hard up. Did he know where the money had come from? Had she extorted it from Fullthorpe in return for her silence?

Thomas was still running possibilities through his mind when DI Grey knocked on his door and entered. 'Sir.' She said nodding.

'Take a seat.' Thomas said. 'Shall we go through our reports first? I think we have issues there to clear up. Firstly, I didn't understand what you meant when you described Mandy Singleton as being 'enigmatic'.'

Grey hung her designer jacket on the back of the office door and took a deep breath as she sat down opposite Thomas. 'I'm not sure I did myself sir. She was well, weird. Very quiet, seemingly shy, and yet some of her answers came across as downright callous. And somehow sitting close to her in a small room unnerved me, I don't mind admitting it. She never took her eyes off of me; she was like a cat watching a mouse.'

'Do you think she was hiding something?'

'Possibly sir but it was difficult to tell; she was so difficult to read. I expected her to show more concern for Reed, after all they had been close friends, but she expressed no regret that her friend had been murdered, and when I questioned her about Reed's relationship with Styles she was quite scathing; she showed more emotion about that than she did about Reed's death.'

'Maybe it was her strict Catholic upbringing; maybe she was unable to hide her intolerance.'

She nodded in agreement. 'Possibly sir; whatever, she definitely gave me the creeps.'

Thomas nodded 'OK, and this section where you mention her saying that she and Anne Goodchild had seen Colin Fullthorpe messing about with Susan Reed in the Fox & Hounds. Are you absolutely certain that's what she said?'

'Yes sir, absolutely.' Grey confirmed.

'She definitely said that Anne Goodchild had seen them?' Thomas pressed the point.

'Definitely sir.'

Thomas scratched his chin. 'Hmm, that is interesting. When I spoke to Anne Goodchild she told me that a few students had complained to her about being harassed by Fullthorpe, but she hadn't reported him because it would have been only their word against his. Now that's odd if she had actually seen him with Susan Reed herself; she could have reported him as an eye witness. I wonder why she didn't and why she didn't mention to me that she'd seen him?'

'Staff loyalty perhaps?' Grey offered.

'Maybe, but Goodchild works on a charitable basis and I suspect she sees the paid help as beneath her; I doubt she would have felt much loyalty towards Fullthorpe. She might have simply decided not to bother but then it was still a strange thing to say if she had seen them. Anyway I'd like you to go over to Brington and see her. As her for an explanation.'

'Sir.' Grey said jotting down a reminder.

'Now I need to update you on Styles. There's absolutely nothing from the searches unfortunately, and we're still waiting on forensics. The good news is Styles has admitted being at the scene but the bad news is he says Susan Reed wouldn't let him in so he slouched off, wandered around a bit and then got drunk in the White Elephant.'

'He also says he's fairly sure Alan Reed knew he had been sleeping with his wife because he almost caught them at it. There's more; Leroy James says Reed knew he had been sleeping with his wife because he'd interrupted them having sex in the hallway. So Alan Reed has lied to us and we have quite a strong circumstantial case against him. That said, we also have quite a strong circumstantial case against Robert Styles. Nevertheless I fear without the weapon or forensics we don't have enough against either of them.'

Grey had been trying to take it all in; Thomas had been speaking quickly and her mind was struggling to keep up when she blurted, 'We need the weapon sir.' Thomas gave her a withering look, making her blush furiously. *'Damn I did it again',* she scolded herself. One of her old mentors had cautioned her once *'Don't just say something, stand there!'* and she couldn't believe she hadn't remembered it before she'd opened her mouth.

Thomas continued. 'We found a kilo of cocaine in James' house plus some lines ready for sale; he'll be charged with dealing and possession but he appears to have an alibi for Monday morning. One interesting thing he did say was that two weeks before Susan Reed died, she had unexpectedly turned up at his door and cleared all her debts, in cash; she'd given him over £1,000 according to James; then a week later she paid him for drugs again in cash, saying he needn't worry about money any more.'

Grey whistled. 'I wonder where she got it.' Then she had a sudden thought. 'What if she'd been blackmailing Fullthorpe sir? That would explain where the money came from, and have given Fullthorpe a motive for killing her.'

Thomas smiled, seemingly impressed. 'That's exactly why I want you to check Fullthorpe's bank accounts and credit card accounts.' Grey flushed with pride and scribbled some rubbish on her pad, hoping to impress Thomas further. 'Meanwhile I'm going to have another chat with Alan Reed. Any luck with Louise Theroux?'

'Afraid not sir, the college has no record of her address, and neither do the current tenants at her old flat. I'm going to have to do some digging.'

Thomas smiled sympathetically. 'Oh well, we have plenty to be going on with. Priority is Fullthorpe, then Goodchild, then Theroux.'

'Sir.' Grey said standing and heading out the door. Inwardly Grey was cursing herself one moment and feeling proud the next. *'Keep your mouth shut and let your brain do the talking from now on.'* She warned herself. On reaching her office she called Fullthorpe at his home and arranged to see him there. She decided to take a uniformed constable with her just in case she needed to arrest him.

Fullthorpe lived in a 1970's built detached bungalow in Berrydale, a small estate on the far eastern side of town not far from the village of Great Billing, once famous for its lace; a few hundred yards to the west was a small woodland, Billing Lings, named after the unique heather found there. Bungalows in Berrydale were roomy three and four bedroom affairs and when Grey pulled up outside Fullthorpe's she guessed his had four bedrooms judging by the large plot and double garage. She parked on the road at the end of the drive next to the plain blue Astra the uniformed constable had been driving.

They approached the front door and Grey rang the bell. Fullthorpe opened it after a few seconds and after Grey had explained they needed to talk to him again he reluctantly invited them in. In the hallway Grey was looking around, admiring the pictures, woodland prints in good quality frames, and expensive looking lighting, when suddenly a small woman, face bright scarlet and fierce with fury, tears flooding her eyes, ran from a side room and screamed at her.

'What are you doing to my husband? Why are you persecuting him? Why can't you leave us alone?' The woman tried to push Grey but she took a step back and the woman stood still, panting heavily after her outburst.

Grey was taken aback but then quickly realised that this must be Mrs. Fullthorpe and she would have taken the full brunt of the search undertaken a few days earlier. She looked about ten years older than her husband. 'Mrs. Fullthorpe.' Grey began but was interrupted before she could continue.

'My Colin is a good man, an intelligent man, he cares about his students. You have no right to hound him like this. He has done nothing; nothing!' She cried, wagging her figure at Grey.

Grey turned to Colin Fullthorpe and said. 'Perhaps it would be better if we did this back at the station sir.' But Fullthorpe ignored her and was already guiding his wife back into the side room murmuring soothing words to her.

'It's alright Aida dear; this won't take long. It's alright.' Distraught, Mrs. Fullthorpe allowed herself to be ushered back into the room.

Grey could see her shoulders shaking and hear her pitiful sobbing as Fullthorpe closed the door gently behind them and she wondered whether he had ever stopped once to consider that his promiscuity might one day cause his wife such distress. Somehow she doubted it.

Colin Fullthorpe came out a few minutes later and said. 'I'm sorry; shall we go into the lounge?'

Grey and the constable followed him into a large room with a low ceiling. On the floor was a plush deep red carpet; an oak coffee table stood in the centre of the room and a sideboard and bookcase lined two walls while a black stereo unit and two speakers adorned a third. Full length double doors led to a well kept back garden. There was no TV. The sofa was cream velour with deep cushions and wooden arms; two matching chairs flanked it either side. Fullthorpe sat on the sofa and Grey sat on one of the chairs; the constable stood at ease near the entrance with his hands behind his back. Grey noticed there was hardly any sign of the earlier search in this room. She doubted others would look as tidy; normally search teams had scant regard for tidiness.

'How can I help you?' Fullthorpe asked, smiling. Grey could see he was putting on a show, but underneath the smile he looked tired and worn, the stress of the past few days ageing him rapidly. His face was drawn and lined, his eyes bloodshot. His trousers were creased and his shirt grubby. The upper edges of his lips were tinted grey. No doubt, she thought, Mrs. Fullthorpe had given him the third degree, demanding answers; it's not often a fully tooled up search party invades your home and the poor woman must have been terrified when it arrived. Judging by her earlier hysterical outburst Fullthorpe had no doubt given her a carefully censored explanation and blamed everything on the Police; a case of mistaken identity and police brutality as a minimum, she guessed. She wondered how Mrs. Fullthorpe would take it if the truth came out in court and her husband lost his job.

'This shouldn't take too long sir; could we see your most recent bank statements and credit card statements?' Grey asked.

Fullthorpe look startled. 'Whatever for?' he asked.

'Please sir, if they are to hand.' Grey insisted.

Fullthorpe shrugged and left the room, reappearing a few moments later with a two week old bank statement and credit card statement. Grey studied both for recent large withdrawals but found none. She handed them back after noting the account numbers; she would double check with the bank later for connected accounts and more recent transactions.

'What's this about?' Fullthorpe demanded.

'Did Susan Reed ever demand money from you?' Grey asked.

'You've already asked me this and I've already told you; no, why should she?' Fullthorpe replied sounding puzzled. He didn't seem to have any perception of how exposed he had been to extortion.

'Did she try to blackmail you; threaten to tell your wife or the college about your relationship?'

Fullthorpe was incredulous. 'Good Lord no; Susan was not like that. No inspector, our relationship was very loving.'

'Did you ever give her money for any purpose?' Grey persisted.

'No never.' Fullthorpe maintained firmly.

'Did you ever give her husband money, or did he ever demand money from you for any purpose?'

'No, never. Look what's this all about?' Fullthorpe replied.

Grey stood up and ignored his question. 'Thank you Mr. Fullthorpe; that's all for now.' She said.

They walked out of the lounge into the hallway and Grey's stomach dropped when she saw Fullthorpe's wife again. She had wiped away her tears but her eyes were burning with a fierce hatred and Grey braced herself for another volley of abuse. But to her surprise Aida Fullthorpe turned on her husband instead.

'A loving relationship; what loving relationship? You told me it was all a mistake.' she ranted and a relieved Grey quickly signalled the constable to leave, noticing as she stepped over the threshold that Colin Fullthorpe had turned a ghostly white as his wife railed at him.

Chapter 27

Grey called Anne Goodchild from her mobile and although she sounded surprised to hear from the police again, she nevertheless agreed to see her in an hour. Grey calculated it would take her about half that to drive to Great Brington and that left very little time to do anything productive so she decided to treat herself to a coffee and doughnut at the Weston Favell Centre. Opened in 1974 and constructed of reinforced concrete, the centre was the largest shopping mall in the town and featured a large almost Gothic vaulted ceiling reminiscent of some Cathedrals, but Grey liked it and parked her car in the multi-story before heading for Tesco's canteen.

She ordered her snack and sat on a blue plastic chair, coffee and doughnut close to her hands as they rested on the red laminate table. Her thoughts drifted to Chris Atherley and her date with him later that evening. He was a dish, no doubt about it, and he seemed so happy to be with her. He was almost childlike in his uncomplicated joy of life. She wondered why nobody had snapped him up before and made a mental note to pry a little into his past when she saw him. Nobody's that perfect, she told herself. She could so easily fall for him. She wondered whether she should sleep with him; she wanted to; she melted every time he looked at her and when they'd kissed the other night she could gladly have eaten him up whole. But perhaps not yet; too early; but then how long would he wait before he moved on? Men! Life was much less complicated without them. She took a disparaging mouthful of doughnut and quickly washed it down with the coffee.

It had started to rain on the way to Great Brington and after she had reached the village it took her a while to find Anne Goodchild's house. Irritated, knowing she was behind schedule, she had a throbbing head-ache when she finally turned into the drive and a few moments later ground to a halt outside Goodchild's manor house, tyres groaning against the sharp gravel stones. Another car, a black E series Mercedes was already parked outside. Grey rang the bell and an attractive fortyish blonde opened the door after a few moments. 'You must be DI Grey.' Anne Goodchild said in greeting.

Grey showed her warrant card and shook her hand. 'I'm Anne; do come in.' Goodchild invited and Grey followed her into a small study furnished with three office chairs and a pine desk on which stood a telephone and fax machine.

A tall grey haired distinguished looking man stood up to greet her as she entered. 'Hello, Arthur Lees, family solicitor.' He said smiling.

'Detective Inspector Grey.' She introduced herself. *The staff quarters and Perry Mason; some welcome*, she thought ruefully.

All three sat and Grey began, addressing Mrs. Goodchild. 'As you know Mrs. Goodchild I'm investigating the death of Susan Reed and I wanted to go over again some of the information you gave to DCI Thomas the other day.'

Silence followed and Grey continued. 'Can you remember an evening you spent recently with your Goddaughter Mandy Singleton at the Fox & Hounds?'

Lees asked. 'Inspector, can you tell me what relevance this has to your enquiry?'

Grey had expected the interruption. 'We are gathering background information on the victim Mr. Lees; we believe the information Mrs. Goodchild can provide will help us build a picture of Mrs. Reed's friends and associations and her movements in the weeks leading up to her death.'

Lees said nothing. Mrs. Goodchild turned to him and he nodded. 'Not vividly; Mandy and I went there one evening for a drink I recall but I couldn't swear exactly when it was.' She said.

'Can you recall seeing anyone there?' Grey continued.

Goodchild thought for a few moments before answering. 'No I'm afraid I can't inspector.' She said.

'Are you sure? Can you try to think back carefully Mrs. Goodchild; it is important.' Grey pressed.

'Inspector,' Lees warned. 'Mrs. Goodchild has answered your question.'

Grey ignored him and pressed on. 'You see Mrs. Goodchild, Mandy told us she saw Susan Reed that night.'

Goodchild blushed from the neck up. 'Oh, really?'

'Please try to think; did you see Susan Reed that night?'

'Inspector, Mrs. Goodchild has already given you her answer.' Lees interjected.

Grey looked at Mrs. Goodchild expectantly. Goodchild appeared reluctant to answer but after a few seconds of silence finally said. 'If Mandy saw her then I'm sure she was there but I'm afraid I don't take an awful lot of notice of people inspector.'

'Can you recall if she was with anybody?' Grey probed, hopeful now that Goodchild might admit seeing her.

'As I said inspector I really don't recall seeing her. Oh wait; yes of course; I remember now. Yes I did see her; she was with Colin Fullthorpe.'

'And can you tell me what they were doing?'

Goodchild sounded puzzled. 'I'm not sure I understand inspector; what do you mean?'

Grey explained trying not to lead; remembering Thomas' warning. 'Were they eating, drinking, talking; what did you observe about them?'

'Oh, I see; well I don't recall anything unusual; perhaps Mandy can tell you more; she notices people but as I said, I don't.' Goodchild replied, blushing more.

'So, to be clear, you recall seeing Susan Reed with Fullthorpe in the Fox & Hounds but observed nothing remarkable in their behaviour?' Grey tried again.

'That's right.'

'Now when you spoke to DCI Thomas he asked you whether you had heard any complaints from students about Fullthorpe in your role as counsellor. Is that correct?'

'Yes, I think he did; I told him a few students had complained.' Goodchild agreed.

'And he asked you why you hadn't reported these complaints to the board. Can you remember you answer?' Grey asked.

Lees sensed this could be dangerous ground and interrupted. 'Am I to understand DI Grey that Mrs. Goodchild has already provided an answer to DCI Thomas?'

'Yes sir.' Grey replied. Lees might have described himself as the family lawyer, she reasoned, but he was probably a thousand pounds an hour family lawyer and he was nobody's fool.

'So you already have your answer.' He said with a sickly smile.

'Yes sir, but that's the problem.' Grey went on. 'We need to make sure we have understood Mrs. Goodchild's answer correctly.'

'Well I think your understanding of Mrs. Goodchild's answer is a matter for you inspector, so if there's nothing else.' Lees said with finality, beginning to stand.

Grey remained motionless. She couldn't understand why Goodchild had called in the cavalry over something as trivial as this, and now Lees was not allowing her to answer the very question she needed her to answer. Why? She asked herself.

'Is there any reason why you don't wish to answer the question Mrs. Goodchild?' Grey asked.

Anne Goodchild looked completely lost. Her face and neck were crimson and her eyes had a bewildered look about them. Grey was sure she was about to say something when Lees said sharply. 'Inspector I think that's about enough. If you have any more questions perhaps you would direct them to my office?' He handed her his card. Grey was desperately trying to think of another question that would allow her to segue back onto the reason why Goodchild had not reported Fullthorpe but she couldn't think of a single one. Cursing herself for not being quick witted enough she reluctantly stood up.

'I will sir, thank you.' She said. Lees quickly ushered her out and had closed the door before she reached her car.

Driving back to Northampton, her head throbbing, she was convinced that Anne Goodchild was hiding something, but she had no idea what it could be or why. It was possible that she had not seen anything happen between Reed and Fullthorpe but Mandy Singleton had insisted she had. And when Thomas had interviewed her and asked her why she hadn't reported Fullthorpe to the College Board, she'd given the reason that it would have been his word against a student's. Even accepting for a moment that she herself had seen nothing, unlikely in Grey's view, Mandy had, and surely she would have mentioned it to her. If so why had Anne Goodchild lied? Had she deliberately lied or had she simply forgotten?

Perhaps Mandy hadn't said anything; she was certainly a strange one so nothing was impossible. One moment she appeared to be shy, the next callous, or at best apathetic. With her kind of upbringing she would have expected her to be full of care and compassion for her dead friend; if nothing else she would have expected her to have been upset over her death. Yet in some ways she had given the impression that she really didn't care what had happened to Susan Reed and that she'd got what she had deserved. And those hypnotic staring eyes; what was behind them she wondered? She shivered; they had given her the creeps. Shaking her head, Grey concluded they were a strange pair and concentrated on her driving.

Chapter 28

Thomas picked Alice up from the hospital on his way home from the station. She had suffered mild concussion but had been given the all-clear earlier in the day, and Bill was safely in care for a few days allowing them a little time to try to decide what to do with him.

He drove her home and made sure she was comfortable on the sofa while he prepared a pasta dish using a pre-prepared Billato and chilli sauce from Tesco. Alice still had a mild head-ache but she hadn't refused a glass of Chablis when Thomas had offered and she was sipping it when he served up the pasta on a tray. Alice made herself comfortable and Thomas sat beside her, taking a sip from his glass of Merlot.

'The hospital said they would keep Bill for up to five days so hopefully that should give us enough time to organise something.' He explained, gathering up a fork-full of pasta.

'I don't like leaving him there on his own.' Alice said. 'He should be here with us.'

Thomas swallowed before speaking. 'And he will be, but yesterday proved you're not safe alone here with him; you need help. He could forget who you are again and attack you anytime, you know that. Next time he might choose something more lethal than a saucepan.'

Alice sighed. 'I know you're right but he's my father, he should be here with me. He cared for me when I was in nappies, why shouldn't I do the same for him when he needs me?'

'Alice,' Thomas said patiently. 'He will be here, and we will look after him, but you can't do it alone. You need professional help; he could turn on you at any time.'

Alice started to cry. 'We can't afford it Brian, you know that. Professional help will cost more than your salary.'

Thomas knew she was right, he had checked. Full time home help would cost far more than they could afford, and part time would be no use. By its nature his job demanded unsocial hours; it wasn't nine to five and that meant they would have to have somebody on standby in case he had to work late or at weekends.

He put his tray down onto the carpet and took her in his arms, kissing away her tears. 'It'll work out alright. Don't worry. Let's try to get NHS support. The paperwork's a bit of a nightmare, I don't even understand half the questions so we'll need help just to fill the forms in, but once we've done that we might have a chance.' He said trying to sound positive but inside feeling helpless.

Alice sniffed, dried her eyes and nestled her head against his shoulder. 'Then that's what we'll get because I am not giving up on him. Tomorrow I'll call the healthcare trust and see if we can get to the bottom of what we can claim and how to go about it.' She said determinedly.

Thomas squeezed her. When Alice got the bit between her teeth there was no stopping her, but he wondered whether her famous determination would be enough; the NHS seemed to want to do only what they absolutely had to.

'So tell me about yourself.' Grey said. She and Atherley were holding hands as they sat together on a padded bench in the Lumbertubs pub drinking pints of Old Speckled Hen. Grey reckoned she ought to be feeling self-conscious about holding hands with a man in public, she was after all no spring chicken, but it felt natural with Atherley, and she squeezed his hand as she spoke.

Atherley reached for his pint and downed an inch from his glass. 'Oh well, not a lot to tell really; boring; left school at eighteen, went to Leicester Uni, got a two-two in Economics, began working at the college and I've been there ever since. It's not a bad job; the salary's OK and there's a decent pension at the end of it.' He said.

'Are you a Northampton man?'

Atherley smiled and turned towards her. 'Oh yes, I was born at the Barratt, lived in Billing Road. I went to Vernon Terrace and then onto the Grammar School.'

Grey had been drowning in his eyes as he spoke and it was a second or two before she came back to the present and probed further. 'Ever married?'

A pained expression passed over Atherley's face for a split-second then disappeared. 'For twelve years until five years ago. It sort of fizzled out somehow and she moved out; finally divorced two years ago; no children fortunately. Perhaps we married too young.' He shrugged. 'Who knows?'

'And since then?'

'I've had the odd relationship but nothing has lasted; not for the want of trying I might add. I sometimes wonder if I've already given all I've got to give emotionally, and women sense it and move on. It's not something I feel myself but maybe there's something hidden in my subconcious.' He said wistfully.

Grey squeezed his hand again. 'I don't sense it.'

Atherley leaned over and kissed her. Again she told herself, I should feel embarrassed kissing him in public, but I don't. 'What about you?' Atherley asked.

Grey sipped her beer. 'Well, I've never married; never found the time if I'm honest; the job has always come first. One thing you'll have to get used to if we carry on seeing each other is that this job can keep me out all hours, and it's totally unpredictable.'

Atherley drew her towards him. 'I want to see you all the time. I'll wait for you if I have to.' He said and kissed her again. 'Are you local?'

Grey felt a warm glow wash over her but wondered if he really would wait when it came to it. 'Yep; same as you, born in The Barratt; my family lived in Harlestone Road. I went to Spencer and joined the Police straight after. I've been with them ever since; I started in uniform as a PC then moved into plain clothes about eight years ago. This is my first murder enquiry though.'

'What about your parents, are they still alive?'

'Yes, they still live in Harlestone Road. I see them most weekends and we're in touch by phone. Fortunately they're still in good health. Yours?'

'Both dead I'm afraid. Dad died several years ago from lung cancer; he was a lifelong smoker, and Mum died of a stroke last year.'

'I'm sorry to hear that.'

'Thanks, makes us appreciate life and good health when something like that happens doesn't it?' Atherley took another sip of his beer. 'Oh by the way I've not had a lot of luck asking around about Louise Theroux I'm afraid; someone said they thought she'd moved to Leicester but nobody I asked knew her address.'

'No to worry, I'm sure I'll trace her somehow.' Grey said and leaned over to kiss him.

Later that night at 23:00 a call came into the Police operations centre at Wootton Hall concerning a disturbance outside a bungalow in Berrydale. Three residents had complained of a drunk stumbling about in the street shouting abusive language, and two claimed they had witnessed somebody throwing stones and bricks at the Fullthorpes' bungalow.

Wootton Hall despatched a squad car to the scene and when the Police arrived a white male was trying to kick down the front door. Fullthorpe's terrified wife was cowering behind a net curtain, peeking out, trying to shoo the assailant away, but he was in a drunken rage and paying no attention to her. Colin Fullthorpe was nowhere to be seen.

The constables could hear the man shout 'Come on out you bastard; I'm going to rip your balls off, come on out!' And then they saw him beating on the door with both fists.

The two constables quickly restrained him; he stank of whisky and was crying as they cuffed him and slung him into the back of the squad car. One sat with him, keeping an eye on him, while the other comforted Mrs. Fullthorpe. Once she had calmed down he took a statement from her and another neighbour and then drove the man back to the cells where he was charged with disturbing the peace and being drunk and disorderly. They decided to lock him up for the night while he sobered up; somebody would talk to him in the morning. He gave his name as Robert Styles.

Excitement over, after a brief huddle in the street as the Police left with the culprit, the residents of Berrydale quickly settled down to their beds and TV's again. Neither they nor Mrs. Fullthorpe had any idea where Colin Fullthorpe was.

Then two things happened in quick succession.

The first was over almost as quickly as it had begun. The 23:00 express train out of St.Pancras to Leicester passed through Wellingborough, about ten miles East of Northampton, just before midnight. It was a fast train and although it had to slow down in order to safely manoeuvre around the sharp bend on the approach to Wellingborough station, it was still travelling at fifty or so miles an hour when, to the heart-stopping horror of the driver, a figure leapt from the platform into its the path. There was no time to react and although the driver stamped on the emergency brake as quickly as he could, he knew it was too late when he saw the figure disappear under the train. The impact of a man colliding with a five hundred ton train travelling at fifty miles an hour is not enough to cause even a ripple of sensation in the driver's fingers, but he almost instantly vomited over his controls as the appalling realisation of what had happened slammed into his senses at the speed of light. He had killed a man; he had been powerless to prevent it but nevertheless he had killed a man, and he was still being sick a few minutes later when the train drew to a shuddering halt. He didn't know the name of the jumper but later police would identify the tangled crushed mess beneath his wheels as Colin Fullthorpe. They closed the line immediately and for the whole of the next day, much to the irritation of the hundreds of commuters who relied on the line every weekday to get to work.

The second passed much more slowly. Mrs. Aida Fullthorpe's peaceful world had begun to crash around her the moment the police had hammered down her door and proceeded to tear her much cherished home apart as they searched for the murder weapon that had killed Susan Reed. Still reeling from the shock of that, her emotions had been pummelled again by the inconceivable revelation that her beloved husband Colin was being questioned by police about the murder of Susan Reed, a student at the college where Colin had taught; but the final mind-numbing blow had landed when she had overheard Colin admitting to the detective woman that he and Susan Reed had shared a loving relationship.

Aida Fullthorpe was a timid loving wife who thought simple thoughts and didn't ask much of life. Her marriage to Colin had been happy enough; they had two children both at university, one at Nottingham, the other at Leicester, and they were comfortably off. Colin was a kind, considerate husband,

and although his job sometimes meant he had to work late, it was a small price to pay for the contented lifestyle they led.

Aida was a member of the Northants County Golf Club and had many friends there, a few of whom had introduced her to the local W.I. and recently she had surprised herself when she had plucked up the courage to join in some of the voluntary activities they undertook. Her proudest moment had been earlier in the year when she had been elected onto the Committee at the County Club and had been nominated as next year's vice-captain.

But Aida had been emotionally crushed by the rapid-fire events of the past few days; the rocks on which she had built her life had been brutally blasted from underneath her and she had been mortally wounded by the lethal fragments. Her husband, whom she had believed had loved her, in truth had been in love with another woman, and worse one of his students; the shame and scandal the police investigation would bring would ruin her reputation at the Club and the W.I., and she would be forever tarnished; she could almost hear the whispers that would circulate around the club; and where would the money come from, how would she live? She could see only loneliness, misery, poverty, and disgrace ahead of her. In her shell-shocked despair she could not think of her children and the support and hope they would provide in her hour of need. Thus it was that shortly after Colin Fullthorpe had thrown himself under the midnight express, Aida Fullthorpe had reached for the ParaceBillol capsules that would kill her several hours later.

Police quickly formed the opinion that Colin Fullthorpe had taken his own life. They identified his body from his driving licence and established that he was a married man so they drove around to his house at just after two in the morning to give his wife the news of her husband's tragic death and to try to establish a motive for what he'd done. At the time they had no idea she was in the house comatose on her marriage bed, and so when there was no reply they left with the intention of trying again in the morning. It was only later, at 4:15 a.m. after someone at the station had made the connection with the Susan Reed murder investigation that they had called Thomas, and it was only a few minutes after that when residents of Berrydale had their peace shattered for the second time that night when police forced entry into the Fullthorpes' bungalow. Inside they found Aida Fullthorpe in a coma on the bed in the main bedroom. Paramedics arrived not long afterwards and she was rushed into Northampton General but despite their best efforts she died shortly after eight in the morning. Leicester and Nottingham police were told and they would have the unenviable duty of informing the Fullthorpes' children.

Thomas had insisted that the children be given his name and number so that they could speak to him if they wished. As distraught as he knew they would be, he was equally sure that they would sooner or later want to know what drove both of their parents to suicide on the same night and he was determined to help them all he could.

Chapter 29

Slightly weary from lack of sleep, Thomas called DI Grey early next morning to let her know what had happened overnight, and then had Alan Reed brought into the station.

Although he had nothing concrete on Reed, he was still his most likely suspect and he had lied when he'd interviewed him earlier in the week. Maybe this time he would crack. Thomas made his way from his office to the Interview Room where Reed, his solicitor, and a constable were waiting. Reed was seated when Thomas entered. He was dressed in black jeans, white T shirt and black leather jacket. With his solicitor by his side he looked much more confident than he had when they'd met earlier in the week.

Thomas switched on the tapes, stood back, and asked. 'In the few weeks before your wife died, did you come into any money?'

Reed looked surprised. 'No, I wish I had.' He said.

'Did she?'

Reed laughed in derision. 'No, she was always broke.'

'Are you certain; no lottery wins, horses, inheritance, anything?'

'No, I'm certain.' Reed said.

'Did you love your wife Alan?'

Reed replied angrily. 'What? Why are you asking, and why am I here again? You've got nothing on me.'

Thomas reminded him candidly. 'You're here on suspicion of murdering your wife. Did you love her?'

'Of course I did; it's a stupid question.' He said truculently.

'Did you love her even when you caught her giving oral sex to Leroy James in the hallway of your house?' Thomas demanded leaning over the desk towards Reed.

Reed gave him a disparaging look. 'What are you talking about? This is ridiculous!' He shouted turning towards his solicitor.

'Did you love her when Leroy James demanded payment for her drug addiction?'

Reed shot out his right arm and jabbed a finger at Thomas. 'I told you, I didn't know where she got her drugs from. I told you.' He repeated.

'Did you love her when you caught her in bed with Robert Styles?' Thomas pressed on.

'You don't have to.' Reed's solicitor began to say but Reed interrupted.

'Styles!' He shouted disparagingly. 'That low life; Susan wouldn't have given him the time of day.'

Thomas straightened and leaned back against the wall, arms crossed over his chest. 'So you knew Robert Styles?'

Reed shrugged his shoulders. 'I knew of him but I didn't know him personally, at least not well.'

'Where did you meet him?'

'I dunno, maybe at college with Sue; I can't remember.'

'Didn't you meet him at your own house?' Thomas continued.

'I doubt it; I can't remember.'

'But I think you can Alan, he was upstairs in bed with your wife when you came home unexpectedly wasn't he?'

'Chief Inspector my client has already answered that question.' Reed's solicitor said wearily.

'Then he won't mind answering it again will he? Well Alan?' Thomas said.

'I told you, she'd never be interested in someone like Styles.'

'So why do you think he has made a statement under oath that one day not long ago he was having sex with your wife in your bed when you came home unexpectedly; does he have a grudge against you?' Thomas pressed on.

'Why would he? I hardly know him.'

'Exactly; he has no reason to lie Alan; you on the other hand have every reason.'

'What reason?'

Thomas shrugged. 'Self preservation against a lifetime behind bars; if you had found them together it would give you a motive for killing her. You came home early one day and found Robert Styles in bed with Susan; isn't that true?'

'It's his word against mine; you can think what you like.'

'Not just his word Alan; three other people say they knew of your wife's affair with Styles. I think you knew about it too.'

Reed put both hands on the table. 'So what if I did?' He asked challengingly.

'So you did find them in bed together; and you came home another day and found her giving oral sex to Leroy James didn't you?'

'So what?' Reed said scathingly but Thomas could see beads of sweat on his upper lip and forehead.

'And Leroy James demanded money from you for drugs he'd supplied to your wife. Isn't that true?'

'You don't have to answer Alan.' Reed's solicitor said. 'In fact I think it's best if you don't.'

Reed ignored him again. 'That bastard James got her hooked on coke; she didn't know what she was doing. He treated her like dirt and me just as badly. He's pond life and I hope he rots in hell.' He said bitterly.

'Did you know she was having sex with Colin Fullthorpe?'

Reed jumped out of his chair again and pointed a finger at Thomas. 'That's a lie. You have no right to say that about her; that's a damned lie and if you weren't a copper I'd knock your bloody head off for suggesting it.' He shouted.

'Why should you be surprised; she'd had sex with Styles and James, why not Fullthorpe? You knew didn't you?' Thomas went on.

'Alan I really don't think you should.' The solicitor tried again but Reed wasn't listening.

'No I bloody well didn't know you bastard. Why can't you let her rest in peace?' Reed cried, his eyes challenging Thomas, his face crimson.

Thomas sounded scornful. 'You knew Alan; you found her blowing James and to add insult to injury he later demanded money from you to feed her habit, then you found her in bed with Styles and the last straw was when you discovered she was having it off with Fullthorpe, an old man; everybody but you eh Alan?'

'I didn't know; I didn't.' Reed shouted.

'Come on Alan, admit it; you killed her; you snapped and killed her. It's understandable; I understand; a jury will understand; Christ no man could put up with all that. Admit it Alan, you snapped and you killed her.'

'Chief inspector you know as well as I do that this is entirely inappropriate. You are bullying my client. Alan don't say another word.' Reed's solicitor said firmly.

Reed was breathing heavily; face scarlet, sweat dripping down his forehead and cheeks. Thomas thought for a moment he had him, he felt so close to a confession he could almost touch it but after a few seconds Reed sat back down again and said nothing.

'Is there anything else Chief Inspector?' Reed's solicitor asked.

Thomas tried one last time. 'Did you kill your wife Alan? If you admit it, it will help you later; did you kill her?'

Reed said nothing.

Frustrated Thomas ended the interview and reluctantly let Reed go. Angry at his inability to break him, he was about to return to his office when he remembered Styles was still in the cells. He would not normally get involved in D&D's but he wanted to see Styles so he decided to have him brought into the Interview Room. Styles' story had checked out; the barman in the White Elephant had remembered him and a DC had been able to track down the taxi driver who had taken him home at 2.30p.m. on Monday. Nevertheless apart from Reed he was the only one they could place at the scene.

Thomas made sure the tapes weren't running before Styles entered. When he did he looked hung over; his eyes were bloodshot, his cheeks pasty and slightly sweaty and he still reeked of whisky. When he saw Thomas he groaned.

Alone with him Thomas asked. 'Not feeling well Robert?'

Styles slumped into a chair hands in pockets. 'No, I feel sick.'

'Never mind; it'll pass. I thought I'd have a little chat; got something to tell you.' He said conspiratorially leaning towards him.

'Oh what's that?' Styles asked seemingly disinterested in anything Thomas had to say.

'You first; where were you last night?' Thomas asked leaning against the back wall, arms crossed.

Styles looked sharply at him. 'You know damn well where I was.'

'Oh yes, that's right, you were in Berrydale weren't you?'

'Yeah.'

'Why were you in Berrydale?'

'You know why; Fullthorpe lives there. I was going to teach the dirty little bastard a lesson.'

'Oh that's right, and how did you find out he lived there?'

'He's in the book.' Styles said.

Thomas knew he wasn't but let it pass. 'I see. What lesson exactly were you going to teach him?'

'He'd have found out if he'd have had the guts to have come out of his house, but he didn't; he shut himself indoors like the little coward he is.'

'The officers who arrested you said you were trying to kick the door down, and neighbours said you'd been throwing bricks at his house and shouting; is that right?'

'Yeah; I was trying to get the bastard to come out and face me like a man.'

'Yes, understandable I suppose given what you thought he had been doing with your girlfriend. Oh, just one question though.'

'What's that?' Styles asked.

'Before you began hurling bricks and trying to kick his door down, did you make sure he was there?' Thomas asked.

Styles looked at him as though he'd gone mad. 'What?'

'Yes, before you began your one man Rambo act, did you check he was at home?' Thomas pressed on.

'He was there; the lights were on; he lived there didn't he?'

'Yes but actually he wasn't at home last night.'

Styles looked incredulous. 'Of course he was; I told you the lights were on.'

'Actually he wasn't. No, he was busy getting run over by a train; but his wife was at home.'

Styles could not take it all in. 'His wife?'

'Yes Fullthorpe was married; didn't you know? Oh yes, for over twenty years. Of course you would understand, being the sensitive creature you are, that even before you turned up she would have been very upset about having her house turned over. You'd understand that because I'm sure your own parents were upset weren't they when we searched your house. On top of that of course she'd had to cope with the knowledge that her husband was a suspect in a murder case.' Thomas continued.

Styles sat stupefied, his mouth open but saying nothing.

'Yes she was alone when you turned up and began throwing bricks, kicking her door and generally making mayhem; naturally she was terrified, she had no idea who you were or why you were there; and on top of what she had already been through, well you can imagine.'

Styles put his head in his hands. 'I didn't know. Christ I didn't know.'

'No I'm sure you didn't; you didn't bother to find out did you? But now we come to that something I promised to tell you.'

'Oh what's that?'

'She killed herself just after you left.'

Styles looked up from between his hands, his face like death; Thomas had moved in so close he could feel the heat from Styles' face. 'Two sons Robert; both about your age; do you want to tell them or shall I?' He whispered.

Chapter 30

Thomas walked back to his office berating himself and silently apologising to Styles. He hadn't deserved what he'd just given him; at least Styles had had an excuse for what he'd done; he'd been drunk. Thomas on the other hand had been stone cold sober just now when he'd laid the blame for Aida Fullthorpe's suicide at his feet when actually he knew it was a combination of many things that had caused it. If anybody had been to blame it had been her husband, not Styles, but he'd allowed his anger and frustration to get the better of him yet again. Judd had already warned him once and just because he hadn't been able to get a confession from Reed was no reason to take it out on a poor schmuck like Styles. The phone was ringing when he reached his office and he snatched it up to his ear in irritation. 'Thomas' he barked.

'Bad business this Fullthorpe mess Brian.' Judd said, sounding reproachful. 'Double suicide; the press are going to love it; it could reach the nationals.'

Thomas sighed. 'I know sir; we didn't see it coming.'

'Hope you didn't push too hard; sure you didn't; the two sons could cause trouble.'

Thomas didn't rise to Judd's bait. 'Let's hope not sir.'

'The Chief's not going to like it Brian; hope you're squeaky clean on this one.' Judd warned.

Thomas got the impression that Judd was distancing himself ready for when the shit hit the fan. 'I think so sir.' he said, seething inside.

'I hope so. We need a result Brian, and fast.' Judd said unnecessarily and rang off.

Thomas spent half a minute staring at the receiver, temper bubbling up like Vesuvius on a hot day. Memories of the racial abuse he'd suffered all his life came flooding back to him and for a moment he had Judd down as just another negrophobe; but then he told himself Judd was just doing his job and actually had done him a favour by tipping him off about the Chief; at least it gave him time to prepare a defence if he needed one; and he had been right; they needed a result, and fast.

Grey was idly clicking on trace websites hoping to find something on Louise Theroux but in the back of her mind dreaming about Atherley. Last night had been one of the happiest she'd spent in years. She'd arranged to see him again and was debating with herself whether or not to invite him to her flat for a quiet meal in with a bottle of wine and what that might lead to when Thomas called her to his office. She picked up her case notes and set off upstairs.

Thomas was staring at his board scratching his chin when she arrived. 'Take a seat.' He said. 'So your meeting with Anne Goodchild didn't go that well.'

'No sir, she had a lawyer, a chap called Arthur Lees with her and he wasn't allowing her to say anything.'

'Strange that she should feel the need don't you think? But then her husband Billy threatened me with your Arthur character when I was there, so maybe she's just following orders.'

'Maybe, sir but there's definitely something strange going on there. I just can't put my finger on what it is.'

'Well we're not much further forward with hard evidence. We have no weapon, still no forensics, and only CCTV and Styles' testimony placing him at the scene. I tried again with Reed this morning but got nowhere. He's hiding behind his lawyer too.'

'We still haven't traced Louise Theroux sir; perhaps she will be able to help us.' Grey said not really feeling very hopeful she would.

Thomas began chewing on the end of a pencil, making Grey gag. Disgusting, she thought, he could get brain damage chewing all that lead and the splinters will stick between his teeth.

'Let's hope so. I wonder if we're missing something. This case could still turn out to be a standard domestic; it's definitely the most likely outcome, but nevertheless there are aspects of it we don't understand, a few questions still unanswered. Perhaps when we do answer them they might give us the break we need. I think it's important we trace Louise Theroux, that's number one priority now, and we need to find out where Susan Reed found the money to pay Leroy James. The telephone number for Louise Theroux is invalid, is that correct?' Thomas asked.

'Yes sir not recognised.' Grey confirmed.

'Ok so check with all the networks, see if they can give you some idea of what that number means. It might be invalid, but it might mean something to somebody.'

'Sir.'

'And let's see if we can discover where Reed got the money from to pay James. Meanwhile I'll find out what's taking forensics so long.'

Grey left Thomas to his board and returned to her office. She studied the name and number Reed had put in her contact list; Louise Theroux –00440273944327.

She knew that 0044 was definitely the UK dialling code, but she thought she remembered hearing somewhere that you needed to drop the leading zero from the area code, so she wrote it down again, this time separating the international code and area code. 0044/ 027/ 3944327. Studying it closely, Grey reasoned Reed could have made a typing error so tried dialling the number excluding the zero before the area code; it was still not recognised; next she substituted the zero with every number from one to nine and tried each one; still no use.

She called all of the mobile phone networks that she could think of but none of them had any record of Louise Theroux, and neither could they make sense of the telephone number in her contact list. All of them confirmed what she had suspected, that if Reed had meant to use the UK international code, then she should have dropped the leading zero from the area code.

She trawled the electronic electoral rolls for districts around the County for any Theroux, but found nothing; there was no sign of any Theroux or any name remotely resembling it. Then she remembered that Atherley had said that someone had thought she had moved to Leicester so she searched the roll for Leicester and much to her delight found a Gaston and Edith Theroux listed as living in the Glenfield area. She tried to find them in the local telephone directory, but they weren't listed so she called BT and enquired whether they had an unlisted number but they had no trace of any number at the address on the roll, or under the name of Theroux.

So she called Leicester police, explained what she was working on and asked them to visit the Theroux's to see if they were related to Louise and if they knew where she was. She didn't need to tell them it was urgent, but she did anyway and they promised to get back to her within the day.

She decided that she might be able to kill two birds with one stone, trace Reed's sudden windfall just before she died, and trace Theroux at Reed's house so drove to Manfield Road in her Astra, the April sun, not quite at it full height, dazzling her through the windscreen as she headed towards it. Grey loved the change from Winter to Spring; the warming air gradually defrosting her bones as the days rolled on and the sun grew stronger, the light brightening and the daylight hours stretching, the parks and meadows awakening from their winter hibernation, people smiling more and gingerly shedding a few winter layers. It made her glad to be alive, especially now that she'd met Atherley. She took a deep breath, contented.

She pulled up outside Reed's house and quickly found a free parking space. *'Must have spooked a few locals,'* she chuckled knowing how difficult it had been to park before the murder. Ignoring the 'Police do not enter' tape she walked to the front door and unlocked it. The hallway was dark so she fumbled around for a light switch and flicked it on, almost stumbling over a pile of post. Obviously police keep out signs didn't apply to Royal Mail staff she cursed as she regained her balance.

In the harsh light the eerie hallway spooked her; the hand prints on the blood-spattered walls seemed to be reaching out to try to grab her, tell her what had happened, plead for her help, and she tried to tip toe around the crimson splashes on the carpet fearful she might somehow desecrate the memory of Susan Reed if she stepped on one. A metallic copper odour that was new to her invaded her senses and made her feel sick.

When she reached the lounge she found more blood on the carpet and SOCO had taped the shape of Susan Reed's body where she had died. Grey walked around it, careful not to disturb it or tread within its area, and headed for the kitchen. She wasn't sure exactly what she was looking for but anything at all that might give her a lead; an address or telephone number, an email address, or even another friend's number or a bank statement might give her what she needed.

She began in the kitchen, checking cupboards containing pots and pans and crockery, tinned foods, jars of sauces, herbs and spices, and then moved onto the drawers, finding cutlery, a few household bills and tea towels.

In the lounge there was nowhere obvious to store any papers but she looked under the sofa and chair cushions and ran her hands down the gaps between the cushions and arms and backs, but found only a few crumbs and coins for her trouble.

She stepped back into the hallway and moved on into the sitting room where she found a sideboard and chest of drawers. She carefully examined the contents of each drawer and cupboard but uncovered nothing relevant.

Beginning to feel slightly downhearted she headed upstairs to the first bedroom. In the centre was a king-sized double bed flanked on both sides by small tables on which stood reading lamps; a dresser with four drawers stood against the far wall, plus there was a built-in wardrobe. Grey looked at the bed and imagined Susan Reed having sex with James, Styles and Fullthorpe on it, not to mention Alan Reed. She shuddered at the thought.

It didn't take her long to whip off the quilt and mattress but there was nothing underneath and she found only dust when she looked under the bed. The wardrobe was empty except for clothes on hangers and although she went through each pocket of each garment, even those belonging to Alan Reed, they were all empty. Next she turned her attention to the dresser, tipping the contents of every draw in turn onto the bed, finding mostly clothes and underwear but also a few papers including a birth certificate, cheque book and a household insurance policy. Remembering that Reed had apparently come into money just before she died, Grey decided to keep the cheque book and made a mental note to ask the bank to provide details of recent transactions.

The other two bedrooms smelled musty and were unfurnished; a few cardboard boxes full of newspapers and magazines were stashed in the corner of one, and the other was empty. *'Very frugal'* she observed.

In the bathroom there was an empty wicker washing-basket and a mirrored cabinet screwed to the wall. She opened it to see a small red plastic aspirin bottle, assorted vitamins, and a shaving brush and razors. SOCO had unscrewed the bath panel but there was nothing of interest there except for a few mouse droppings. There was a built in airing cupboard which Grey emptied finding only towels and sheets and more mouse droppings. *'Must be breeding fast; wonder if she could hear them scurrying about while she was screwing her boyfriends.'* She asked herself idly.

She stood for a moment and collected her thoughts. Only the loft and garden to go. Which one? Tossing a coin in her mind and opting for the loft, she moved out of the bathroom and onto the landing. Looking up she could see the loft-hatch was secured by two small batons that rotated on a central screw. She had noticed a four foot long broom-handle with a rubber tip in the airing-cupboard and she went back to fetch it before lifting it up to release the batons. The hatch dropped down on its hinges revealing an aluminium loft ladder that she managed to pull down by hooking the rubber tipped broom-handle over one of its rungs.

Grey took off her jacket and carefully folded it on the bed in the main bedroom before climbing up the ladder. Feet on the third rung from the top and eyes peering over the hatch she found a light switch and pressed it. A four foot long fluorescent illuminated the cavernous space, exposing millions of specks of dust floating in the stuffy air. *'God, I'm going to breathe that.'* She fretted.

She looked around; the roof joists were covered with loft boards on which stood two water tanks and about twenty boxes. SOCOs had not been so careful up here and they had left papers and books strewn all over the floor. In fairness they had been looking for a weapon and blood-stained clothes so they wouldn't have been interested in papers; still in her opinion they could have been tidier. Pipe work extended precariously from the water tanks and disappeared through holes in the floor, and electric and TV cables snaked around the beams and joists, pinned to them every four or five feet.

Mouse droppings littered the floor and there was a stench of stale mouse-urine.

She climbed up the last few rungs and stepped onto the boards. For the next hour she inspected each box thoroughly and made neat piles of the papers, scan reading each one but finding no mention of Theroux or trace of Reed's windfall. Next she took a slow walk around, peering into each darkened corner for any sign of documents that might help her. There was nothing. Disheartened she stepped back onto the ladder, made her way down, and closed the hatch.

Having rescued her jacket from the bed she went back downstairs through the lounge and kitchen and into the back garden. There was no shed, she noticed, and no sign of any garden tools. A concrete path ran down one side of the narrow lawn and she tracked along it, peering amongst the overgrown flower beds and grass, but unearthing nothing.
Thoroughly dejected she closed the front door behind her, making sure the lock engaged properly and trudged back to her car. In the two hours she had spent at Reed's the warm sun had been replaced by a depressingly dark damp drizzle.

Thomas at last had a preliminary report from forensics and he began reading it with hope in his heart. It began encouragingly; on the carpet in the hallway they had found traces of Susan Reed's hair in quantities that suggested they had been tugged from her head.

On the back of her blouse, the front above the breastbone, the collars, and right shoulder, were traces of a natural fibre, mohair, coloured charcoal; source unknown. They had found similar fibres in Reed's congealing blood on her chest.

On the carpet in the hall, smaller traces of the same mohair were found, together with samples of various stones and soil that had probably been picked up on the soles of shoes and carried in by persons unknown.

Thomas read the report with increasing dismay; none of the searches he had ordered so far had found any sign of mohair garments, and the stones could have been carried in by anybody. In frustration he stood up out of his chair and threw the report down onto his desk. He paced around his office for a few minutes, breathing deeply, calming himself, wondering where next to turn.

Chapter 31

Arriving back in her office Grey found no messages from Leicester police so decided to cast a wide web in her efforts to trace Theroux; she began by trawling the electoral rolls in surrounding counties, and put out a general enquiry to Registrar's offices. Drawing a blank from the rolls she decided to check Companies House Direct, the Registrar of Companies' online service, to see if Theroux had any corporate interests; unlikely for someone that young she thought but worth trying. Under Directors Search she typed in Theroux's name and the address she had shared with Reed, and to her astonishment Companies House listed a Louise Theroux as a Director of LT Consultancy Ltd.

Heart beating suddenly much faster, Grey downloaded the Directors registration documents from the Companies House files. Excitedly she began to read the results on her computer screen, but sank back in her chair in despondency when she found herself reading the address she already had for the flat Theroux had shared with Susan Reed.

She had been sitting and staring glumly at the document for several minutes, wondering where to look next when her telephone rang.

'DI Grey.' She answered gloomily.

'DI Fallon, Leicester police,' a voice said, 'calling in response to your enquiry about one Louise Theroux.'

'Oh, yes, thanks for coming back so quickly.' Grey said gloomily.

'No problem; bad news I'm afraid.'

'In this enquiry', Grey wondered, *'will we ever get any good news?'* 'Tell me.' She said.

'Well we managed to get hold of Mr. Gaston and Mrs. Edith Theroux, and you were right, they were related; they were Louise Theroux's parents.' Grey sat up straight, suddenly all ears, heart picking up pace again. 'We confirmed that we were talking about the same Louise Theroux and in fact they remembered the name of your victim, Susan Reed; their daughter had spoken about her quite often.' Fallon said.

'So what's the bad news?' Grey enquired.

'She's dead I'm afraid; died in a motorway accident a year ago; multiple car collision in thick fog; I remember it well; four people killed including her; very sad.'

'A year ago you say?' Grey asked suddenly deflated again.

'Yes, last May; I can send you a copy of the death certificate if it helps.'

Grey let out a deep sigh. 'Yes, please, you've been most helpful. Many thanks.'

'No trouble at all.' Fallon said and rang off.

Grey rested her chin on both hands and sat glumly staring at her screen feeling utterly miserable. Theroux, the only plausible new source they had, was dead. Buggeration!

But at that moment something began gnawing at the back of her mind, trying to tell her something; something she had missed; something obvious, so obvious she could see it right there in front of her. And then suddenly she *could* see it and straightening her back began tapping away furiously at her keyboard. Five minutes later she was rushing into Thomas' office without knocking.

'Sir this is weird, really strange; I'm sure it means something but I don't know what.' She blurted, waving papers in front of his face. Thomas looked mildly surprised and calmly took them from her. 'Sit down.' He said smiling, one eyebrow raised.

Grey sat patiently waiting, her heart beating wildly as Thomas read what she had downloaded from Companies House. 'Why don't you tell me what all this means and save me from taking the mystery tour?' He suggested, putting the papers on his desk.

'Well sir, if you look at the date the Company was formed you will see that it was formed a few weeks ago, and if you look at the date Louise Theroux was appointed Director, that was the same date.' Grey said excitement in her voice.

'Yes, so?' Thomas asked.

'Well sir, I couldn't find Theroux from any of our usual searches, so I tried some of the surrounding counties and came up with a Gaston and Edith Theroux in Leicester. Leicester police went to see them earlier today and they reported back about twenty minutes ago.' Grey was speaking too quickly and willed herself to take a deep breath and slow down.

'Go on.' Thomas encouraged.

'Gaston and Edith Theroux were Louise Theroux's parents sir; they told Leicester police that Louise had been killed in a motorway accident last May, nearly a year ago sir.'

Thomas whistled and leaned forward, suddenly understanding why Grey was so excited. 'So, a dead person registered this company?'

'So it seems sir.' Grey said.

'Could it be a mistake, a clerical error?' He asked.

Grey shook her head. 'No sir, those are downloads of the original documents; they're handwritten; and there's more sir.' Grey pressed on.

Thomas nodded. 'Carry on.' He said.

'Well sir, as you'll see from the Directors Form, the address given is the address Theroux shared with Susan Reed, but if you look at the Registered Office address you'll see it's in Kettering Road Northampton.'

Thomas read the papers again finally looking up and smiling. 'Well well, well. So let's see,' He summarised, 'we have a company, LT Consultancy, registered less than a month ago, the sole director of which died a year ago. Someone is passing off as our Louise Theroux, and provides a false address; we know it's false because it's the address Theroux once shared with Susan Reed and they are both now dead. Now why would anybody want to do that?' He asked.

'To hide their true identity sir?' She offered.

'Exactly;' Thomas said, standing up, 'this might be too much of a coincidence to be unconnected to our case. Come on; let's go and pay a visit to this address in Kettering Road.'

The address in Kettering Road turned out to be a newsagents shop. Thomas showed his card to the shop-assistant, a small thin Asian girl no more than sixteen he guessed, and asked to see the owner. The young girl eyed him suspiciously before picking up the telephone and speaking rapidly in what he guessed was Urdu.

After a wait of a few minutes a small Asian man, about fifty years old with black hair greying at the temples, appeared from behind the curtain at the back of the shop.

He held out his hand. 'I am Mumtaz.' He said in a thick accent. 'How can I help you?'

Thomas shook his hand. 'Detective Chief Inspector Thomas and this is my colleague Detective Inspector Grey. Perhaps we could speak in private?' Grey shook his hand too and Mumtaz ushered them towards the curtain at the back. They passed through it into a small sitting room furnished with a much worn orange sofa, matching easy chair, three bar electric fire, and a colour TV which was tuned into an Asian channel with the sound on very low. Mumtaz sat on the chair and Thomas and Grey on the sofa.

Thomas said. 'We are investigating the murder of Susan Reed and information has come to light that suggests you might be able to help us. Does the name Louise Theroux mean anything to you Mr. Mumtaz?'

Mumtaz shook his head. 'No sir, I'm afraid not. I do not know that name.'

'How about LT Consultancy limited?' He tried.

Mumtaz nodded his head. 'Oh yes; I know that name. Sometimes I offer a mailbox service for small businesses. LT Consultancy is one of my customers.' He said.

'What kind of service exactly do you offer?' Thomas probed.

'Well it depends; sometimes I forward on mail, or I can hold mail until it is collected; sometimes I can provide a fully secure service.' Mumtaz explained.

'And what do customers get from your fully secure service?'

'A safe, here on the premises and a mail box; it is very secure sir; yes very secure and very discreet. I do not advertise the service and people use it at their own risk.' Mumtaz assured him.

'Can you tell us what kind of service you provide for LT Consultancy Ltd.?'

'A fully secure service I think.'

'So you provide a safe and a mailbox for LT Consultancy Ltd.; is that right?' Thomas asked.

'Yes, that's right.'

'And who has access to that safe?'

'Only the client sir; only the client. We give each client a membership card which they must produce each time they access their safe. It is very secure sir, very secure.' Mumtaz repeated, sounding confident.

'Does the safe have a key lock or digital?' Thomas pressed, deciding not to enlighten Mumtaz on how secure he thought his membership system really was.

'Digital sir; all my safes are digital. Only clients know their own code. It is very secure sir.' Mumtaz said proudly.

'But presumably you have a pass code in case somebody forgets their code?' Thomas asked hopefully.

Mumtaz eyed him warily. 'Yes sir; customers do forget their codes.'

'So you could open the safe for LT Consultancy Ltd on your own, without them being here?'

'Yes sir, I could.' Mumtaz admitted, suddenly sounding unsure, 'but I would never do that without my customer's permission.'

'Yes I'm sure. Mr. Mumtaz, this is a murder investigation and I have reason to believe that the contents of the safe you hold for LT Consultancy Ltd. might help us with our enquiries. Can you open the safe please?' Thomas said.

Mumtaz looked very worried. 'Chief Inspector, my business depends on discretion; is this really necessary?'

'It is Mr. Mumtaz. I could come back with a warrant if you insist but then we would have to close your shop and inspect every item of stock; it could take days sir. Don't you agree DI Grey?' Thomas explained.

'Days, at least sir.' Grey added in support.

Mumtaz was already getting up out of his chair. 'No no Chief Inspector that will not be necessary; come.' He said and Thomas and Grey followed him up a narrow staircase to the first floor landing from where Mumtaz turned into a room on the left and Thomas and Grey followed close behind. On entering Grey whistled out loud. Amazingly it was a mini bank vault; all four walls were lined with small light grey built in safes. She counted twenty in each row, five deep; one hundred per wall, almost four hundred in all. Grey was finding it hard to believe that something like this could exist in such a run down place.

Mumtaz bent down to one of the safes on the second row and punched in a code. He pulled the door open and stepped aside. Thomas knelt and peered inside but couldn't see the contents clearly; he did not want to handle them so asked Mumtaz if he had a torch. Mumtaz hurried out and returned a minute or so later carrying a thick orange plastic model and passed it to Thomas. Thomas switched it on and shone the light inside the safe. In it he saw a large quantity of twenty pound notes, a bank card, and some bank statements. 'Well well.' He said aloud.

He stood up and asked Grey if she had an evidence bag on her. Grey fished two out of her pocket plus a pair of tweezers she always carried for emergencies and handed them to him. He had one himself, knelt again and, using the tweezers, gently pulled out the notes, the bank card, and bank statements before sealing them in the bags.

'Do you have a record of the last time someone accessed this safe sir?' Thomas asked.

Mumtaz shook his head sadly. 'I'm afraid not sir; customers pay in advance; cash.' He said. 'After that they are free to come and go as they please.'

'But you must know how long in advance they have paid?' Thomas pressed.

'Oh yes sir. I will look.' Mumtaz said and disappeared again returning a few minutes later with a small ledger. Quickly flicking through it he stopped suddenly and said. '£200 cash was paid three weeks ago sir. That would be for two months in advance.'

'Did you record who gave it to you?'

Mumtaz shook his head. 'No sir, only that it was LT Consultancy Ltd. I offer a very discreet service; no questions.'

I'll bet you do Thomas said silently imagining the type of person who would find Mumtaz's little bank vault useful. With enough time he was willing to bet some of his colleagues from the fraud squad would have a field day in there. 'Can you recall who gave it to you?'

Mumtaz thought for a few seconds before saying 'I'm afraid not; I have many customers as you can see.'

Thomas gave Mumtaz a receipt for the contents of the safe, thanked him, and returned to the station with Grey. Once there he handed them over to forensics for fingerprinting and fibres. He waited for copies of the bank statements then returned to his office where Grey was waiting for him

'There must have been over £5,000 in that safe sir.' Grey estimated.

'At least;' Thomas agreed, 'and the bank statement shows a balance of over twenty thousand. Presumably our identity thief doesn't entirely trust Mr. Mumtaz. Can't say I blame him, it's the sort of place you'd use only if you had to, for example if you had something to hide. So what have we got? A false name and address on a company's registration, a quantity of cash and a bank account, but no direct connection with our case except the name of Louise Theroux.'

'It can't be a coincidence sir.' Grey asserted.

'Unlikely I agree but we need to prove a connection somehow.' He said. 'Let's begin with what we know; Theroux shared a flat with Reed, Theroux is dead and someone has stolen her identity. I think it's safe to assume that whoever has stolen her identity is the same person who rented the safe from Mr. Mumtaz; agree?'

'Yes sir, I agree; whoever it was recorded the address at Companies House, presumably because they needed it in order to open the bank account. It's worth remembering that Susan Reed suddenly had money just before she was murdered so maybe she took on Theroux's identity?' Grey offered.

'Yes it would fit wouldn't it? My wife told me a story the other night about a man who had defrauded Barclays bank out of two hundred thousand pounds by stealing other people's identities. He did it by using their utility bills as proof of who he'd made out to be. It's possible that Reed took on

Theroux's identity using utility bills from the flat she had shared with Theroux.'

'It is sir, but why?' Grey asked, simultaneously registering the fact that Thomas had actually mentioned his wife for the first time since they'd been working together.

'Well assuming our hypothesis is correct, and we still have to prove it, then the obvious answer is to make money without anybody knowing. How, is another question; we tested the blackmail theory with Fullthorpe but got nowhere. Perhaps our thief is defrauding the banks.'

'Perhaps but maybe our mystery person was blackmailing somebody else sir.' Grey suggested.

Thomas shook his head. 'We're getting way ahead of ourselves. First we need to establish a credible link, any link, between this discovery and our case. It might have nothing to do with it. Unless we can we have nothing except a simple case of fraud; so Tomorrow DI Grey I want you camped on the doorstep of Barclays Bank until you know everything there is to know about the opening and operation of LT Consultancy Ltd.'s bank account.'

'Yes sir.' Grey said.

Chapter 32

Grey had arranged to meet Atherley that evening and was soaking in a warm bath, a large glass of chilled Sauvignon Blanc balancing on the rim. This would be their third or fourth date that week, she wasn't sure which, she'd lost count, and she was fretting whether they were moving too fast. When she was with him she became lost in his world; work hardly crossed her mind and she felt a joy and contentment completely new to her. He could make her laugh one minute and light-headed the next, especially when he gazed at her with those deep blue eyes. But what did he want from her; was it a bit of fun or a long term commitment? And what did she want from him? The job had always been her first love; she'd put it above everything else in her life for so many years. She couldn't remember the last time she'd had a serious relationship. Now that Atherley had arrived on the scene would she allow him to change that? Did he want more of her than she could give? What would happen when the job clashed with him as it surely would? What would she do? What would he do? Men!

Thomas confused her as much as Atherley, but in a different way. One minute he was treating her like the office go for, the next he was allowing her to almost run the investigation. One minute he was praising her, the next fixing her with one of those scornful looks that made her want to curl up and hide in the nearest dark corner. He was an insensitive bastard, but she couldn't help but respect him. He hardly ever seemed to get flustered and she was learning a lot from him. Yet he was so impersonal, almost machine-like; one of the DC's had told her he was married but until earlier that day she'd never heard him speak about his family, and he never spoke about day to day things like the weather, where he was going for his holidays, or the football results, the kind of things most people chat about when they meet. Maybe he was scared his guard would drop and she would lose respect for him if he shared his private thoughts with her.

She stood up, stepped out of the bath and began towelling herself dry. Alan Reed was another conundrum. How could he have put up with so much and done nothing about it? What man would stand idly by and watch his wife commit adultery with one man after another? Surely any man worth his salt would have either walked away or thrown her out? But if his statements were to be believed, he had done nothing. Ok, he'd said he'd argued with his wife, but she would have expected more. Maybe he had done her in; at least if he had he would have shown some passion, some semblance of self-respect. But then again maybe he was just a weak bastard.

She padded barefoot from the bathroom to the bedroom and sat in front of the dressing table. She took a sip of her wine, put down the glass and reached for her make-up. Fullthorpe had been another odd character. Seemingly for years he'd risked his career, his marriage, and his whole station in life for a twitch in his pants, and yet the moment he'd been rumbled he'd topped himself. While he'd been busy philandering with his students, hadn't he stopped to think just once where it all might lead? Hadn't he had any idea how vulnerable he'd been? Someone had once told her crudely that a standing prick had no conscience, and maybe they'd been right. Oh well Fullthorpe's chickens had come home to roost eventually and when they had, he'd turned out to be a selfish coward.

Satisfied with her make up she slipped into her best Diane von Furstenberg wrap dress in black, which had cost her a week's wages, sat down again and began combing her hair. Styles was another strange bird; why had he been so hot on someone like Susan Reed? She'd had almost as many men as the Grand Old Duke and yet he'd somehow managed to blot all that out and fall in love with her. What man in his right mind would hold a candle for a woman like that? Even after she'd rejected him he'd come back for more! Incredible!

And as for that low-life James; well he'd be out of circulation until he wouldn't be able to tell his dreadlocks from his nasal hairs, and he deserved all that was coming to him. What drove a man to prey on a vulnerable woman for the sole purpose of getting her hooked on the drugs he was selling? And where did he find the gall to demand money from Alan Reed even after he'd caught his wife giving him a blow job? Outrageous! Mary Ann Evans had been right when she'd written something like 'cruelty didn't need motive, just opportunity.' On the other hand, somebody else had said 'Men are cruel, Man is kind.' In her view whoever had said that had probably been a bloke and he had definitely never met Leroy James.

Having allowed her mind to ponder for the last hour on the imponderable nature of man, and having concluded that they were all a complete waste of space, Grey was finally satisfied that she looked good enough to go and meet Atherley.

'The hospital is sending someone round Tomorrow to talk about Dad.' Alice said placing a hot wet plate onto the drainer.

'About time;' Thomas said picking it up and rubbing it dry with a towel, 'finding a way through those forms is a nightmare, and I don't like this postal code lottery. Where does Northampton stand on Primary Care?'

'I spoke to a woman at the Primary Care Trust earlier today and she told me that care for the elderly with Alzheimer's is much better than it was a year ago. The

Government was lambasted in the press last year when an 84 year old man came into the town from Swindon and was told he'd have to pay £165 a month for the drugs he'd been getting free in Swindon. He created a real stink and the papers got behind him. Eventually it went national and Milburn got wind of it; he stepped in and changed it all.'

'Hmph, so it had to hit the papers before anybody moved off their arse.' He said derisively, grabbing a handful of forks.

'Afraid so; still at least it will have put them on their guard; surely they'll think twice before they mess around with anyone else.'

Thomas dropped the forks into the cutlery draw with a loud clatter. 'Don't you believe it; the only effect that episode will have is to make them more careful next time.'

'They are at least making an effort; they're trying to come up with the best way to help us with full time care. The difficulty is the flexibility of cover we need. With you working long hours sometimes, they're not sure what to do. One day we'll only need somebody for say ten hours, but the next it might be sixteen hours. Plus there are the weekends. It's not easy for them.'

'I'm sure it isn't but we can't be the only family in the county who needs flexible cover. From what I've seen the problem with the NHS is that they'll only do as much as they have to; they work in silos. Once they're faced with a problem that demands a little bit of lateral thinking they bury their heads in the sand, do nothing, and hope it goes away.'

'Well let's hope not in our case; we need them. I went to see Dad today. He says he understands why we can't have him here until we find some help, but I can tell deep down he's hurting.'

'We all are Alice; the sooner he's back here the better, but it has to be right, you can't be alone with him.' He could sense another long discussion about Bill coming on so tried to change the subject. It wasn't that he didn't want to talk about it, but they had gone over it a hundred times and there was nothing new to say. 'Hey I ran into an identity fraud today, quite like the one you were telling me about the other night.' He said, hanging up the tea towel and pouring a glass of Merlot for himself and Chablis for Alice.

'Oh really; was there much money involved?' She asked taking a glass from him and heading from the kitchen to the lounge.

Thomas followed behind her, admiring her backside. 'Quite a lot; we're not sure exactly how much yet, but it's a very similar MO to yours on the face of it.'

'According to the papers it's becoming more and more common; people are so careless with their own security.'

'Guess so; maybe we should take up bin raiding after we retire.' He offered, sitting down next to her on the sofa.

'How's your case coming along?' Alice asked placing her glass on the coffee table.

He let out a deep breath. 'Slowly so far but we might have got a break today. DI Grey turned something up that might help. Who knows? I think the Chief's getting impatient; it's breaking his budget, plus some high-powered shit is rattling his cage, screaming police brutality.'

Alice snuggled up to him. 'You need to relax more.' She murmured.

'That I do;' He said, 'any suggestions?'

'I've got a list too; maybe we should compare notes.' She said, reaching up to kiss him.

Chapter 33

Thomas was in the office early next morning; he had awoken with the idea that he needed to study the CCTV list more carefully and he'd been trawling down it for almost an hour when his telephone rang.

'Chief wants to see you now; Billy Goodchild is with him together with his brief. Meet me outside his office in five minutes.' Judd said.

Thomas' stomach dropped a few inches. *So,* he thought bitterly, *Billy boy really does want to make something out of nothing.* Worried but determined he headed for the Chief's office where he found Judd waiting for him.

'Let me do the talking.' Judd advised before reporting to the Chief's secretary. A few moments later she was leading them into his office, a large square room with a teak bookcase running the length of one wall and two matching filing cabinets against another. Half a dozen plush leather chairs filled the centre of the room, and the Chief's huge leather topped desk stood in front of the window. Photographs of the Chief at different stages of his career hung on the walls, and a family portrait stood on one corner of his desk. *No budget worries here then.* Thomas observed churlishly to himself.

The Chief was sitting in one of the chairs chatting amiably with Billy Goodchild and Arthur Lees and he stood and introduced Judd. 'DCI Thomas I think you know already.' The Chief said to Goodchild and Lees. Goodchild gave Thomas a look and Thomas returned it with a bitter sweet smile.

The Chief was all smiles. 'Now DCI Thomas, Mr. Goodchild here has kindly agreed to give up some of his valuable time to visit us in person. He wonders why we have found it necessary to interview his wife not once but twice. She is clearly not a suspect in this investigation and I must admit I'm struggling to understand it myself. Perhaps you can explain.'

'Thanks for the support.' Thomas said to himself bitterly.

Judd stepped in. 'Sir, this is a difficult murder enquiry and DCI Thomas has been simply verifying statements other people have made. As you know it is standard practice.'

Lees chipped in. 'But it isn't standard practice to hound my client Chief Constable. Nor is it standard practice to make the kind of racist remarks DCI Thomas made.'

'I hardly..' Judd began but the Chief interrupted him in his thick Yorkshire accent.

'Mr. Lees DCI Thomas is a well respected and experienced officer and to my knowledge is not racist at all. Do you have any proof of this accusation?'

Thomas was apoplectic, blood pumping up through his neck into his face at the speed of a flash flood. Judd could tell he was about to explode and gave him a cautionary look.

'My client is not in the habit of carrying around recording devices on the off chance he might be faced with a racially abusive police officer Chief Constable. There was no recording of the conversation for obvious reasons,' Lees said sarcastically, 'but my client is a well respected businessman of international repute; his word is his bond. Why would he make up such a story? He only wants to help.'

'Your client wants to help?' Thomas repeated challengingly facing Lees. Thomas could see Judd watching him warily out of the corner of his eye but ignored him.

'That is his wish DCI Thomas.' Lees said eyeing him warily.

'Then perhaps he can tell us how it came to be that a car registered as being owned by his company was recorded on CCTV being driven along Wantage Road at 10.02 a.m. last

Monday morning heading East, and later at 10.24 a.m the same car was recorded heading West along Wellingborough Road. Perhaps Mr. Goodchild could supply us with the name of the driver as well.'

Billy Goodchild jumped out of his chair. 'This is outrageous!' he shouted, pointing a finger at Thomas. 'Arthur, this black bastard is outrageous.'

'Billy!' Lees cautioned. 'Billy this is not the way.' He said trying to calm his client. Goodchild sat back down with a face like thunder.

The Chief spoke in a conciliatory tone. 'Gentlemen please, this is all unnecessary; Mr. Goodchild clearly wants to help us all he can and DCI Thomas is only doing his job. Mr. Lees I think you will appreciate that in a murder investigation we need to leave no stone unturned. Now surely it won't be difficult for Mr. Goodchild to provide this information?'

Lees said. 'No Chief Constable, I'm sure it won't if you think it is relevant but you must surely be aware that Mr.Goodchild's company owns hundreds of vehicles and so I'm sure it isn't unusual to see one around Northampton. What relevance would this information have to your enquiry?'

'Susan Reed was murdered at her home on Monday between ten and ten thirty. Wellingborough Road runs to the south of her street and Wantage Road to the North. There are no other ways in or out of the street where she lived. We are checking all vehicles seen in the vicinity.' Thomas explained.

Lees looked pensive for a few seconds. 'In that case we will do our best to help if we can.' He said guardedly.

'Good well that's settled then. DCI Thomas will liaise with you Mr.Lees and then I'm sure we won't need to bother Mr. Goodchild or his family again.'

Goodchild and Lees got up to leave and shook the Chief's hand. Judd offered his and Goodchild and Lees took it, but when Thomas offered his both ignored him.

After they had left Judd said to no one in particular. 'That could have turned nasty.'

The Chief sat down in the chair behind his desk. He looked sternly at Thomas 'DCI Thomas don't ever pull a stunt like that again. Do I make myself clear?'

'Yes sir.' Thomas said regretting allowing his temper to get the better of him once again. He knew he could and should have dealt with Goodchild's complaint first and then asked for the driver information later but Goodchild had rankled him and he had been unable to control himself; again. Now his temper had given him a reputation with the Chief as someone who was irascible, a maverick who didn't understand the niceties of dealing with complaints from high powered shits. The Chief would have recognised Goodchild for what he was straight away and understood what was needed and how to talk to him. What he had been looking for in Thomas was a way to smooth over the troubled waters. It was his opportunity to shine, create a good impression in the Chief's eyes; instead he had come across as a smart arse and he had blown it. Well done Brian, go to the top of the class.

'Good, well carry on.' The Chief said in dismissal.

Judd and Thomas trooped out of his office and back towards their own floor. Judd said. 'Glad that's over. Do we have any new leads Brian, apart from the CCTV?'

'Maybe sir; we'll know more later today.' He said. 'Sir, in light of the CCTV evidence, I will need to check Goodchild's alibi.'

Judd thought for a moment. 'Let's wait and see who Lees tells us was driving that car before we jump. Maybe it will be somebody we know.'

'Sir.' Thomas agreed.

'Oh and Brian, don't take it too much to heart. The Chief was only doing his job.'

Thomas said. 'I know sir that's what worries me.'

He returned to his office to find a brief report from the team searching the Racecourse awaiting him; they had found nothing and called it off earlier that morning. *That'll send me straight to the top of the Chief's class, I'm sure.* He thought ruefully.

Sheila Grey had arrived at Barclays Wellingborough Road branch at ten and asked for copies of the application documents for the accounts in the name of LT Consultancy Ltd. and Susan Reed. She also wanted full details of any accounts connected to those two. The smartly dressed woman on Barclays' cusBiller help desk looked nonplussed, it wasn't the sort of request she dealt with every day and she didn't know whether she could or should give Grey what she'd asked for, but after a few seconds of indecision she disappeared to consult someone higher up the banking hierarchy.

She returned after about ten minutes with a promise that faxed copies would be available within the hour. Grey said she'd wait and the woman ushered her into a waiting area out of sight of the many cusBillers wandering in and out of the branch. Grey sat on a chair and began to study the photocopy of the LT Consultancy Ltd bank statement that forensics had provided earlier.

The first entry had been a deposit of three thousand pounds cash paid in two weeks earlier, followed by similar and larger amounts paid in at almost daily intervals thereafter. She wondered whether the bank staff had bothered to complete money laundering reports and send them off to NCIS. They were required to do that under FSA regulations as part of the anti-terrorist initiative, but she decided it wasn't her problem and dismissed it from her mind. There had been no withdrawals and the balance on the statement she was looking at was just over twenty thousand pounds, but it was not up to date and the balance could have changed since it had been printed.

A question suddenly formed in Grey's mind and she called the help desk woman over.

'Can you tell from your records exactly what time of day these deposits were made?' She asked, pointing to the entries on the bank statement.

The woman said 'Yes, the exact time and date of deposit is recorded by computer.'

'And can you also tell from your records which cashier handled the deposit?'

'Yes, again that is recorded.'

'So,' Grey said looking towards a camera pointed at the cashiers, 'your CCTV cameras will have images of the person making these deposits.'

'Yes, they should have.'

'Good' Grey said; 'I need the exact times and dates for each of these deposits and I need the CCTV data corresponding to them. Do you think you could get that for me?'

Again the woman seemed uncertain but she took the statements away and a few minutes later returned with more copies and said the information would be available later that day.

Grey waited, idly thumbing the LT Consultancy bank statement and reading the details before putting it down again. It was then that she noticed something about the account number that looked familiar. She couldn't place where she had seen it before but she knew she had, and it was on the tip of her tongue, she almost had it, but it wouldn't come out. Frustrated, she knew from experience that the best way to remember something like that was to forget about it and wait for it to surface when it was ready, so she went back to studying the paperwork.

After about half an hour the documentation she'd asked for arrived wrapped in a manilla envelope, and she quickly thumbed through it to make sure she had what she needed. Satisfied, she left, promising to return later that afternoon to collect the deposit and CCTV information.

Chapter 34

Thomas had requested close up images of the car registered to Goodchild's company and they had arrived soon afterwards, but to his disappointment, there was no clear image of the driver. Whoever had been driving it had their head down and the outline of their face was cloaked by a baseball cap. Nevertheless, the grainy image did loosely fit the description given by Clare Trussler so he was hopeful it would have some relevance to the case. If this was the person Clare Trussler saw, the person who had knocked on Susan Reed's door at ten ten, and if Styles and Reed were to be believed, then this person could hold the key to the case. He needed Lees to provide the driver's name urgently but he didn't want to push him too hard in case he made another complaint to the Chief. The car though was a silver Land Rover Discovery. *Somebody senior* he reasoned.

He was not relishing his next meeting. John and David Fullthorpe, Colin Fullthorpe's two sons, had telephoned earlier asking to see him and he had agreed to meet them. It had been a commitment he had made when both their parents had died in such tragic circumstances earlier in the week, and as hard as he knew it would be, he was determined to honour it. But he also knew that meeting them could be dangerous; if he said the wrong thing or in any way incriminated the force, then his offer could easily backfire on him. He hadn't asked the Chief for permission to speak with the them and doubted he would have granted it if he had, so if it all went wrong, he would be in deep water. For that reason, to protect himself he decided he needed a witness and asked Grey to join him.

Thomas introduced Grey and shook hands with the two young men before they all sat down. He had arranged the chairs so that there would be no barrier between himself and the Fullthorpes; normally he would sit behind his desk and visitors in front, but he wanted them to feel as relaxed as possible and so sat beside them. It was not going to be a contentious interview; he was simply going to do his best for two distraught young men who were looking for answers.

'This must be a very difficult time for you both.' He began. Both young men looked reasonably calm on the surface, but underneath he imagined they must have been at breaking-point, the double tragedy of losing both parents and not knowing why impossible to bear.

David spoke first. 'We are grateful for your time Chief Inspector; as you can imagine we are still trying to come to terms with what has happened. We are hoping you can help.'

'I'll do my best but I'm afraid neither of your parents left any note to indicate what they had been intending.' Thomas offered. 'We have found no explanations that would directly indicate why they should have done this. Within the family did you have any clue? Was there anything either of them had said or done that looking back might have led you to realise what they had been thinking?'

'No, I spoke to Mum on Monday and she sounded her usual cheerful self. I didn't speak to Dad but she said he was fine.'

John said. 'Neighbours told us police had searched the house earlier in the week; can you tell us why?'

Thomas had been waiting for this question and knew he would have to handle his reply very carefully. 'There had been a murder earlier in the week, a student at the college where your father worked, in fact one of your father's students. We think a weapon was used and, for a while, we were investigating the possibility that we might find it at your parents' house. Now, before you jump to any conclusions, I need to tell you that it isn't unusual in a murder enquiry for lots of different locations to be searched, and this case has been no exception. I can tell you that we found no weapon at your parents' house.'

'Was Mum upset?' David asked.

'I imagine so.' Thomas said gently. 'It's a natural reaction. Someone unexpectedly invades your home; goes through your private things. When it's a burglar it's bad enough; when it's the police it's worse because they have the right to do it and you don't really know what they're looking for or what they're going to find.'

'And did Dad know you were searching the house?' John asked.

'Yes he did.'

'Chief Inspector was my father the murderer?' David asked.

'The enquiry is ongoing, but at this stage I have no evidence that would lead me to believe he was.' Thomas said.

'Did he think he was under suspicion?' John pressed.

'He had been questioned,' Thomas answered truthfully, 'as had many other people, but no charges had been brought and he had been released. That said, he could have been worried; he might have made more of it than he should have; that's entirely understandable, people generally don't understand police procedures and it is difficult not to be concerned after being questioned over such a serious matter.'

'Can you tell us why he was questioned?'

'Not in detail, but he was the victim's tutor, and he did know her. If it helps I can tell you we also questioned many other people from the college. Your father wasn't singled out in any way.'

'Neighbours said there had been a disturbance the night they died. Somebody had been shouting abuse and throwing things.'

'As I understand it there was a drunk out of his head, I believe he was arrested.'

'But why would a drunk pick such an out of the way place? And neighbours said he seemed to be targeting our house. It doesn't make sense.' John asked.

'Who knows; maybe he got lost? When he was sober I doubt if someone asked him why he'd ended up in Berrydale he'd have any idea either.'

'So you don't think this had anything to do with the murder investigation.'

'No'. Thomas lied.

He felt bad about lying to them but the truth would have served no purpose except perhaps to cause more trouble for the young Fullthorpes and for Styles. He was still feeling pangs of guilt over how hard he'd come down on Styles and now, he told himself, he'd lied to the Fullthorpes. On top of the beatings he'd been giving himself about losing his temper, he didn't have a very high opinion of himself at that moment. What a wonderful thing hindsight is, he thought; if only I'd been born with it.

'Is there anything else you can tell us Chief Inspector, anything at all?' David asked.

'I'm afraid not. I am really very sorry for you both; it's a tragedy and I can't even imagine how you must feel. I can promise you that if anything turns up in our enquiries that I think will help you, then I will call you.' Thomas assured them.

Chapter 35

Shortly after the The Fullthorpes left Grey updated Thomas with what she'd collected from Barclays and what she'd arranged for later that day.

'Do you have the documentation with you?' He asked.

Grey had brought it with her and had placed the envelope on Thomas' desk before the meeting with the Fullthorpes had begun. She reached over, opened it, and extracted the copy statements and application forms. Thomas spread them out on his desk.

'So now there's over thirty thousand in the LT Consultancy account; our fraudster has been a busy bee. I wonder if the cash we found in the safe was all there is or whether there's more stashed away somewhere else. I can't see anything interesting in Susan Reed's account, certainly nothing to suggest she was involved in any way.' He said thoughtfully.

Grey was studying the handwriting on both application forms. 'The handwriting on her application looks very similar to the handwriting on LT Consultancy's sir.' She said.

Thomas studied both forms carefully for a few minutes. 'It does I grant you but we're no experts; there's nothing concrete here that we can use to link these accounts to our case. It looks like we'll have to wait for the CCTV.' He said disappointed; he had hoped to find some connection from the documentation so that they could get on. He sensed he needed to increase the pace of the investigation.

'I checked with Fullthorpe's bank as well sir; there have been no large withdrawals.' Grey added. 'So where this money has come from is a mystery.'

She did not need to pour over the bank papers any longer, she'd already seen what she could, so she turned her attention to Thomas' board and was absent-mindedly reading what he'd written when suddenly the thought she'd almost had in the bank came to the front of her mind.

'I think I know why Louise Theroux's telephone number wasn't recognised by the networks sir.' She announced excitedly in a loud voice.

Startled Thomas sat up straight in the chair, not quite registering what she had said. 'Telephone number?'

'The number on Susan Reed's mobile sir; the number against Louise Theroux's name; it's the number of LT Consultancy's bank account; it's not a telephone number, it's a bank account number.'

Thomas looked at her in astonishment. 'Are you sure?' he asked unnecessarily.

Grey blushed and double checked. 'Look sir, she's reversed the sort code, but the account number is exactly the same. The number on the bank account is 20/44/00 73944327 and the number in the contact list 00/44/02 73944327. Surely it's too much of a coincidence sir.'

Thomas double checked and then puffed out his cheeks, exhaling as he spoke.

'I think you're right, and if you are we have our connection, Reed is our mystery identity thief after all. Presumably she used her mobile phone to store the number in case she needed it in an emergency. I suppose that would make sense; she wouldn't have wanted to keep any obvious record of it and it would have been insurance against Mumtaz ripping her off. The CCTV will clinch it beyond any doubt.' Thomas said eyes alight.

'She went to a lot of trouble to conceal what she was doing sir. I wonder why she opened a bank account in the first place; after all she could have simply hidden the money under the floorboards or somewhere similar.'

Thomas thought for a few minutes before he spoke. 'It's a lot of money to hide like that and I'll bet she would have been worried that somebody like James might have stumbled upon it. Don't forget she was still sleeping with him. I don't think she would have trusted Mumtaz enough to leave the whole stash with him and I can't say I blame her; after all he could have stolen everything from her and she couldn't have complained to us without having to tell us where the money came from. Laundering the money through a bank made good sense; firstly it kept her money safe and secondly, because she set up the bank account in a false name, she could keep it completely secret.' He said.

'I wonder if there'll be anybody with her on the CCTV sir.'

Thomas scratched his chin. 'That will be interesting won't it? I don't know; I suppose it depends on what she was up to. If she set all this up in order to launder cash from extortion I think she'll be on her own. I suppose extortion is still a possibility even though we drew a blank from Fullthorpe's finances; maybe she had been blackmailing somebody we haven't considered yet. If she had it's unlikely anybody was working with her, blackmailers they like to keep things very close to their chest. On the other hand if it turns out to be a bank scam she could have been part of a much wider network and I won't be surprised to see her with somebody else.'

'If she had been blackmailing somebody sir, why would he have killed her?'

'There could be lots of reasons, but the most likely is greed. Blackmailers normally go back for more. Perhaps she pushed her mark too far and he bumped her off.'

'Which begs the question who?'

'Well, whoever it was, they had access to plenty of money; we know there's over thirty thousand pounds in the bank and there was over five in the safe, that's thirty five, and we know she gave James over a grand. Not a bad haul for an out of work college student. But we still don't have any proof that she had been blackmailing anybody. She could have got the money from a credit card scam or some other means. All we really know is that she stole Theroux's identity and set up this phoney company through which she was laundering a lot of cash.'

'Well if she was blackmailing somebody, the only person we know with that kind of money is Billy Goodchild.' Grey said.

'Indeed he is but as I said we have no proof; we need evidence. Let's wait for the CCTV; if that proves the money was deposited by Susan Reed then we will move on.'

Later that day Grey collected the tapes from Barclays and as Thomas had suspected they showed Susan Reed alone depositing the money. Grey and Thomas looked at every tape corresponding to every deposit and there was no sign of anyone else with her on any of them.

Chapter 36

In his office Thomas scrubbed out most of his board and began afresh.

- Timeline 10.00 – 10.20 Susan read murdered

- 10.00 + Reed says he left the house
- 10.00 + Mrs. Stephens sees 20-30 year old male knock on door/probably Styles
- 10.10 Miss Trussler sees mid forties male knock on door
- 10.22 Alan Reed calls ambulance

- Susan Reed admitted her killer into her home or she was dead already.

    - takes on LT's identity
    - forms company LT Consultancy Ltd through which she launders large sums of cash.
    - Rents safe in Mumtaz' shop in which cash and bank card stored

- Susan Reed's mobile phone contacts;

    - Vanessa Vokes – friend of SR and MS

- Mandy Singleton – friend of SR and VV and Goddaughter of Anne Goodchild Statement inconsistent with AG's
- Colin Fullthorpe – deceased-SR's lover and tutor
- Bob Styles – SR's lover
  - CCTV puts him close to scene at 09:57a.m.
- Louise Theroux – deceased
  - SR stole her identity
- Leroy James – SR's lover and drug pusher

o Anne Goodchild
- Susan Reed's counsellor at college
- Mandy Singleton's God mother
- Statement inconsistent with Mandy Singleton's

o Billy Goodchild
- Husband of Anne
- Promised alibis not yet provided.
- One of his company cars on CCTV

o Alan Reed
- Knew his wife had been sleeping with LJ, RS, CF possibly
- LJ had demanded money for SR's drugs
- Motive and opportunity

Grey sat studying the board as Thomas was writing it. She summarised what they already knew. 'So we have three suspects; Alan Reed, still perhaps the most likely but we can't find the weapon so we have no proof; Robert Styles who we can place at the scene but again we can't find a weapon, and now possibly Billy Goodchild if our blackmail theory is correct.'

Thomas was silent for several seconds deep in thought. 'Don't rule out Fullthorpe; even though he's dead he could have done it. But I agree with you about the most likely culprit. Nevertheless we need to check out this blackmail theory.' Turning to Grey he said. 'I'd like you to go back over all of Susan Reed's property; check her computer first, then delve into her mobile, her papers everything; if she was blackmailing somebody then she had to have something on them, a photograph, a letter, something. Try to find it.'

Thomas had begun to formulate a theory in his mind and he was debating with himself whether he had enough to go to Judd with it. On balance he decided he hadn't; he needed something more. Making a quick decision he dialled Vanessa Vokes' number and crossed his fingers that she would be at home.

To his relief Vokes answered on the fourth ring and he arranged to meet her at her flat in twenty minutes. Driving through the rain to Westone he couldn't decide whether to risk the shuffle again. He was on a roll; Jolene, The Emperor, Comfortably Numb, Freaker's Ball, Telegraph Road and On The Moon. It was an impressive run, tantalisingly close to his record; just two more needed to equal it, three to beat it. Should he shouldn't he? His finger hovered over the button for a brief moment while he made up his mind; finally he pressed shuffle and held his breath. A second later Willie Nelson began singing 'Crazy' and Thomas shouted a loud 'Yes! The run continues.' In his mind Crazy Jolene had met The Emperor and they were Comfortably Numb having been to the Freaker's Ball on Telegraph Road On The Moon. That made seven, one shy of equalling his record. He thumped the wheel with joy.

He parked his car and ran to the entrance to Vanessa Vokes' block with his collar turned up and his hand on his head to protect it from the rain which was sheeting it down. By the time Vokes had unlocked the door to her block his coat and shoes were wringing wet, and he stood in the lift brushing rainwater off of his clothes while water dripped down his nose and neck. Finding apartment 4B he rang the bell and Vokes answered a few seconds later. After carefully checking his warrant card she stood aside and let him in.

'You look wet through Chief Inspector; might I take your coat?' She asked.

Thomas said. 'Yes please. If you don't mind.' And slipped it off.

Vokes took it from him and disappeared to find a hanger, returning a few seconds later. 'I've hung it above a radiator so it should dry out quite quickly.' She said. 'Please take a seat. Can I get you anything?'

He sat on a leather sofa facing the window. 'Thanks, but this shouldn't take long.' He said. 'It's good of you to see me at such short notice.'

Vokes smiled. 'Not at all Chief Inspector; how can I help you?' She asked sitting opposite him.

'DI Grey came to see you and you were able to provide her with some useful background information about Susan Reed. In the course of that conversation you mentioned that one of her friends was Mandy Singleton. Is that correct?'

'Yes, both Mandy and I were friends of Susan.'

'I wonder if you could tell me more about Mandy.' Thomas said.

Vokes looked surprised. 'Mandy; she's not in any trouble is she?'

'Not that I'm aware,' He said, 'but it will help our enquiries if you can tell us what you know about her.'

Vokes looked taken aback but offered. 'Well, Mandy is very quiet but very bright; academically at least she is much brighter than Sue and I. She's also a very devout Catholic; she lives with her uncle, he's the priest at St.Gregory's, and she hardly ever misses Mass. Her mother more or less brought her up on her own. I think her father left home several years ago for another woman. She seems to live quite a sheltered life, for example I know she spends an awful lot of her time helping her uncle out at the church.'

'Did she ever tell you how she felt about Susan Reed; how she felt about her taking up with Leroy James for example?'

Vokes furrowed her brows looking pensive for a moment. 'Not in so many words. Mandy keeps herself very much to herself, but by her expressions I'm sure she disapproved. She would disapprove of any form of adultery, I'm sure.'

'But she never actually challenged Susan about it?' Thomas probed.

'Not in my presence.'

'What about when Susan took up with Styles?'

'That was completely different. She tried to warn her off of him. For some reason she became quite animated when she found out she was seeing him. My impression was that she thought Sue's relationship with James was a fait-accompli whereas I think she thought she might be able to talk her out of doing anything with Styles; save her soul as it were.'

'You heard her try to talk her out of it?'

'Yes, as I say she became quite emotional; for her that is. I remember at one point she pleaded with her, said if she wouldn't ditch him to help herself then she should give him up for her sake. Sue didn't listen of course, although I must say she didn't stay with him for long so perhaps she did take some notice of what Mandy had said after all.'

'Did Mandy ever discuss it with you, out of Susan Reed's earshot?'

'No, not directly, but I was with her when she challenged Sue. As I say she became quite animated.' Vokes said.

'Do you know why she became so excited about Styles in particular?'

'No I'm afraid not. As I said Mandy doesn't say much which is why her reaction to Styles was so unusual.'

Thomas paused for a few seconds, trying to organise his thoughts. He brushed his fingers through his wet hair then leaning forward asked. 'To your knowledge has Mandy ever had any emotional or stress related problems?'

Vokes was silent for several seconds. Finally she said. 'She is very highly strung; I think partly it's her intelligence but also I think she needs an outlet; she's quite repressed as you can imagine given her domestic circumstances. She is so quiet you see, so shy, and yet sometimes she can come alive. She needs space to be herself, I'm sure she would relax more if she could find it, but of course, living where she does, with her mother and a priest, well.' Vokes left the sentence unfinished but Thomas thought he understood.

'Do you know whether she ever had any counselling at college?'

'Not really although I know she sees Anne quite a lot, I think they get on well together. But Anne is her Godmother so I can't imagine it's ever been on a formal basis, she could discuss her problems with her at anytime.'

'Did Mandy react at all when she found out Susan had been seeing Fullthorpe?'

'Yes with horror and distaste; horror I think that Susan could even consider going with somebody that old and who had such an appalling reputation, and distaste because I think Mandy was of the opinion she only went with him for what she could get out of him.'

'Did she tell you that?'

'Not in so many words, but then she wouldn't. Mandy tells you what she's thinking by the look on her face; she doesn't need to say anything.'

'Does Mandy have any boyfriends?'

Vokes exclaimed. 'Good lord no Chief Inspector; Mandy is far too shy. In any case what would mummy say unless he turned out to be a monk?'

Thomas thanked Vokes for her time and made his way back to the office deep in thought. He had found out what he needed to and had decided he would go to see Judd and discuss his theory with him; if Judd accepted it he would ask for approval for a search and arrest knowing that if he was wrong his career would be on the line. He didn't risk the shuffle on the way back; he didn't want to push his luck. He'd had enough for one day.

In Judd's office he explained his theory and the reasoning behind it. He began by admitting that unwittingly he'd made a huge blunder earlier in the day when he'd told Billy Goodchild about the CCTV image, and followed it up by telling Judd why he believed that unless they conducted the search now vital evidence could well be lost, assuming it hadn't been lost already. Thomas knew that his theory was quite a jump from the evidence they had but he was banking on the search uncovering more evidence to support it. The atmosphere in Judd's office became quite heated and Judd made it abundantly clear that if Thomas was wrong, he would make sure they both went down together, but in the end he approved the search warrant and the arrest subject to sanction by the Chief, which he also made clear was no certainty. But Thomas knew Judd had a first class relationship with the Chief and it would be unthinkable for him to overrule Judd's recommendation.

Grey was trawling through the files on Susan Reed's computer. She was no computer expert but she knew her way around Windows and thought she could cope as long as she wasn't confronted by any passwords that Susan Reed had set. Fortunately there hadn't been one when she'd logged on as Reed, and she had her fingers crossed that she wouldn't stumble across anything that would bring her night's work to a sudden halt. In her own mind she felt that she had made a crucial discovery when she had uncovered Reed's fraud, and it might yet be the spark that would blow the case apart. If Thomas had been right and somewhere in her possessions there was something she had used for the purpose of blackmail, she wanted to find it; if she did then it might lead them to her killer and promotion to Chief Inspector would surely follow.

Grey began tapping away on the keyboard scanning the photographs on Susan Reed's computer. To her way of thinking everything was beginning to fall into place. Susan Reed had not committed any bank fraud, she had been blackmailing somebody. Alan Reed hadn't killed his wife, even though it had looked at one stage as though he must have done. Neither had that wimp Styles; he really had turned up at the door and sloped off miserably when Susan Reed had told him to 'F off'. Fullthorpe hadn't done it, she was sure now, and James had an alibi, so that only left Billy Goodchild or person or persons unknown. But to Grey's mind it had to have been Goodchild; he was the only person they knew who could have given Reed the kind of money they'd traced to her.

Suddenly the computer sounded a bleep and a file she wanted to scan wouldn't open. The cursor was blinking and a message had popped up on the screen. 'Password required.' Cursing, she looked at her watch; 19.22. Way out of normal office hours and so more in hope than expectation she called Technical Services; amazingly a young male voice answered on the second ring.

'I've got a problem' she said.

An hour later, after the pimply faced young wizard from Technical Services had unlocked the password, Grey was sitting staring at the screen, eyes wide, mouth agape, not believing what she was looking at.

'C'can you print that?' She asked.

'Oh sure.' He said and pressed a couple of buttons as if he did it every day, which he probably did she suddenly realised.

A few minutes later she was running up the stairs to Thomas' office.

Chapter 37

Thomas arrived in the office early the following morning despite still being at his desk until almost eleven o'clock the night before.

Less than an hour after Judd had approved the search warrant Arthur Lees had been on the telephone to the Chief and he had been putting severe pressure on Judd to call everything off. Thomas could almost hear Billy Goodchild's foul mouth barking out orders to Lees, and Lees turning them into the legal stick to beat the Chief with. Thomas had known when he went to see Judd that apart from the connection Grey had found between LT Consultancy and Reed the rest was pure conjecture. But his interview with Vanessa Vokes had convinced him his theory had been right even though it had been just a theory. Yes they had the CCTV, but Billy's business was nationwide and anybody could have been driving that Land Rover, so he had been beginning to wilt under the Chief's pressure until the moment when Grey had rushed in with the photograph. Thankfully, after that everything had gone very quiet.

Thomas imagined that Lees would have been with the Goodchilds all night, working out a strategy, wondering what Thomas had; well they would find out soon enough.

Thomas asked Grey 'Ready?'

Grey blushed, bursting with pride that Thomas had invited her to help him, and said. 'Yes sir.'

Together they headed for the Interview room where Anne Goodchild was waiting with Arthur Lees. When they arrived, Goodchild and Lees were already seated. Thomas went through the formalities and sat down opposite with Grey next to him.

Anne Goodchild looked tired and frightened; not at all like the relaxed, confident, well dressed woman he had met in Great Brington earlier in the week. But Lees was sitting beside her and Thomas knew that he would have a battle on his hands if he was to break her.

'Mrs. Goodchild, I would like to begin by asking you where you were between ten and ten thirty on Monday morning.' Thomas said.

'I was at home.' She said.

'Can anybody verify that?'

'No, I'm afraid I was alone Chief Inspector.'

'Do you own a silver Land Rover Discovery?'

'No.'

'Do you sometimes drive a silver Land Rover Discovery?'

'No.'

The monosyllabic nature of Anne Goodchild's answers confirmed to Thomas that Lees had done a good job of coaching her throughout the night.

'Are you Godmother to Mandy Singleton?'

'I am.' Anne Goodchild replied. She was sitting with her back ramrod straight and her hands clasped tightly together resting on the desk.

'Did you ever counsel Mandy Singleton at college?'

Goodchild cleared her throat. 'Mandy came to see me once or twice.' She admitted.

'Why did she see you?'

'She was under stress, from her studies.'

'And how many times did she see you?'

'Two or three times I think; no more than that.'

'Did you ever counsel her other than at the college?'

Thomas noticed blotches appearing on Goodchild's neck. 'Once or twice but it was more like a social thing; it helped her to relax.'

'Were you counselling her when you went with her to the Fox & Hounds in Great Brington six weeks ago?'

Anne Goodchild hesitated before she answered. 'I don't remember; perhaps; we often went to the Fox & Hounds.' She said sounding unsure.

'I'm referring to the occasion when you saw Susan Reed and Colin Fullthorpe.'

'I don't recall that occasion.' Goodchild said.

'But you do recall seeing Reed and Fullthorpe?'

Lees jumped in. 'Chief Inspector my client has already answered these questions.' He said.

Thomas ignored him and pressed on. 'Can you tell me what you observed about Reed and Fullthorpe?'

'Observed? Nothing.' Anne Goodchild said.

'Are you sure?' Thomas persisted.

'Chief Inspector I really must insist you stop badgering my client.' Lees said firmly.

'Do you own a charcoal grey mohair jacket?' Thomas asked. The overnight search had produced a blood-stained mohair jacket, which Thomas hoped would eventually be matched to the fibres found on Susan Reed's body. The blood was hard to see in normal daylight, it had seeped deep into the fabric and merged with the dark colour. Under a microscope however, it was clearly visible.

Goodchild seemed to check before she answered. 'Yes.' She said. Her expression was one of perplexity and Thomas could almost hear her mind turning, wondering what was coming.

'Can you tell me how it came to get blood on it?'

Clearly Goodchild had not realised the jacket had blood on it, he reckoned, because she blushed furiously and repeated 'Blood?'

'Yes we recovered a blood-stained charcoal grey mohair jacket from your house last night. Can you explain how the blood got there?'

'I really can't remember Chief Inspector; perhaps I cut myself.'

'Do you know what your blood type is?'

'No, I'm afraid I don't.'

'The blood type on the jacket Mrs. Goodchild is type AB negative. Less than one percent of the population have it. Susan Reed had it.'

'That only leaves about half a million possibilities.' Lees offered smugly.

Thomas nodded in agreement. 'That's right Mr. Lees, but of course forensics will determine if the DNA matches Susan Reed's.'

Lees looked as though he was about to say something more but thought better of it.

Thomas lifted a sheet of paper from a pile he had placed on the desk. 'A second item was recovered from one of your kitchen drawers, a Swann-Morton retractable craft knife. This is a photograph of it.' Thomas passed the photograph over so that Goodchild and Lees could see it. 'Do you recognise it?'

Goodchild picked up the photograph, saw a royal blue crescent shaped knife with a retractable blade, and nodded. 'Yes.'

'Does it belong to you?'

'Yes.'

Thomas pressed on. 'This too had microscopic traces of blood on it Mrs. Goodchild. Do you know how blood came to be on this knife?'

'No, I can't say.' She said. Thomas noticed that Goodchild's hands had begun to shake and her right eye had developed a twitch. She seemed to be trembling.

'The blood is type AB negative, the same as Susan Reed's.'

Thomas extracted another sheet of paper from his pile and passed it over to Goodchild and Reed. 'This is a copy of a bank statement; the name on the statement is Anne Goodchild; is it your bank statement?'

Goodchild examined it briefly. 'Yes.' Perspiration was beginning to run down her cheeks, and her neck was covered in scarlet blotches when she answered.

'Can you explain the cash withdrawal of £50,000 one month ago?'

'It was a charity donation.' Goodchild said.

'Which charity?' Thomas fired back quickly.

Goodchild brushed the hair away from her face with her hand. 'Not a single charity Chief Inspector; there were many.'

'Do you have receipts?'

'I'm not sure; I don't think so.'

'Did you give the money to Susan Reed?'

Goodchild raised her eyebrows, looking surprised at the question. 'Susan Reed, why should I?'

'Did you?'

'No of course I didn't.'

'Was Susan Reed blackmailing you?'

'Of course not; why on earth should she?'

Thomas was tempted to show Goodchild the photograph Grey had recovered from Susan Reed's computer. He had it with him and had placed it at the bottom of his pile of papers, but he decided against it. Instead he stood up and paced around the room. 'So let me summarise; from the search of your house last night we have recovered a mohair jacket and a craft knife, both bloodstained with blood type AB negative; Susan Reed was type AB negative. You admit to owning both the jacket and the knife. Plus we have a bank statement showing the withdrawal of £50,000 cash which you say you donated to various charities but you haven't any receipts. DI Grey, would you like to continue?'

'Did you kill Susan Reed?' Grey asked.

Goodchild laughed nervously. 'Of course I didn't.'

'Did you slit her throat with the craft knife in the photograph?'

Goodchild put a hand to her mouth, as if horrified. 'No, of course I didn't; how horrible!'

'Did you drive a silver Land Rover to Wantage Road on Monday morning, walk to Manfield Road, enter Susan Reed's house, and kill her?'

'Inspector my client has already said she did not kill her.' Lees said tiredly.

'When you were in the Fox & Hounds with Mandy, did you see Colin Fullthorpe kiss Susan Reed?'

'Inspector, my client has already answered.' Lees repeated.

'Why did you not report Fullthorpe to the College Board after you saw him kissing Susan Reed in the Fox & Hounds?' Grey asked; her questions were quick fire; she intended to give Goodchild no time to collect her thoughts.

Lees said. 'My client has already said she did not observe them doing anything inspector.'

'Did they see you?' Grey asked. It was the question she now knew she should have asked Mandy Singleton when she had first interviewed her, and the question Thomas should have asked Anne Goodchild when he had interviewed her earlier in the week.

Goodchild's face contorted into an ugly shape; Grey had seen it before when someone was under extreme pressure; people sometimes couldn't control their features. She noticed too that Goodchild was trembling and her hands were shaking. Perspiration was running down both her cheeks and her neck had turned bright red.

'I don't know.' She managed to say.

'How long was it after you had seen them before you and Mandy left?'

'I can't remember, not long I think.'

'Had you walked or driven to the pub?'

'Driven; we always drive; it's safer.'

'Did you notice whether Reed and Fullthorpe followed you out?'

'No, I have no idea whether they did.' Goodchild said.

Thomas had been leaning on the wall, arms crossed. Grey turned to look at him and he nodded. Grey uncovered the photograph from the bottom of the pile and slid it across the desk. It was the photograph she had discovered on Reed's computer.

Goodchild looked at it briefly and, stunned, turned white and sank back in her chair. Lees took a quick look at it and said. 'Chief inspector I really think my client is unwell. I request that we terminate this interview until she has had time to recover.'

Thomas nodded and Grey switched off the tapes. They left the interview room and Thomas asked the duty sergeant to have the duty doctor attend to Mrs. Goodchild.

They returned to Thomas' office to hear the telephone ringing. Grey waited while Thomas answered it; he listened for a few minutes then punched the air. He listened for a few minutes more then said. 'Ok thanks.' And put the phone down.

'They matched the fibres.' He said quietly.

Grey beamed, her face beginning to blush from the neck up.

Two hours later they were back in the interview room; Goodchild and Lees were seated across the desk from Thomas and Grey. The tapes were back on. Goodchild still looked pale but she had regained some of her composure and was sitting up straight, her eyes clear.

Thomas began 'I'm going to tell you what I think happened and then DI Grey will ask you some questions. I think it began at college. Susan Reed was a drug addict but could not afford to buy the cocaine she craved. She was also an emotional wreck and her studies suffered. Fullthorpe offered to help but as you know Mrs. Goodchild Fullthorpe had a reputation amongst the students and Susan Reed allowed herself to be seduced by him. One night they went to the Fox & Hounds in Great Brington where you and Mandy Singleton were having a drink. Both you and Mandy saw them playing cupid. All that I've said so far is fully corroborated so I don't think we need to spend time arguing about it.'

'Now when I interviewed you we touched on the subject of Fullthorpe and his predilection for students and why when you had heard complaints you had not reported him to the College Board. You told me it was because it would be his word against theirs. You didn't tell me you had seen them together with your own eyes. So I began to wonder why you had lied to me, and I must admit that when we tried to find out why, DI Grey and I followed completely the wrong line. You see we were asking you and Mandy what you had seen, but we should have asked Fullthorpe what he had seen.'

'I think Susan Reed and Fullthorpe saw something happen between you and Mandy in the Fox & Hounds. You had counselled Mandy at college and at sometime during that period the two of you had begun an affair. You didn't report Fullthorpe because you were frightened he would report you.'

'From your sessions with her, Susan Reed would have known something about you; that you worked pro bono, that you were married to a rich man, that you are Mandy's Godmother, and I think, desperate and drug addled as she was, in that moment when she saw you with Mandy in the Fox

& Hounds, she saw an opportunity to make money and fund her addiction.'

'On the off chance I think she followed you home that night and struck gold, because she saw the two of you in a passionate embrace and took a photograph of you on her mobile phone, that photograph.' Thomas said pointing at the photograph on the desk. 'Later she transferred it onto her computer and somehow, I don't know how, made contact with you and demanded £50,000 in return for her silence.'

'All you could see ahead of you was ruin and shame; Mandy was your Goddaughter, lifeblood of your lifelong friend, a very devout Catholic lifelong friend who would never understand your affair with her daughter no matter how hard you tried to explain it. You had pledged to look after her, but instead you were having sex with her; you had betrayed her. You were the wife of the Chairman of a Public Company, you served on several charity boards, and you were counsellor to young students at the college. You had counselled Mandy; she had come to you for help and in return you had seduced her. Public disgrace was a real possibility. In short you had so much to lose and so you agreed to pay her. But then she got greedy; she asked for more, and when she did you decided enough was enough and killed her.'

'Now DI Grey is going to ask you some questions but before she does I am going to tell you that forensic examination has matched the fibres from your mohair coat to fibres found on Susan Reed's body. DI Grey?'

While Thomas had been speaking Anne Goodchild had begun to cry and when Grey began she was still sobbing with her head in her hands.

'Did you kill Susan Reed?' Grey asked.

Goodchild sniffed and then sat up straight, gathering herself. 'Yes, I did; I killed her.' She admitted. Grey felt adrenaline pulse through her, every nerve tingling, her heart picking up speed, senses on full alert.

Lees quickly put his hand on Goodchild's arm. 'Anne I don't think you should say anymore.' He said.

Goodchild shrugged his hand away. 'It's no use Arthur; they already know.' She said.

'Do you want to tell us about it?' Grey asked tenderly.

Goodchild blew her nose and nodded. 'Much of what you have imagined is correct Chief Inspector. Although Mandy is my Goddaughter, we had hardly seen one another since she was a child. I met Linda, her mother, regularly over the years of course but Mandy was always busy doing something else. So she was almost a stranger when she came to see me at college. At fist she was stressed and confused and for obvious reasons it took a lot of courage on her part to admit why.'

'You see she was in love with Susan Reed; Susan didn't know it of course, Mandy was far too frightened to tell her. She was her best friend and she was petrified that she would somehow let her feelings show and turn her against her. Reed had got herself in a bad way with Leroy James and Mandy was desperate to help her but didn't know how to without giving herself away. Then Reed turned to Robert Styles and Mandy was beside herself with jealousy. She tried so hard to steer Reed away from him but without success. Mandy was completely heartbroken and didn't know who to turn to. So I began to talk to her, counsel her if you like, initially at the college but then soon she began to call me at home and plead with me to see her; she needed a shoulder to cry on. She couldn't unload her feelings onto her mother or her uncle of course because she feared they wouldn't understand or tolerate how she felt; and I think she was probably right, they wouldn't understand at all; the Catholic Church is not very tolerant of gays. So she kept everything bottled up inside and that made her feel worse.'

'It had also been a very difficult time for me; Billy was spending nights away from home and he would often return stinking of cheap women and alcohol. We hadn't slept together as man and wife for several years. But you were wrong when you assumed I had seduced Mandy; in fact it was the other way around. One night we had both had too much to drink and I became emotional; I told her all about the problems Billy and I were having and she just listened without saying anything. Then she kissed me and somehow we ended up in bed together. I don't know how I allowed it to happen but I did. I think perhaps I needed someone to hold me and understand how I felt. Of course at the time I wasn't thinking about the possible consequences, I was so happy. It was simply wonderful to feel loved and wanted again.'

'The Fox & Hounds is a very quiet place in the week and we would often go there for a drink and something to eat. Mandy couldn't handle drink very well and she could get giggly and silly after only one glass of wine. On the night Reed and Fullthorpe saw us the place was empty and Mandy was quite tipsy. She was being shall we say mischievous; it was all very silly but also I admit I found it exciting being wanted in that way again. Until that is I noticed Susan Reed staring at us. Before that moment I had not known she was there but the expression on her face left me in no doubt that she had been watching us and understood completely what had been going on between Mandy and I.'

'Did Fullthorpe see you?' Grey asked.

'I don't know; perhaps although it would have been difficult for him to see us from where he was sitting, but of course even if he didn't there was a risk that Reed might have told him what she had seen. Anyway neither of them spoke to us and we didn't speak to them. To be perfectly honest I just wanted to get out of there, I was so embarrassed, but Mandy was completely oblivious to what had happened and I didn't want to alarm her so did not mention the incident to her. Reed and Fullthorpe carried on as though they hadn't seen us, and we left shortly afterwards. I hoped that the whole episode would blow over. I reasoned that Fullthorpe would say nothing for obvious reasons and of course neither would I. I also believed that Reed would show us both some respect and keep quiet because I had tried to help her and Mandy was one of her close friends. How wrong I was Inspector!'

'Where was the photograph taken?'

'From the garden; there are glazed double doors leading into the lounge. Mandy and I were making love on the sofa. As you know our house is quite secluded so it's not unusual for me to leave the curtains open at night. I can only imagine she must have followed us home and taken the picture, perhaps using her mobile phone. As you know the house is only a stone's throw away from the Fox & Hounds.'

'She knew where you lived?'

'Yes we had talked about the house and gardens when I was counselling her. I had shown her photographs too. I think you will agree it's quite ironic in the circumstances. I always tried to put my students at ease and found that a little personal detail sometimes helped. As it has turned out, well, it was obviously a mistake.'

'You weren't to know.'

'No I wasn't was I? Anyway two days later a copy of that photograph was delivered to my home together with a demand for £50,000. There was no threat describing what would happen if I didn't pay but there didn't need to be; it was obvious; I stood to lose everything that was dear to me; my reputation, my best friend, my marriage, my charity positions; everything. Although I had a good idea who had sent it I couldn't believe she could be so callous; after all I had tried to help her and she had shared some of her deepest fears with me. My first reaction was to go and see her but the more I though about it, the more I realised what a precarious position I was in. So I paid.'

'Looking back the arrangements were ridiculously theatrical. I was to put the money in a Nike bag which I would find in Foot Meadow under the Railway Bridge near the river at midnight three days later. In the pitch dark it is a very forbidding place inspector and I was very frightened. However I did as instructed then hurried off but quickly doubled back and hid a few yards away. A few minutes later Susan Reed, dressed in a long coat, hat and a very long blonde wig picked up the bag and hurried off with it. It was the sort of outfit one would buy for a fancy dress party and I recognised her straight away. I felt ridiculous and was very close to calling call the police there and then.'

'You should have.'

'Yes, well, as much as I was enraged that she could be so vindictive after all I'd done to try to help her, and that she should take me as such a fool that I would not recognise her, I kept quiet thinking that it would be the end of it.'

'It rarely is.'

'No, you're right; it wasn't. Last Saturday another demand arrived; I was to pay another £50,000 on Monday night. Inspector I felt an indescribable rage, a fury that I could not control. This drug addict, this promiscuous little guttersnipe was trying to cheat me out of my fortune and threatening to ruin my life. After all I had tried to do for her! It was too much to bear. I spent the rest of Saturday and all day Sunday trying to imagine a way out but the only way I could think of was to stop her somehow.'

'Why didn't you come to the police?'

'I couldn't; I had too much to lose if it ever came out and there was Mandy to consider don't you see? I had to protect her; nobody could know about us. I was fairly sure that Reed didn't know I had seen her so over the weekend I found out where she lived from college records. On Monday morning I had made up my mind to confront her, so I drove to Wantage Road and walked to her house. In case I met someone I knew I tried to disguise my appearance by pinning my hair up and wearing a baseball cap. I knocked and she answered. She looked quite shocked to see me on her doorstep and I can't imagine what thoughts went through her mind, but I smiled and asked if she could spare a few minutes as I happened to be passing. I think she must have imagined I wanted to enquire after her well-being and she invited me in.'

'I had wanted to talk to her, tell her how ungrateful and callous she was being, but when she turned her back on me all I could think about was how this little slut was trying to ruin me. For a moment I had no conscious thought of what I was doing; Even now the whole thing is more like a nightmare than reality and I fully expect to wake up at any moment. I remember grabbing her hair and yanking back her head before slashing her with the knife. Then I stabbed her with it in the back. Blood was spouting everywhere and I was horrified at what I'd done. I hadn't even realised I had the knife in my hand. I froze for a moment but then quickly came to my senses and hurried out.'

'Did you notice anybody else in the house?' Grey asked astonished by Goodchild's candour. She seemed to have recovered completely from her earlier fear. She was sitting upright and talking quietly and steadily as if they were having a cosy chat over afternoon tea.

'No.'

'Did you wait until you thought she was alone?'

'No I was too angry; I hadn't planned anything and didn't even consider whether there might be anybody else in the house.'

'And yet you had the knife with you. Surely you had intended to use it?'

'I think that will be quite enough inspector,' Lees interrupted determinedly, 'my client is exhausted.'

It was a smart move Thomas reckoned. In that moment Lees had earned every penny of his fee however much it was. Thomas could imagine he was already planning a defence as he spoke. She had said she had been in a frenzy and had had no conscious thought of what she had done, it had all been a kind of dream. Lees wasn't going to give her the chance to admit she had planned it before she left Great Brington. He probably thought he could get her off with manslaughter. Thomas closed the interview shortly afterwards and Goodchild was escorted back to the cells leaving him alone with Grey in the interview room.

'Did you work it out last night sir?' Grey asked.

'I had an idea but I wasn't sure until you found the photograph.' He said.

Grey ran a hand back though her hair. 'I must admit I thought Billy had done it.' She said.

'Earlier you had Fullthorpe down for it.' He chuckled.

'I did sir,' she admitted, 'at one time he seemed the obvious choice if Alan Reed hadn't done it.'

'There was no evidence against him. Theories are all well and good but never forget, let the evidence lead you.'

'Yours was only a theory sir, surely.' She shot back.

Thomas smiled sheepishly. 'Yes well, practice what I preach; I've been doing it a lot longer than you have, but you're right it was only a theory. For what it's worth here's what I thought.'

'Firstly you will remember that Styles was still in love with Susan Reed even though she had rejected him. For that reason I really didn't think he had killed her. So I believed him when he said she had turned him away at just after ten on the morning she died. Now, if she really had turned him away, it meant that she was still alive when Alan Reed left the house to buy his paper. That meant he probably hadn't killed her either. Of course it was still possible that he had seen Styles leave and had killed her in a fit of jealousy but somehow I didn't think so; he didn't have the weapon to hand for one thing, plus he was very confident that we would find no forensic evidence against him. So I ruled him out.'

'Of the other potential suspects, James, Vokes, and Singleton all had cast iron alibis.'

'Once you uncovered the identity fraud then blackmail seemed to be the most likely motive and so I started to wonder who could be the likely mark. Of course there was Fullthorpe but he was too weak to have killed her; it takes courage to murder someone and Fullthorpe didn't have it. He was a serial philanderer but he had no backbone; evidence for example his suicide at the first sign of trouble. Also we had checked out his finances and found nothing unusual.'

'That left Billy but Billy has no shame; if Susan Reed had tried to blackmail him he'd have laughed in her face then sent the boys round to scare her to death. No, Billy is a street-fighter, that's how he's got to where he is. Plus there was absolutely no evidence to connect him to Susan Reed at all. Frankly if he had wanted a woman he could have done better.'

'So then I gave a lot of thought to your report on your meeting with Mandy Singleton. You had said she had made you feel uneasy, that she had a hypnotic way about her. So I went back to see Vanessa Vokes and asked her about Mandy. Vokes is a very perceptive young woman and I think she suspected that Mandy had been in love with Susan Reed but was not prepared to share her suspicions with us. She did tell me though that Mandy was repressed and had sought counselling with Anne Goodchild so it wasn't much of a leap to imagine them having an affair. I suspected that Anne's marriage to Billy wasn't very good by the way he spoke to her when I first interviewed her so it was a possibility.'

'I began to theorise that perhaps Anne Goodchild had been the mark. She had wealth, she also had a lot to lose, and she had access to Billy's company cars so circumstantially she could have done it, but was she the type? Well in my view Billy is a hard case but Anne comes from a different stock altogether. I think she thought she had married beneath her class when she married him but went through with it for the money; she knew she would be able to act the lady of the manor with his money behind her and Billy wouldn't demand much from her in return, he would be too busy making millions. That shows a certain determination, courage if you like.'

'And unlike Billy she knew the meaning of shame; the shame of losing her name, her reputation, her wealth, her station in life. Susan Reed threatened all of those things, everything she held important in her life, and that's why she killed her. Ultimately I think class had a lot to do with it, or at least Anne Goodchild's perception of class. She was enraged at being affronted by someone as low down the food chain as Susan Reed. I think she had shame in spades, but no guilt. I don't think she has felt guilty about what she's done for one minute.'

'And what about Mandy?' She asked.

'There's always a loser DI Grey. It'll all come out now, the whole sorry story. We can only hope that her mother will provide her with the help and support she needs. It's a pity she didn't confide in her first and then perhaps none of this would have happened.'

'It's a pity neither Colin Fullthorpe nor Anne Goodchild considered what the consequences of their liaisons might be; if they had then three people might still be alive.' Grey added.

'Who said 'live in such a way that you would not be ashamed to sell your parrott to the town gossip'?' Thomas asked himself out loud.

'Will Rogers sir, very famous film star and wit; he was a Cherokee Indian, pretty good with a lasso too.' Grey said, and Thomas looked at her in astonishment.

Chapter 38

Thomas had decided to allow Grey to formally charge Anne Goodchild; she had after all done almost all of the groundwork on the case and he was fairly certain she would have eventually got to Anne Goodchild even though he suspected she would have arrested Billy first. Chuckling to himself, he imagined how that would have gone down with Billy boy and the Chief. It could have queered her pitch for a DCI in one fell swoop.

He was driving to meet Alan Reed in the bed sit he had rented in Bostock Avenue while the police investigation was continuing. He needed to inform him of Goodchild's arrest.

Thunder clouds hung black and heavy overhead and raindrops were drumming on his bonnet and bouncing off of the road like bullets as he drove east along Wellingborough Road towards Bostock Avenue. Approaching headlights shimmered in ink-like puddles and the spray from oncoming traffic sheeted against his windscreen. His wipers were on full speed but even so he could hardly see a yard in front of him.. His heater was on full blast and inside the car it was hot and damp, but outside, the thunder rolled and people were scurrying along the pavements, hiding under umbrellas, trying to dodge the occasional jet spray from passing traffic.

Thomas was listening to Sergei Rachmaninoff's piano concerto number 2 in C minor. Composed in 1900 for piano and orchestra, Rachmaninoff had dedicated the piece to his doctor Nikolai Dahl who had helped him overcome a bout of depression bought on by the disastrous unveiling of his first symphony. Thomas particularly liked the sostenuto second movement with flute and arpeggio piano; the slow hypnotic melody always carried him away and although he had always hated it, he couldn't stop himself singing the words from Eric Carmen's 1976 hit 'All By Myself', which had been based on the second movement's theme.

He pulled up outside Reed's flat and rang the bell. Reed answered after only a few seconds and looked angry and astonished when he saw Thomas on his doorstep. 'What do you want?' He growled.

Thomas had expected the reaction and said quietly. 'We need to talk Alan; there have been some significant developments in the case.'

'What do you mean by developments? If you're here to start on me again you can bugger off until my solicitor can be with me.' Reed shouted ready to slam the door in his face.

Thomas raised a hand in the manner of a policeman stopping traffic. 'We need to talk Alan; it's important.' He said in a conciliatory tone.

Reed thought for a moment or two and then said begrudgingly. 'You'd better come in then.'

Thomas followed him into a large bay-windowed room in which stood a bed along one wall and a new looking maroon sofa along another. Opposite the sofa, perched on a low pine table was a flat screen TV and portable CD player. The windows were dressed with deep red curtains and nets for privacy. The walls were freshly painted in magnolia. The air was thick with smoke and Reed lit a cigarette.

'So why are you here?' He asked.

Thomas said 'Mind if I sit down?'

'Suit yourself.' Reed replied shrugging. He remained standing as Thomas sat on the sofa.

'As I said, there have been developments in the case, and I thought I'd better come and tell you before the newspapers got wind of them, but first I wanted to apologise.'

Reed looked puzzled. 'Apologise?' He repeated.

'Yes, you see I'm afraid I completely misjudged you. Given the facts of the case I was fairly certain that you had both motive and opportunity to murder your wife; after all you had witnessed her affairs with Leroy James and Robert Styles and I think you suspected she had been seeing Colin Fullthorpe.'

'I knew nothing about Fullthorpe until you mentioned him.' Reed said sharply.

Thomas nodded in acceptance. 'OK, but still I think you would agree that many men would have cracked under that sort of provocation.'

'Well I didn't.' Reed said firmly.

'No, you didn't; we know that now; but one thing did puzzle me, still does, and it's this. Why did you stay together; why didn't you just leave her? You knew she had lovers after all.'

Reed stubbed out his cigarette and brushed some stray ash from his trousers. He glared disparagingly at Thomas. 'You don't get it do you? I told you; I loved her. Don't you understand what love is? I loved her and didn't want anybody else. Why should I leave her? Everything she did she did after she was hooked on drugs; she had no idea what she was doing, so why should I blame her for it?'

'But surely the marriage was dead; she was sleeping with other men.'

Reed flushed in anger and frustration. 'It wasn't dead! I loved her and she loved me. We still had a full marriage; we slept together, ate together, and we talked; I understood her and she understood me; we helped one another all the time. Look, she met James when we were going through a bad patch and yes she was infatuated by him, but she never loved him. She clung to him because he got her hooked on cocaine, but believe me she was trying her hardest to get off of it. She never loved him.'

'What about Styles?'

'Styles was nothing to her.' He spat. 'He caught her in a weak moment when she didn't know what she was doing, that's all. If she'd have had all her faculties she would never have given him a second glance. She never forgave herself for getting involved with him.'

'And Fullthorpe?'

'Yeah well,' he said evasively, 'I didn't know about him; she never told me; James and Styles we had discussed and I was trying to help her get herself back together, get off the drugs, so we could be together again, like it was at the beginning. It was what she wanted.'

'Are you sure Alan? Why would she get involved with Fullthorpe if that's what she really wanted?'

Reed slumped down into an easy chair. 'I don't know; it doesn't make sense in some ways but then again she was desperate to get through the college course; she saw it as our future; maybe she was using him. I just don't know; her mind wasn't straight in the last few weeks.'

'So you really didn't know about Fullthorpe?'

'No I didn't.' Reed said bitterly.

'So on the night she came home and showed you the photograph of Mandy Singleton locked in a passionate embrace with a near naked Anne Goodchild, she didn't tell you she'd been out with Fullthorpe?' Thomas asked eyes drilling into Reed.

Reed was outraged. 'What photograph; what are you talking about?' He demanded.

Thomas stood up. 'I'm talking about the night she came home from the Fox & Hounds in Great Brington six weeks or so ago; the night she'd been out with Fullthorpe and had arrived home excited, carrying the answer to all your prayers.' He said.

Reed took a pace towards him and jabbed a finger into his shoulder. 'You're doing it again aren't you? What is it you have against me? I've done nothing to you. I don't know what you're talking about. I know nothing about any photograph, and neither do I know anything about Fullthorpe or Great Brington. You're living in fantasy land.'

Thomas ignored the jab and said quietly. 'It's no use Alan; you see I know what happened. She came home that night with the photograph stored on her mobile phone, but you said yourself that she was a wreck, unable to think straight. Nevertheless some instinct had told her to follow Goodchild and Singleton and take the picture. I bet she couldn't believe her eyes, and you couldn't believe your luck.'

'So over the next few days, you hatched your little plan to blackmail Anne Goodchild. It was you who dreamed up the phoney bank account; you needed it to launder the money didn't you; and it was you who knew about Mumtaz's little side line wasn't it? In the state she was in she wasn't capable of concocting such a detailed plan. No it was you Alan; you worked it out, masterminded it; Susan was just the carry horse. She collected the money from Goodchild, she opened the bank account, she arranged for the safe in Mumtaz's vault, while you stayed in the background.'

'When I interviewed you on Monday, you suspected that Goodchild had killed her didn't you? But you weren't going to say anything because you thought that as long as she was still around, she was still fair game. You were going to carry on weren't you? Only now the stakes were higher. She'd committed murder, so the price of silence was going to go up wasn't it?'

Reed was laughing in derision. 'You're mad; what are you on?'

Thomas leaned against a wall and put a hand in his pocket. 'You know, I really do believe that you two loved one another despite her many affairs. Why else would you have stayed together? And I believe you when you tell me that she was trying to get off of the coke and you were helping her. I think you were much closer than anybody realised; if nothing else you were soul mates; that's why you stuck together. But you were desperate for money, first to fuel her addiction, but also just to live and be comfortable. By the way that's a nice TV Alan, is it new?'

Reed scowled. 'That's none of your business.'

Thomas raised an eyebrow. 'You think not? Oh well, let's continue shall we. The trouble with blackmailers Alan is that they get greedy; they're never satisfied, always have to go back for more. I think you're no different. I bet when you came home and found Susan dead it really upset all your plans didn't it? After all you were expecting another £50,000 later that night weren't you? Susan was going to collect it again wasn't she? And what was worse she was the only one who knew the combination of the safe in Mumtaz's vault; she was the only one with access to all the cash. Alive you trusted her to share it with you, but with her dead you had no way of getting to it.'

'You're a sad bastard Thomas; you ought to work on CSI or Cold Case; you'd make a great script writer.'

'I had wondered how you had known about Mumtaz's little side-line and then I remembered you had worked as an articled clerk at Dove's. So I checked and I found out that while you were there you kept Mumtaz's books. That's how you knew about the safe. Maybe I am a sad bastard Alan but it did occur to me that you would be worrying about how to get your hands on the cash and you wouldn't be able to resist trying to convince Mumtaz that he should allow you access to the safe. You would have had no idea that we had found the money and emptied it. So I paid a visit to Mumtaz earlier today and I showed him your photograph.'

Reed was disdainful. 'What photograph? You don't have a picture of me.'

'Ah but I do Alan; you're forgetting the photograph we took when we arrested you on suspicion on Monday. I showed it to Mumtaz and he remembered you were the person who came to his shop and asked him to open the safe belonging to LT Consultancy Ltd. earlier this week. So you see the question is, if you know nothing about this little scam then how do you know about the existence of LT Consultancy Ltd and the safe?'

Reed jumped at Thomas screaming 'You bastard, you bastard,' but Thomas stepped to one side and grabbed his arm, pulling it hard up behind his back with one hand while putting him in a headlock with the other. Reed was cursing and struggling to free himself but quickly Thomas forced him face down onto the floor and put a knee between his shoulders while he handcuffed his hands behind his back. Then he hoisted him up to his feet and said. 'Come on Alan, we've got a lot of talking to do.' as he bundled him out of the room towards his car.

Later that night after he had safely secured his seat belt and begun the short journey home, he decided to risk the shuffle. He felt that the case had come to a successful conclusion and he was feeling lucky. Would this be the big one? Would he equal his record? Holding his breath he pressed and waited an agonising second before shuffle selected the third movement of Beethoven's Pastoral Symphony. Panic stricken Thomas could think of nothing that went with being Comfortably Numb having met Crazy Jolene and The Emperor at the Freaker's Ball along Telegraph Road On The Moon. His mind was working at light speed, sifting possibilities and rejecting each one but nothing came to mind that would continue the string and he slammed the steering wheel in frustration.

'Damn.' He shouted out loud. But then he remembered that Beethoven's Pastoral had five movements and the third was called Lustiges Zusammensein der Landleute which translated as 'happy gathering of country folk'. So he could be Comfortably Numb having met Crazy

Jolene and The Emperor at the Freaker's Ball, 'a happy gathering of country folk', along Telegraph Road On The Moon. 'Oh yes! Oh yes!' He sang as the scherzo danced merrily along.